DURING THE FLIGHT

EMMA ALCOTT

During the Flight © Emma Alcott 2020.
Edited by Courtney Bassett.
Cover design by Terram Horne.

To Michelle Faulkner, whose kindness is unparalleled.

PROLOGUE

WARREN

Doucheweasel

Gender-neutral word for a scheming, arrogant, jerkfaced
prick who likes to pretend he's hot shit, but who isn't. At
all. Ever.

*"Did you hear the only reason that jerk passed biology is because he
copied off the hard-working, smart, REASONABLE guy next
to him?"*
"God, really? What a doucheweasel."

#Asshole #Douchebag #Delusional #Poser #Chris Donnelly

Okay, so maybe it was a *little* immature to draft a definition
defaming a classmate on Urban Dictionary, but it wasn't like Chris
didn't deserve it. He was, and had always been, a *dick*.

The reigning champ of chode.

Grade-A wielder of man-meat—and not the good kind.

There was no redeeming the kind of guy who, in first grade, had
knocked Warren into a puddle—*totally on purpose*—with the express

1

intention of ruining his school picture. And even if there was, the time in seventh grade when Chris had slammed into Warren's cafeteria table while roughhousing with his crowd of meat-headed orbiters and "accidentally" spritzed Warren's pizza lunch with AXE was inexcusable.

Who the *hell* had AXE fights? Let alone in the cafeteria.

But today? Oh, today had been the last straw.

Today, Warren had found out that Chris—who bragged about never studying—had scored an 89% on his biology final.

Fat. Chance.

The only reason he'd done so well was because he'd rigged the seating chart so he'd be placed next to Warren, who had *also* scored an 89%. Coincidence? Unlikely. Even Warren, who took pride in his education, had found the exam tough. There was no way Chris could have scored as highly without resorting to some underhanded tactics, and Warren wasn't going to let that stand. The problem was, Warren wasn't a snitch. He also wasn't as strong or as popular as Chris, so physical confrontation was out. That left the final frontier —the internet. It was the one place where Warren could win.

Which had brought him to Urban Dictionary.

All he'd had to do was come up with a word befitting of Chris's level of douchery. "Douche" was too obvious. Too plain. Too expected. "Shithead" was tired and old. "Dick" was accurate, but didn't pack enough punch. "Doucheweasel," on the other hand, was evocative. Powerful. Apt. It was perfect and, best of all, it was original. There was no entry for it on Urban Dictionary.

Not yet, at least.

Propelled by teenage indiscretion, Warren proofread his work, then submitted it. Internet algorithms would no doubt bury his post so no one would see his genius, but it was probably for the best. If Chris didn't know, he couldn't get even. After years of doing nothing because he was too afraid of retaliation, it was good to let off some steam.

The screen reloaded, booting to a confirmation screen that

2

assured Warren the definition was live. Warren followed its link to the doucheweasel entry and spent a while twisting idly in his swivel chair, refreshing the page every now and then to see if it was getting any traction. It attracted an up-vote or two—which he'd figured would happen—then died down. When there was no change for a handful of minutes, Warren powered off the screen and stretched, then rose from his chair, content in knowing that justice had been served.

What a happy ending.

Satisfied with his harmless internet shenanigans, Warren left his desk and headed to bed. It was getting late, and he had to be up at five to make it to work before the first pallets arrived. Unlike *some* people, he had ambition, and college wasn't going to pay for itself.

A text woke Warren before his alarm did.

Libby: Um, Wren? You up?

Warren squinted through the dark at the time displayed on his phone. It was just after three in the morning—a little too late to go back to sleep, but a little too early to get out of bed. It was going to be a long-ass day.

Warren: I am now. What's up?
Libby: So there's a weird... thing... happening, and people are starting to talk. Did you do anything out of the usual in the last, oh, six hours?
Warren: What do you mean?
Libby: I mean, like, did you make a post on Urban Dictionary?
Warren: ... Why?
Libby: So... there's this hashtag trending rn, #doucheweasel,

and um, well, it links back to an Urban Dictionary post that
kinda name-drops CD
Libby: Like, OUR CD
Libby: And the way it's written makes it sound like you were
the one behind it

Shit.

Warren threw back the covers and bolted for his desk, jabbing
the power button on his monitor with such force, he was afraid he'd
broken it. The screen buzzed, then flickered to life. On it was the
doucheweasel entry he'd been tracking the night before—the one
that was supposed to have faded into obscurity.

It had over twelve thousand up-votes.

"Oh, *fuck.*"

Over on Twitter it was even worse. #doucheweasel was trending. New tweets were being made every handful of seconds, and
likes and retweets were pouring in.

**Doodlebug | commissions open!! DM me @loveylu_png -
51m**

The newest insult in my vocabusweary: #doucheweasel

Don't call me Batman @vodka4me - 2h

#doucheweasel, not the insult we need, but the one we
deserve

4

Socklint was wrong—*Warren* was the one whose life was about to be blown to smithereens. If Chris caught wind of this, it was a one-way ticket to pound town.

And *not* in the good way.

Not that he'd ever want something like that from a jerk like Chris.

Warren: Libby, tell me this isn't the end of the world
Libby: I mean, he DID totally cheat by copying your test answers… it's not like you're WRONG
Warren: Libby
Libby: And the whole asshole and douchebag thing is true, too. Dude's a total prick. I don't know how Free stands him
Warren: Not helping
Libby: I know, I know
Libby: But what do you have to worry about? It's summer. So what if Urban Dictionary entries can't be edited or deleted? It's no big deal. You don't hang out with the same people, so it's not like you're gonna bump into each other. And if he's ever at my place beating his chest in the hopes it'll convince

5

Free to drop her panties, I'll give you the heads up so you don't come over accidentally. Easy. Besides, the internet moves on from things super fast. Everyone will have forgotten this happened by next week

Warren: You promise?

Libby: I promise

If only she'd been right.

That summer doucheweasel went viral, and while Chris Donnelly never dragged Warren behind the auditorium to introduce him to his fists or dunked Warren's head in a toilet bowl, there was unmistakable frost in the air when they crossed each other in the hallway that academic year. Worse, Chris seemed to have taken it upon himself to sit next to Warren in as many classes as possible, where he spent the majority of his time attempting to murder Warren with his eyes. It was a relief when they finished their senior year and went their separate ways—Warren to college and Chris to basic training. The distance between them marked the end of a year-long cold war that Warren was happy to never think about again.

Until, twelve years later, he came home early after a long shift and found an eight-year-old stationed in front of his Xbox.

"Libby," Warren called uneasily from the front door, eyeing the kid, "why is there a child in our living room?"

Libby poked her head out her office door and offered him a sheepish grin. "Well, about that…"

Before she could finish, an all-too-familiar voice spoke from somewhere deeper in her office, and all the pieces fell into place. "Is that your roommate?"

No.

Oh, no.

Not here. Not now. Not in his fucking house.

Warren jerked his gaze away from Libby to look at the kid on the couch.

Dark, messy hair. Shocking blue eyes. An infuriatingly charming smile that hearkened back to times long past. It was like a rift had opened in the space-time continuum and brought the worst part of Warren's childhood into the present.

But that was impossible.

What was possible was...

"Hi," said the kid on the couch. He set down the controller and smiled sweetly at Warren. "I'm Jack. What's your name?"

Warren took a good, long look at the kid, then fixed Libby with a glare that would've put Chris Donnelly to shame. Libby didn't die, but she did flash him an apologetic toothy grin before swinging the door shut, leaving Warren alone with a miniature version of the doucheweasel himself.

1

CHRIS

Nothing good ever came out of Liberty Owen's toothy grin—Chris had been its victim often enough to know it to be fact. On Jack's second birthday, she'd flashed it his way while sidestepping out of the kitchen, where he discovered the cupcakes she'd been charged with delivering had met with an untimely fate. Liberty had apparently tripped on the half-step leading into the kitchen coming in from the garage, crushing Free's dreams of a perfect party as effectively as she had the buttercream.

Jack hadn't minded—he'd been too busy smashing cake into his face to notice it was squished.

On Christmas the year of Jack's fifth birthday, Liberty had arrived on Chris's doorstep wearing that same grin. He later found out she'd been caught speeding through the neighborhood by Chris's CO, who lived two houses down.

And of course, there'd been the *incident* on their trip to Disney World. The one they'd all agreed never to bring up again. It'd been years since it happened, but the shriek-scream of traumatized children haunted Chris to this day. So when Liberty slammed her office door shut and showed him her teeth, Chris knew that something was up.

"Liberty?" he asked in a warning tone.

Liberty laughed nervously and brushed a wayward lock of hair away from her face. It'd tumbled from the misshapen bun atop her head when she'd slammed the door shut. "Sorry about that! You know how roommates are. Or, uh, actually, you probably don't, but that's okay. Just, um, you know... pretend he doesn't exist."

"You're serious right now?"

"Yeah! Totes. Totes serious. So serious I'm unironically using 'totes' in a sentence."

The toothy grin persisted. Liberty stayed stationed in front of the door.

Their eyes met. Liberty's grin wobbled. The skin between her brows creased with what Chris perceived to be worry and tension, until at last she crossed her arms over her chest and looked away. Chris had her. Unlike every other time she'd grinned her way out of trouble, this time she wasn't able to run.

"Liberty," he said in that same stern tone, "what the hell is going on?"

"Nothing."

"Somehow I'm not buying that." Chris jerked his chin in the direction of the door. "Your roommate—he doesn't know about our arrangement, does he?"

Liberty tucked her chin against her shoulder like a swan who'd come to Jesus and found it within herself to feel guilt. "Maybe."

"Why didn't you tell him?"

"It wasn't like I wasn't going to." Liberty sighed loudly and deflated into her office chair, which she'd thrown across the room in her haste to get to the door. Once she was seated, she rolled back to her desk, dragging herself along with pitiful kicks of her heels. "It's just... he works a lot, and I haven't had the time. Important work," she added quickly before Chris could cut in. "Like, super-official health stuff. If I'd interrupted him when he was on shift, people could have *died*, Chris. Like, actually kicked the bucket. Do you *really* want me to distract the guardian of the bucket over one teensy detail? I think not."

Chris's eye twitched. If there'd ever been any doubt in his mind that Freedom and Liberty were sisters, it'd now been cajoled to death. *"Liberty."*

"Hey! It's not like he'll *never* know. If he hasn't figured it out already, he'll figure it out soon."

Chris glared at her.

"Because I'll tell him," Liberty hastened to add. She splayed her hands apologetically. "I'm sorry, Chris. I promise everything will be okay. My roommate is, uh, well... he knows how I am, and he'll be cool with Jack being here. Besides, it's not like you'll end up seeing each other much, since he works all the time. In fact, I'm pretty sure you'll never see each other. Ever. So why don't we pretend he's not even here?"

"Lib, are you seeing this guy?"

Liberty gagged. "God, no! I'll have you know it's possible to live with a member of the opposite sex without boning them. He's just a roommate."

"Then why don't you want me meeting him?"

"Well..." After a few nervous moments spent picking at a loose string on her pajama bottoms, she plucked a hair clip that looked like it should be starring opposite Sigourney Weaver from the middle of the chaos on her head and repinned her hair. Several new loose locks tumbled out in the process, but if she noticed, she didn't let on. "It's just... he can be cranky after a long shift. Forty-eight hours on the job will do that to a guy. I don't want you to get a bad first impression."

Out came the grin. Chris winced.

For some strange reason, he didn't believe her.

Before he could call her out on her bullshit, there came a frantic knock at the door. Liberty yelped and sprang out of her chair, both hands braced in front of her in prime karate chop position.

"Liberty?" It was her roommate, Chris assumed. Either that or

puberty had hit Jack like a truck over the course of the last five minutes. "I need a word. *Now.*"

"Coming!" Liberty trilled, then locked eyes with Chris. She held a finger to her lips and narrowed her eyes in warning. The look said it all—if Chris intervened, he'd be getting chopped.

Not interested in starting yet more drama with an Owens, Chris leaned on Liberty's desk and watched as she bolted for the door.

"And Chris?" Liberty said with one hand on the doorknob, body turned at a slight angle so she could face him.

"Yes?"

"I'm serious about this, okay? Please don't come out when I'm gone. I know I screwed things up by not clearing this with my roommate first, and I'm trying to fix this the best way I can, but the only way that's gonna happen is if you do what I'm telling you to do."

A hint of something serious sobered her face, and it convinced Chris to take what she'd said as the truth. He relented. "Sure. Why not? I'll stay here. You go deal with your roommate."

"Thank you."

Liberty blew him a kiss, opened the door the smallest sliver, and shoved herself through.

2

WARREN

Five years ago when Warren and his best friend Libby had closed on their current home, they'd done so with the understanding that certain rules were to be followed at all times, no matter the circumstances: all repairs, major appliance purchases, and other homestead-related expenses were to be divided evenly between them unless the damage was caused by gross negligence; no fish was to enter the microwave, *ever*; and Chris Donnelly was forbidden from entering their house—trespassers would be shot on sight.

There was a chance Warren had conflated that last rule, but it didn't change the fact that it'd been broken. Chris was both inside the house and, as far as Warren was aware, not being used for target practice. Libby had some explaining to do.

"What," Warren seethed in a hushed whisper as Libby squeezed her way out of her office, "the ever-loving hell is going on?"

As she struggled to escape the clutches of the latch—which'd snagged her baby-blue cami—she pressed a finger to her lips and shot a pointed look in Jack's direction. The kid had popped up over the back of the couch to watch them like a drama-hungry meerkat, which didn't surprise Warren in the slightest, since he was a carbon copy of his father. The urge to fuck up Warren's life probably already had him in its grasp. If they didn't hurry, it wouldn't be long before nature took its course and he griefed Warren's Minecraft base or came over to "accidentally" kick him in the shin. Disturbed by the thought of Chris-clones torturing him for the rest of his life, he locked eyes with Libby, who added, "We'll talk in the kitchen, okay?"

It took a tug or two to free her cami, but once liberated Libby shut the office door, sealing away the evil within. Warren, unfortunately, was not as easily contained. He grabbed her hand and dragged her out of the room.

"Well?" Warren asked once they were in the kitchen.

Libby slid her hand out of his and opened the pantry, which not only housed their sundries, but was large enough for two adults to stand in simultaneously. Better yet, it had a door. She stepped inside and beckoned Warren to follow, shuffling in until her backside bumped a can of soup, which rattled in disapproval.

"Sorry," Libby muttered, apparently to the can, because to Warren she said, "Get inside and close the door!"

While Warren dodged the surplus pack of toilet paper that stuck out at calf-height from a shelf, Libby yanked the ball chain dangling from the ceiling. Harsh light flooded them from above. Libby half sat, half leaned on a shelf occupied by a sack of sprouting potatoes while Warren stood near the cans of things they always meant to eat, but forgot they had on hand. It'd been a while since their lives had been screwy enough to warrant a pantry talk, but here they were. Again.

God, why'd it have to be Chris Donnelly?

Why couldn't Libby just have brought home another raccoon?

"No more excuses," Warren said as he closed them in. "What's going on?"

"Well..." Libby grinned at him, but it was toothy like it always was when she was trying to weasel her way out of something. "You already know *most* of what's going on."

"*Libby.*"

Libby sucked in a breath and rubbed the back of her neck, her elbow almost bumping a box of potato flakes in the process. "Do you want the short version or the long version?"

"I want the version where you explain to me why Chris-*fucking*-Donnelly is in our house!"

"Okay, okay!" She trumpeted her lips. "Short version it is. Chris kind of got divorced and it's really messy and I need to babysit Jack for at least the next little while until the dust settles. Chris's parents can't do it because they work nine-to-five jobs and won't be available to pick Jack up from school."

Warren stared at her.

"But it's not like you're ever gonna have to see him!" she added with a flap of her hands. This time she did hit the box of potato flakes, which she apologized to as well. "Chris, I mean. You'll probably have to see Jack, although just for a few hours at a time—he'll be chilling out here after school until Chris is available to pick him up in the early evening. But it's not like you have to spend time with him. You could, um, spend that time in your room! Masturbating."

Warren's stare intensified.

Libby sighed. "Not even a pity laugh? Okay, okay. I get it. We're not in a jokey mood. That's cool. Just, for the record, that *was* a joke, okay? I'm not trying to perv on you. I'd prefer to think you're perfectly smooth down there. Not like, hairless—although that'd be better—but like a Ken doll, you know? Just a… shapely, dickless bulge of androgyny. Friends shouldn't have genitals."

"Libby," Warren said with a sigh. "Focus?"

"Right. Um." She pursed her lips and narrowed her eyes, locking her gaze on a can of chili. "So… here's the deal. You're not obligated to spend time with Jack. That's all on me. And you don't have to worry about Chris, because he'll only be stopping by in the evenings, so you'll either be at work, or you can arrange to be in your room or out on the town. I'll use my powers of ultimate persuasion to talk Chris out of coming to meet you today, and every

15

time he brings it up after that you'll magically be too busy, or at work, or otherwise indisposed. Sound good?"

Warren scrubbed his face. "And where's Free in all this? Jack's her kid. What's keeping her from looking after him?"

When there was no reply, Warren dropped his hand to find Libby looking crestfallen.

"It's a long story," she admitted after a prolonged moment of silence. Another short silence followed, in which she sucked her bottom lip between her teeth. "It's not really pantry conversation. I'll fill you in on the deets some other time. The gist of it is, neither Free nor my parents are able to look after him, so Jack's gonna be staying here for a few hours a day Monday through Friday, and I'm gonna be the best weird aunt I can be."

It wasn't like Libby to get serious, and it unsettled Warren enough that he didn't push for further details. There was no love in his heart for Chris, but he did love Libby, and seeing her so torn up over the situation brought down his indignation a notch or two. "Lib…"

"I'm okay," she promised, but flashed him a tremulous smile that suggested otherwise. "The whole situation's one big mess, but it's not *my* mess. I'm just helping with cleanup. Jack is a sweet kid. I know he's weasel spawn, but he's still family, and I love him."

Before Warren could say anything, a child coughed somewhere just beyond the pantry door.

"Aunt Libby?" came Jack's voice shortly after. "Are you hiding in the pantry because of that rude guy? Was he mean to you? I'll make my dad go kick his butt if he was."

"Nope." She eased off the shelf and picked her way over a large bottle of vegetable oil, apologizing to Warren with her eyes as she did. It looked like their conversation was over. "That rude guy wasn't mean to me at all. In fact, he's my best friend, and he lives here with me." Libby squeezed past Warren, bumping into a few cans and almost tripping on the pack of toilet paper hanging off the shelf. Warren caught her arm to keep her upright, which earned him a dazzling smile. When she was steady on her feet, Libby opened the pantry door a sliver—presumably to keep Jack from seeing him—and squeezed out, shutting it behind herself. "He wanted to talk to me so badly because he thought I'd eaten his chili, but I hadn't, so I had to go into the pantry to find it. Turns out it was right there on the shelf this whole time."

There was a pause. "You're *weird.*"

"Yup."

"Does that mean I'm gonna grow up to be weird, too?"

"Only if you believe in yourself and get really, *really* into macramé. Now let's go release your dad from my office."

"Why's he there?" Jack asked. Their footsteps and voices faded into the distance. As long as Warren stayed where he was, he wouldn't be disturbed.

"I asked him if he'd wait there for me while I took care of the chili emergency. The pantry's too small for both me and a big, strong guy like your dad. I didn't want either of us to get stuck."

Big and strong?

As if.

Bigheaded, maybe. Headstrong, sure. Anything else was hearsay.

While Warren waited for Libby to wrap things up, he perched on the shelf she'd recently occupied and dragged the sack of potatoes forward, snapping off one of the sprouts. Not all things shunted into dark, forgotten corners decayed—some of them flourished. Hatred, Warren discovered, was one of them. In the years since he'd last thought of Chris, his feelings had germinated and grown into something far more complex. Yes, they were adults. Yes, time had passed, and they'd grown into different people. But at his core, Chris would always be the kid who'd gone out of his way to make Warren's life miserable and made it all look like an accident. Warren wouldn't forget, and Chris wouldn't skirt his way back into his good graces by using his child as a shield. Lethridge was a small town, but it was big enough that Warren didn't have to make peace with douchewesels, no matter how "big and strong" they were.

17

3

WARREN

As much as Warren hated to admit it, Chris was really fucking big and strong.

Goddamn.

It wasn't that he was built like an ox. Not from what Warren could see, at least. The smooth bulges of his biceps and the definition of his chest spoke to a sleeker kind of power—a demonstration of physical prowess that was both understated and impossible to overlook. In the years since high school, he'd lost the trappings of his youth. Gone were the soft angles of his chin and jaw, and his eyes... god, his eyes. Warren pinched outward, zooming in on the picture displayed on his screen. The insufferable glint in Chris's blues was gone, and in its place was...

Warren squinted.

Maturity?

It was probably just a trick of the light.

That said, even if the picture of Chris had been taken on the dark side of the moon, it wouldn't change that—objectively—he was a good-looking man. The kind of guy Warren wouldn't have minded meeting during a Grindr hookup. Maybe even someone he wouldn't mind seeing more than once. With a build like that, Chris

19

would have no problem pinning Warren down and taking whatever he wanted from him, even if Warren struggled. *Especially* if Warren struggled. And once he'd wrestled Warren onto his back and splayed his legs, he looked like the kind of guy who'd push in rough and without warning, clamping a hand over Warren's mouth to dampen his cries of outrage. The more Warren struggled, the more Chris would lean into him until, balls deep, he'd fold Warren in half and growl into his ear that it didn't matter how much he fought—he was getting fucked.

Warren's cock twitched.

Disturbed by his dick's lack of discretion, Warren tore his eyes away from the Facebook profile on his phone and looked to Libby for guidance, but she was too busy cussing at her current commission piece to notice that he was going through an existential crisis.

Chris couldn't be hot.

That was crazy.

It had to be Photoshop, or Facetune, or... Muscletune... or something. If an app could plump lips, widen eyes, and blend away pimples, there was no reason it couldn't give a man drool-worthy biceps and pecs that wouldn't quit.

"Libby?"

Libby stopped swearing at her newest monstrosity of a project to look at him. "Ahoy-hoy?"

"Could you kindly remind me about the disaster that was my last Grindr hookup?"

Libby ditched the endless yards of macramé cord she'd been working with to rocket toward him and fling herself over the arm of the couch. Warren tented his legs so he wouldn't be crushed, and Libby took advantage by claiming the empty space, dropping into a cross-legged position while she peered at him. "Who is it?" she asked, leaning forward like they were kids sharing secrets. "Is he hot? Do you have a pic that's not a dick pic so I can see what he looks like? You're not thinking of driving to Des Moines just to get laid, are you? Because last time you did that you had to drive a couple towns over to get your driver's seat detailed, and I don't think the guy was convinced when you told him they were yogurt stains."

Just like he'd hoped, Warren's semi met with an untimely death. "Thanks."

"No! Noooo. You can't ask me something like that and then not tell me what's going on!" Libby leaned in a little closer. "If you can't show me his picture, at least tell me what his profile name is. Not because I wanna stalk him, but because a guy's Grindr profile name is like the window to his soul."

Warren wasn't sure that it was a window into anything other than a guy's mind when he was too horny to think straight, but he let Libby dream. "I can't give you his profile name because he doesn't have one."

Libby blinked. "So… there isn't a guy?"

"Not really."

Her eyes narrowed. "Then why are you asking me to remind you why Grindr is a bad idea?"

"Because I have an urge to distract myself with something—preferably a man—and you know pickings are slim here in town."

"Oh." She seemed disappointed. "Well, okay. You already seem to know that it's a bad idea, but I'm happy to help you avoid the sweet siren song of anonymous dick. Do you remember that time you drove like, two hours out and the guy canceled on you fifteen minutes before you were supposed to arrive at his place? Or the time you walked in and, surprise! It was a couple, and there were video cameras everywhere?"

Warren winced. "Yeah."

"So don't do it." She sat back heavily and hooked her elbow over the arm of the couch. "Rando-dick is never worth it. Stay here with me instead in our house of friendship and fun. You can play video games and I can swear at my stupid macramé hammock, then we'll order pizza and drink beer. In a couple hours you'll be having such a blast you'll never want to leave."

21

While pixels and coronary artery disease *did* sound like a rip-roaring good time, Warren wasn't sure it was what he needed. If he was going to strike the idea of Chris as an attractive man from his mind, he was going to need a bigger distraction than that. "What time is Jack supposed to be here tomorrow?"

Libby cocked her head to the side curiously. "Um, three-ish. It'll probably be around quarter past when we get back to the house."

"And what about work? Is there anything urgent you need to get done?"

"Wren, I'm self-employed. If my world isn't constantly on fire, I'm not burning the candle on both ends hot enough. There's *always* work I should be doing." Libby arched her back, effectively curling over the arm of the couch to peer at the macramé project she'd abandoned to sit with him. "Buuuut I think if I don't give myself some space from this goddamn hammock, I'm going to lose my mind. So... yes." She snapped upright. "Kind of. I'll catch up later. What were you thinking for tonight?"

"The one man who can distract us from anything. Two words. Five syllables. One international sensation. De-rek Zoo-lan-der."

With a yelp of excitement, Libby sprang off the couch. "I'll pull out the DVD. I'm putting you in charge of the orange mocha Frappuccinos. Do you think we could still do pizza? Because as hyped as I am for this, now I've got cheese on the brain."

Libby didn't need to ask—they did pizza—but not even Blue Steel was enough to keep Warren's thoughts from drifting. Later that night, buzzed on dirty Frappuccinos and stuffed with enough grease to make his arteries weep, he wondered what Chris might look like with his chest bare and sheened with sweat while he dominated the runway. As the credits rolled and Warren blinked in and out of sleep, a ruggedly handsome Chris reached the end of the catwalk, hopped off the stage, and straddled Warren right there in his front row seat. All eyes on them, Chris leaned forward and whispered hot against the lobe of Warren's ear, "I'm gonna fuck you the same way you fucked me all those years ago—hard, merciless, and where everyone can see. Now are you gonna make it easy for me, or am I gonna have to rip your fucking clothes off?"

Warren woke with a start to find lazy golden light pouring in through the living room windows. He'd slept through the night on the couch and suffered for it—his body was stiff. Worse, his head throbbed. It'd been a mistake to let Libby fix him the last dirty Frappuccino of the night—she loved trying to murder his liver. Groaning, he rolled over to bury his face against the couch back when an odd sound directed his attention south. A paper towel covered in Libby's flowery handwriting had been affixed over the crotch of his sweatpants with duct tape.

BONER ALERT

Because I'm so thoughtful, I've provided you with a FREE modesty cover.

PS: I cleaned up because I'm the best
PPS: is your dick #TeamDerek or #TeamHansel?

The answer was neither—Warren's dick was #TeamSeriously-Misguided, and now that Chris was back in town and looking hot as hell, it was only going to get worse before it got better.

———

The first time Warren crossed paths with Jack was a week after the babysitting arrangement began. He'd managed to avoid the kid by sequestering himself in his room and being *very* quiet on trips to the bathroom, but his luck ran out one Monday when, half-dazed from his most recent forty-eight-hour shift, Warren shuffled into the kitchen to discover his pantry had been raided. The culprit? The eight-year-old sitting just short of its door, a largely empty box of Thin Mints between his thighs.

Warren came to a stop.

Jack lifted his head mid-chew.

Their eyes locked.

Jack chewed a few more times, then swallowed.

It was like Chris really had gone back in time to ruin his life. Libby had perfectly good Oreos stashed away in the pantry, ripe for the taking. Why did it have to be his Thin Mints?

"Hi," Jack said when his mouth was empty. "I'm Jack. Do you remember me?"

"Yes."

"I'm here because Aunt Libby is looking after me," he continued, apparently not caring in the least that Warren had answered him. "You're her roommate, right? I keep looking for you every time I come over, but you're never here. You must be really busy. What's your name?"

Warren looked on in dismay as Jack filled the lapse in their conversation with another Thin Mint and said, "Wren."

"That's a weird name." Jack lifted another cookie out of the packaging. "What do you do as a job?"

"I'm a flight paramedic."

"A what?"

There were only three Thin Mints left, and open season on Girl Scout Cookies didn't start again until February. Dismayed, Warren crossed the kitchen and sat on the floor in front of Jack, who handed him a consolatory cookie. Warren considered it. On one hand, the pathogens from a child's hands had the potential to seriously fuck him up. On the other, Jack had only just lifted it out of the packaging. It *probably* wasn't going to knock him flat on his ass. He shrugged and took a bite. "A flight paramedic. When people get hurt and need more help than we can give them here in town, my partner and I fly them to hospitals where they can get better."

"So you're a doctor?"

"Nope."

Jack's brow furrowed. Warren might as well have told him that he was a sham.

"But part of my job involves saving people's lives, just like a doctor would."

"Really?"

"Yep." Warren finished the Thin Mint, and Jack rewarded him with another. "I do know quite a few doctors. And firefighters, and police officers, and nurses."

Jack was silent for a short while. The way he pinched his brow suggested that he was digesting what Warren had said. At last, he lifted his chin and looked Warren in the eyes again, the uneaten cookie held loose in his hand. "What about soldiers?"

"No. No soldiers."

"Oh." Jack frowned. "I was hoping that you knew my dad. He's a hero, like you—a soldier—and I think he's been lonely since we moved here. It would've been good if he had a friend to talk to."

Even though Warren's heart had long ago outlawed feeling any sympathy for Chris, hearing his kid worry about him like that hit him hard. "Your dad's tough," Warren told him. "It'll take him a little while to adjust to life in town, but once he does, I'm sure he'll make friends."

"You think so?"

"I know so."

Jack smiled, and it was nothing at all like Chris's simper from way back when.

That day all of Warren's Thin Mints bit the dust, but so did Warren's apprehension over having weasel spawn in his house. The kid was trouble, but he had a good heart. As long as his dad didn't come sticking his nose where it didn't belong, it wouldn't be so bad to have him around.

4

CHRIS

The call came that night while Chris was pushing spaghetti noodles into a pot of boiling water. Before answering, he glanced over his shoulder at Jack, who was several feet away and spaced out in front of the television. Still, Chris couldn't be sure he wouldn't overhear, so he wrestled open the balcony door and stepped out into the cool October air. "Chris Donnelly."

There was static, then a pop, like the line had only just connected. Chris pushed an empty flowerpot left behind by the previous tenant out of the way with his foot and went to lean on the railing, looking out across the parking lot at the next building over. A pattern of lights zigzagged irregularly from window to window. In one of them, Chris spotted a woman in a robe—probably a Briggs sister, judging by how deathly skinny she looked—sitting down for a meal at her tiny kitchen table. She'd forgotten to close her blinds.

"Chris Donnelly," Chris repeated when he received no reply. "Hello?"

"Good evening, Mr. Donnelly," came a gruff male voice from the other end of the line. "This is Sheriff Sinclair, over at the Howard County Sheriff's Department. I'm calling pursuant to the interview you had here last week."

Steve Sinclair was no stranger—he'd been sheriff for as long as Chris could remember. His bushy handlebar mustache and red cheeks showed up on yard signs across the county once every four years when elections rolled around, and every year like clockwork he gave an anti-drug presentation at the high school. But Steve wasn't calling today to ask for Chris's support in the next election or scare him with scrambled eggs. There was a chance, as minute as it was, that he was calling to usher in Chris's future.

Chris took a second to collect himself before speaking, shifting his position so more of his weight rested on his arms. The cold metal railing bit into his skin, but the sting was a pleasant reminder to stay calm and grounded. "Good evening, Sheriff. Thank you for following up."

"I'm gonna cut to the chase, Mr. Donnelly. I want to offer you the job."

Chris shut his eyes in silent celebration and grinned into the night. "That's fantastic. Thank you, Sheriff."

"I'd like for you to stop by the department tomorrow, say around one. There are some details we'll need to go over before we sign any paperwork, and I'm sure you've got questions of your own to ask me. I figure it'll be easier to get that all sorted in person."

"One works great. I'll see you then."

"Lookin' forward to it."

The call ended not long after that. Chris took a deep breath and blew it out slowly, letting his shoulders slump. What little money he had left after getting divorced and uprooting himself from Fort Hood had been drained by security deposits, and his financial security net had been destroyed years ago thanks to events he preferred not to think about. The fact that he'd landed a job back home was a blessing. He'd get to keep his shoebox apartment and have enough left over to keep Jack clothed, fed, and entertained. It looked like life was done kicking him in the balls.

The balcony door jostled, then was yanked open.

"Dad?" Jack said, calm as could be. "The spaghetti's on fire."

Fuck.

Chris flew back into the house and dealt with the burning pasta, then dropped onto the couch next to Jack, who'd gone back to watching his show. The smoke detector hadn't tripped—thank god —but a charred, wheaty death smell hung in the air and put the kibosh on trying to make anything else. Chris could only imagine what it'd taste like if a stink like that got into his next attempt at making dinner. As he came off his adrenaline high, he ruffled Jack's hair to get his attention and asked, "What do you think about order-in pizza for dinner tonight?"

Life might not have been done kicking Chris in the balls just yet, but that night they toasted a future where it might not with cheese and Italian seasoning.

———

Jack pulled a slice of pepperoni pizza out of the box, breaking off stretchy strings of melted cheese that wouldn't snap with his finger before dropping it on a grease-spotted paper plate. With his spoils in hand, he returned to the kitchen table and sat opposite Chris, who'd been keeping an eye on him to make sure no pizza or pizza-adjacents ended up on the floor. Jack shifted his weight from thigh to thigh to settle, then lifted each of the hanging strings of cheese so they rested on top of his slice.

"I made a new friend today, Dad," Jack said before taking a bite.

"Oh yeah?"

"Yeah. He's like a sky doctor. He says he's not *really* a doctor, but I don't know if I believe him."

Chris gaped at his son, not that he noticed. He'd been expecting Jack to tell him about a friend he'd made at school, but unless protocol had changed since he'd last been in Lethridge, they weren't handing out medical degrees to elementary school kids. Something wasn't adding up. Hoping to get to the bottom of it, he put forth a simple question. "A sky doctor? Where'd you meet someone like that?"

"At Aunt Libby's house." Jack took a big bite out of his pizza and made Chris wait until he'd finished chewing for further explanation. "He's her roommate, but I didn't get to meet him until today because he's been really busy saving lives and stuff. I think you should be his friend. He's fun. We ate cookies together, and then he sat with me and watched me play Minecraft."

Much better. Chris issued an internal sigh of relief. For a second, he'd been worried that someone unsavory had been in contact with his son, but while Liberty was... *unique*... he didn't think she kept bad company. Except for Warren Reaves, who could fuck directly off. "He sounds like a good friend to have. He didn't let you eat too many cookies, did he?"

Jack shook his head at a breakneck speed that sent his hair flying —a surefire sign too many cookies *had* been eaten. Chris let it slide. Leaving Fort Hood had been tough on both of them, and if a couple extra cookies could help smooth the transition, so be it.

"What's your friend's name?" Chris asked, because even if Liberty's roommate was on the up and up, Chris was going to stalk the hell out of him to make sure he was fit to be around his son.

"Wren."

"That's it?"

Jack shrugged. "That's what he told me. I thought it was a weird name, too, but also kinda cool. Like *Star Wars*."

"Wren" wasn't enough to do much stalking, but Chris would wrangle more details out of Liberty the next time he saw her. She'd been oddly cagey about the whole roommate situation, and he'd sleep better knowing why that was.

5

CHRIS

By the time dinner had concluded and leftover pizza had been put away, it was starting to get late. Chris oversaw Jack's bedtime routine and was about to tuck him in when Jack sat bolt upright in bed, startling them both.

"Whoa! Jack, what's going on?"

"My math homework," Jack breathed. He scrambled out from beneath the sheets and launched himself across the tiny room to where his backpack hung on his closet door. Chris watched as loose pencils flew in all directions and... were those *orange peels?* Whatever they were, bits of something desiccated, orange, and sad-looking hit the ground, followed closely by the green-blue crust of a long-ago-eaten sandwich neatly preserved in a resealable bag. A few more food scraps followed, and for every one that emerged, Chris's heart clenched that much more.

He thought they'd left that behavior behind in Fort Hood.

A brown, wilted banana peel joined the mess on the floor, and the sight of it spurred Chris into action.

He grabbed the garbage pail from Jack's bedside and braved the barrage of junk to pick up his son's trash. The little sad pieces of

31

shriveled awful? Yeah, they were orange peels, and to Chris, it looked like they'd been in there for way longer than a week.

It was worse than he'd thought.

"Champ," Chris said in as level a voice as he could muster. "Why is your backpack a lunch graveyard?"

Jack was too busy rifling through god-knew-what to answer.

"Champ?"

Jack took out a loose stack of printouts and carried them mournfully to his bed, where he laid them out one by one. When Chris was done cleaning up the corpses of meals long since passed, he went to see exactly what those papers were. For the most part, they were homework sheets—some old, some new. Jack's large, somewhat erratic handwriting filled gaps in sentences testing his vocabulary and added numbers to balance addition and subtraction problems, and while everything looked right to Chris, Jack's shoulders slumped.

"Oh no," Jack whispered, voice sad and small in a way that broke Chris's heart. "Dad... I forgot my math homework at Aunt Libby's house, and if I don't hand it in tomorrow, my teacher's gonna give me a zero."

Chris set the garbage pail back where it belonged and squatted next to Jack, tugging him into a side-hug. "You're sure it's not here? This isn't it?" He lifted the only math sheet that hadn't been touched by the teacher's green pen. "Your teacher hasn't seen this one yet."

"That one was one we did in class," Jack lamented. "Homework is different."

"And you're *sure* it's not in your bag?"

Jack nodded.

Considering the backpack had gone from Chris's SUV to the hook on Jack's closet door without being tampered with, Chris figured Jack was right. He rose and let a beat of silence pass, then jerked his thumb over his shoulder. "Okay. Grab a sweatshirt and let's go get it."

Jack's once morose face lit up.

"But just so you know," Chris added, holding his son's gaze and trying his very best not to let him see how shaken he was by the scraps in Jack's bag, "tonight's last-minute trip out to rescue your homework comes at a price. You and I are going to cleanliness boot camp this weekend, and we're starting with your backpack."

Jack wrinkled his nose but didn't otherwise protest. All things considered, he was a good kid. With a little guidance, he'd get back on track. Chris would make sure of it.

———————

Lethridge, Iowa wasn't big, but it was the kind of place where it was easy to get turned around. Split down the middle by the babbling waters of Deer Creek, it was a fever dream of one-way streets, stone road bridges, and quaint brick buildings that inspired déjà vu. Tucked away in a copse of trees that shielded it from the dust pollution of miles of surrounding corn fields, it'd often felt to Chris like a microcosm of days long past—somewhere folks came when the world felt like it was moving in all the wrong directions.

It was no wonder he'd come back.

Once Jack had donned another layer, Chris led him down the stairwell of their apartment building and across the parking lot to the old Acura RDX that'd seen them from Fort Hood to their new home. Dirt stuck between its treads and a spattering of rust plagued the wheel well, but otherwise she was still in good shape. Chris saw his son into the car, made sure the door was shut, then climbed in and started the engine. While he did, Jack pulled his sweatshirt up and over his nose and tucked his hands into its sleeves.

"You doin' okay back there, kid?" Chris asked as he planted a hand on the back of the passenger seat and checked the way was clear.

"Mm."

"Mm?"

"Yes." His grating exasperation was joined by the crackle of tires

rolling over asphalt. Chris backed out of their parking space and headed for the road. It hadn't been all that long since he'd gained full custody of Jack, but he'd already learned a few tricks of the parenting trade—if used effectively, silence was often more useful than asking pointed questions. Case in point: the child now shifting restlessly in the back seat.

After a long while, Jack rested his head on the window and finally said, "I'm sorry. I didn't mean to be mean."

The SUV jostled as it made its way over the first stones of the bridge connecting them with the east bank. Another car passed them by, headed in the opposite direction. Chris made sure it was gone, then shifted his gaze momentarily to the rearview mirror to see the boy in the back seat. "I figured. You wanna talk about it?"

Jack mumbled something incoherent and sank deeper into his sweatshirt, but whether it was out of frustration, defeat, or a combination of both, Chris wasn't able to tell. The bridge was narrow, and it demanded his full attention. He needed to keep his eyes on the road. "Champ, if this is about the homework, you're not in trouble. It was an honest mistake, and I'm gonna help you make sure it doesn't happen again when we clean out your backpack this weekend. You don't have to feel bad."

No answer.

On the other side of the bridge, Chris turned left at the intersection and continued on his way. It wouldn't be long before they got to Liberty's place—just a few more turns to go.

"Well," Chris said when he was met with silence. "If you wanna talk about it, I'm here to listen." They turned onto Liberty's street, where Chris parked curbside near her driveway. The porch light was off, but the living room lights were on. Liberty never seemed to sleep, so it didn't surprise Chris that she was awake. "You stay here, okay? I'll go grab your homework, then we'll head home to bed. You remember where you left it?"

"Yeah," Jack mumbled. "In Aunt Libby's office. She was helping me."

"Okay. Got it. You sit tight—I'll be back in a sec."

Chris killed the engine and left the car, locking it behind him. It didn't take long to jog across the patchwork yard, and even less time to clear the three steps leading to the stoop. There was a round backlit doorbell to the right of the door, which he buzzed. Liberty didn't know they were coming, so he assumed it'd be a hot second before she came to answer. To bide his time, he slid his hands into his back pockets and took a closer look at the house his former sister-in-law called home. Like many of the other buildings in Lethridge, it was made of brick, and while it could use a good pressure wash, it was cheerful and, more importantly, sturdy. If her roommate knew what he was doing, he could really make the place shine. Chris couldn't say the same about Liberty, who he'd be nervous trusting around a hairdryer, let alone a power tool.

After a brief delay, the porch light flicked on. The lock clicked. The doorknob turned. Chris stood a little straighter out of habit and readied himself to rescue his son's math homework as quickly as possible, but his plans were derailed before they could even get started.

Libby hadn't answered the door. A man had instead.

For a long, tense moment they stared at each other. Long, side-swept blond hair. A solid but not overly muscular frame. A tapered waist. Legs hidden behind cartoon sheep pajama pants. If Chris had run into him from behind, he wouldn't have had a clue who the guy was, but his face... there was no mistaking it. Chris had stared down those dark, foreboding eyes more than once. Liberty's roommate and his son's new friend, Wren, was none other than the king of all assholes—Warren Reaves.

35

6

WARREN

There was a douceweasel on Warren's doorstep. Warren gave him a good, hard look, then promptly shut the door.

Nope.

No way was he going to deal with that. It didn't matter if it was the setup for a Dr. Seuss story—Warren's heart was perfectly happy at the size it was, thank you very much.

He wished he could say the same about his cock.

Only a few seconds had passed between when he'd registered that Chris was standing on his doorstep and when he'd shut the door, but a few seconds was all it took. An influx of inappropriate thoughts rushed into his head. Yes, Chris was public enemy number one, but *damn* was he hot. Not even his Facebook photos had prepared Warren for what he'd look like in person. The military had sculpted his body into a work of art, chiseling his features and refining his imperfections until even they were gorgeous—like the stupid cleft in his chin that Warren had always hated, and the little indent on the right side of his forehead that was most probably a scar from chickenpox. To make matters worse, the way the porch lights gleamed in Chris's eyes made him look human instead of pure evil, and that... that was troubling. It made Warren feel things beyond arousal—things he'd rather not have to think about.

Like that Chris had looked surprised—not angry—to see him.

Which was stupid. Really stupid. Because Chris hated Warren more than Warren hated Chris.

It was a good thing Chris so graciously started to pound his hammy fists on the door, because Warren had been on the verge of accepting that maybe—*maybe*—there was a chance he'd been wrong. "Open up, you asshole!"

Ah, much better. That was the way things were supposed to be. Big, tough Chris would pound at the door and hurl insults until he got his way, only to play it off like he was the one who'd been wronged when a third party stepped in to intervene. If Warren hadn't been so pissed, he might've smiled. While he wasn't glad that Chris was still an asshole, it was good to know that he'd been right. "Fuck you. Bite me."

"Say that to my fucking face!"

"I am. I'm just doing it through a door. *My* door. AKA: a piece of my property you have no control over. And you know what? I kind of like it closed."

"Are you fucking serious right now?"

"No, but I could be if you give me his number."

"What the hell?" Chris sounded both disgusted and confused. "Open the damned door! *Liberty?!*"

Warren was a second away from telling him that Libby wouldn't be able to save him when she came barreling out of the living room like a stampeding bull. Warren yelped and leapt back to avoid a collision, which turned out to be the right thing to do, since Libby immediately filled the space he'd vacated and yanked the door open. On the other side was Chris, who glared over her shoulder at Warren.

"Chris," Libby said with a forced laugh. "You didn't tell me you were coming over. What an... unexpected surprise. I see you've met my roommate. Guess you can see why I warned you about him being so grumpy. He can get so surly when he doesn't get his beauty sleep."

If it'd been any colder outside, steam would've been visibly rising from Chris's head. Warren scoffed and opened his mouth to argue when Libby kicked her leg backward, almost slamming her heel into his groin. To save the family jewels, he leapt back and kept his distance, which was more than likely her intention.

It didn't stop Chris from glowering at him.

"I'm here because my son forgot his homework," Chris growled, ignoring everything Libby had said in favor of ocular homicide. "Apparently it's in your office. Could you please go get it for me? I'd come in and get it myself, but I'm not going to risk having another door slammed in my face."

There it was: the spin that'd make all this look like Warren's fault.

Which it *wasn't*.

Well, maybe it was a little bit, but it wasn't Warren's problem that Chris was butt-hurt over a door. He'd shown up without having texted first—what was he expecting, a parade?

"Doors *are* hard, aren't they?" Warren seethed in reply. Yeah, he was making things worse, but he'd be damned if he let Chris walk all over him as an adult, too. "Opening and closing at will—how does the world put up with them?"

Chris squared his jaw. "What the hell is your problem?"

Warren was a second away from replying, "You," when Libby whipped her head around and glared at him from over her shoulder. "Wren, you're not helping. We'll talk about this later, okay? Right now I need you to go get Jack's homework while I stay here with Chris. Got it?"

"Fine." Warren challenged Chris with his eyes one last time, then headed for Libby's office. Chris's gaze burned holes into his back the entire way there. Before stepping over the threshold, Warren lifted a hand and raised its middle finger high. Was it petty? Yeah. But at this point, he didn't give a fuck. Chris could suck his dick.

Not *that* way.

Although…

Ugh.

Before his lizard brain could get the best of him, he shut himself into Libby's office and out of sight of a fantasy that could never be.

There was a sheet of math homework tucked in between Libby's macramé scribblings. It didn't take long to find, partly because Libby liked to use cutesy stationary with fancy borders and pastel hues, and partly because her business dealings had very little to do with the even distribution of blueberry pancakes between Jill, Stacey, and Sally. It didn't hurt that her office was tiny. The short side of an L-shaped desk occupied the entire back wall opposite the door, and the longer side gave way with just enough space so she'd have clear passage into the room. The walls were covered with corkboard, onto which she'd pinned patterns, pictures of past products, and handwritten notes Warren didn't stop to investigate. The sooner he got Chris out of his neighborhood, the better.

Math homework rescued, Warren left macramé central and returned to the disaster by the front door. He handed the sheet to Libby, who delivered it to their unwelcome guest. Chris looked as pissed as ever, but he accepted the paper and stepped away from the door, boring into Warren with his eyes one last time before Libby stepped out after him and blocked him from view. Unfortunately, her body didn't shield Warren from their conversation.

"What the hell are you doing living with that jerk?" That had to be Chris, since Libby didn't sound like a man. Or an asshole. "I swear to god, if I find out he's said *anything* hurtful to Jack—"

"He hasn't."

"How can you be so sure? This is the guy who tried to ruin my life for no goddamn reason."

Oh, really?

How convenient for Chris to have forgotten every miserable thing he'd done to Warren while they were in school. Warren clenched his fists and was about to step forward when Libby shut the door. It was probably for the best. The less Warren saw Chris, the sooner he'd forget about him. Chris would know not to come back to the house without advance warning, and their lives would go in totally opposite directions. It'd be just like when they'd been in high school, only now they wouldn't have to share the same hallways. Apart, Warren could enjoy his crush in peace.

… Fuck.

It was *not* a crush. Not in the slightest. Not even if someone steamrolled the definition to stretch it paper-thin.

If anything, it was crush…ing anger.

Yeah, that was it.

Resentment.

Years of pent-up rage.

It was also the result of Warren's abysmal sex life and his three-year relationship dry spell. As soon as he got laid, he'd stop thinking about the look in Chris's eyes. The shape of his body. The way he'd feel on top of Warren while fucking him into submission…

"Christ," Warren muttered under his breath, half to himself and half to the erection getting up close and personal with the front of his sweatpants. He needed to get this under control before Libby came back in and dragged him into the pantry. The last thing he needed was for her to connect the dots.

No one could know.

No one.

Which was how Warren found himself coming hard into his hand not even five minutes later in the privacy of his bedroom, Chris's extremely punchable face in the forefront of his mind.

7

CHRIS

Liberty stepped outside and closed the door, the porch light catching all her flyaways and spinning them into gold. All she was wearing was a t-shirt—Warren's, by the look of it. It was far too big for her, and bunched when she crossed her arms over her chest. The chilly night air locked in around them, but the shiver that coursed up Chris's spine and brought him to pinch his shoulders wasn't related to the temperature. The sight of Warren had set him on edge, reawakening sour feelings he'd shelved years ago.

"Well?" Chris asked when Liberty failed to speak. "How can you know he hasn't said or done anything to hurt Jack?"

Liberty sighed and dipped her head, tucking her cheek against her shoulder. Her arms remained crossed, but her body language didn't come across as aggressive. If anything, she looked sad.

"I know because he's my best friend," Liberty said softly. "I get that things between you are... *weird*... but I promise Warren's not a bad guy."

It was like she wasn't grasping the entirety of the situation. Chris prickled, but he tried not to let it show. If Jack saw them fighting, it'd mean having an uncomfortable conversation that Chris would rather avoid. "I don't care what kind of a person he is to you, or to his parents, or even to the guy down the street. I care about the kind of guy I *know* he is, and that's the kind who's gone out of his way to hurt me in the past. Why should I believe you when you say he's not going to do anything to Jack?"

Liberty lifted her head. Her shoulders sagged. "Because he's not a monster. What happened was a mistake."

"A mistake?" Chris choked back a laugh. "Lib, you don't just trip and fall onto your keyboard and 'oops!' doucheweasel. He did what he did on purpose. It wasn't an accident."

"He didn't mean for it to go viral," Liberty bit back. It wasn't like her to argue, and the conviction in her voice disarmed him. "You weren't exactly great to him, either, you know. He suffered in silence for years before doing this, and, yeah, that doesn't mean that it was okay for him to retaliate, but you know what? He needed to get it out. It was supposed to be a blip on the internet that went away forever. It's not his fault it turned into a thing."

The sound of a car door opening stopped Chris from replying. Jack climbed out of the car and stood hesitantly by the curb, his hands tucked into the sleeves of his sweatshirt. "Dad?"

"I'm okay, champ. I'll be there in a sec." Chris turned his focus onto Liberty. "I need to go. We can pick this up later. Thanks for the homework."

"You're welcome. Just, before you go... know that time changes people." Liberty met his eyes and held his gaze. "It's changed you, it's changed Free, and it's sure as hell changed him. If you'd just give him a chance, you'd see it. We're not the kids we used to be."

Chris shook his head and looked away. "Goodnight, Liberty."

Liberty sighed. "Goodnight."

Chris left her where she stood and headed for his SUV, but no matter how far he got, he couldn't separate himself from what she'd said. Yeah, things were different now, but not *that* different. Time was more likely to strip someone down and expose their true colors than it was to fundamentally change them. That's what had

44

happened with Free. At his core, Warren would always be the jackass who'd dragged Chris's name through the mud.

Chris took one last look at the house once he'd reached the car. An upstairs light had blinked on since he'd arrived. Warren strode into view, and Chris had a second to get a good look at his enemy before he drew the curtains closed. The quiet, kind of weird kid Chris had never paid much attention to in high school was gone. In his place stood a man—solid, athletic... handsome.

The curtains closed and Chris turned his head away.

It didn't matter what Warren looked like, because Chris was going to do everything in his power never to see him again.

"Was Aunt Libby mad?" Jack asked when Chris climbed back into the car and handed him his homework.

Chris shook his head. "No. She knew it was just a mistake."

"Good. I was really worried." Jack sighed in relief and sank into his seat much less glumly than before. "When we get home, can I watch YouTube before bed?"

"Nope."

"Please?"

"Negative."

"Daaaaad."

Chris turned the keys in the engine. "You can catch up on YouTube tomorrow. When we get home, you're putting your home-work in your schoolbag, then going straight to bed."

Jack grumped and grumbled, but in the end did what he was told. Chris was less easily settled. Cold pizza and thoughts of a boy he'd used to know kept him up late into the night.

The Howard County Sheriff's Department was housed in a small brick building at the end of the east bank's section of Main Street, distinguishable from those around it by the weatherworn brass letters affixed above the entryway. Despite having spent his childhood in Lethridge, Chris had never been inside, and he found himself less than impressed. Not only was the lobby small, but it smelled dusty and somehow also artificially floral. It wasn't long before he discovered the source of both scents—an ancient creature stationed behind the front desk whose nameplate read "Kathleen." She peered at him from behind Coke-bottle glasses, which she adjusted a moment later as if to get a second opinion on whether he was really there.

"Howard County Sheriff's Department," she said while squinting. "How may I help you?"

"Is, uh, is Sheriff Sinclair available?" Chris asked. "He asked me to come in for a one-o'clock appointment. Name's Chris Donnelly."

"Crista Nelly?" Kathleen's eyes narrowed. "Sounds made up to me. You're a hooligan, aren't you?" The old phone on her desk was out of its cradle a second later. Grandma could *move.* She held the receiver like a weapon, no doubt waiting for the chance to call in reinforcements who'd bust Chris's hooligan ass. "We don't take too kindly to those types around here."

Chris held up both hands in surrender. "No, ma'am. You've got the wrong idea. My name's Christian, not Crista. Christian Donnelly. I'm here about a job."

"Chrissy-Anne?"

"Christian."

Kathleen glowered and held the phone to her ear. "Stevie? There's a troublemaker here to see you calling himself Kristen. You'd better come out quick. I don't like the looks of him."

Chris's eye twitched. This... wasn't going well. It was no wonder the application had been online only. At least Sheriff Sinclair was on the way. When he saw what was going on, he'd understand.

Sure enough, Sinclair emerged from one of the back rooms with his brow furrowed and his lips pinched, but relaxed upon spotting Chris. He was a little fuller than Chris remembered, both in body and in mustache. The former strained the buttons of his shirt, each one a potential piece of plastic shrapnel that'd no doubt assault

Chris when he was least expecting it. The latter twitched jauntily as Sinclair smiled. "Chris! Thanks for comin' in."

"Thank you for having me."

Kathleen looked between the two of them, then scrutinized Chris with increased intensity.

"It's all right, Mom." Sinclair clapped her on the shoulder, startling her. "I invited Chris here. If all goes well, he'll be taking over Erika's dispatch shift."

Kathleen made a small, somewhat curt sound of acknowledgment, then scowled and set her sights on Chris anew. While she didn't say anything, she kept a close eye on him and mouthed, "I'm watching you."

"You ready to come on back?" Steve asked him. "I'm sure you've got some questions for me, and I'll be glad to answer 'em."

Anything to get out from beneath the watchful eye of the department's guard dog. Chris nodded, and off they went through the door Sinclair had come from, leaving the lobby behind.

Sinclair had a small, cluttered office. Paperwork was stacked haphazardly in a wooden cubby-style organizer on his desk, in piles next to his desktop computer, and—curiously—on the seat of his office chair. Chris watched without saying a word while Sinclair moved his chairwork onto the dusty top of a mini fridge and took a seat. The chair groaned beneath his weight.

How much paperwork did the sheriff of a town of less than a thousand people have to do? Apparently everyone in Lethridge led a life of hardened crime.

"So, here's the deal," Sinclair said as he folded his hands over his belly. His buttons glinted menacingly in the office's fluorescent light, daring Chris to play a game of chicken he wasn't confident he'd win. "We're losing a member of our dispatch team, and we need someone to take her place—someone with a good understanding of

Howard County and the surrounding areas. Our emergency services here in Lethridge respond to calls in every Howard County town and all the remote parts in between, and when shit really goes south, we'll sometimes dispatch medivac services to neighboring counties. Since we're so rural out here, when we get folks callin' up to report they've been in an accident on Highway 9, we need a dispatcher who'll be able to pinpoint their location based on landmarks, not street signs. With the Donnelly family havin' been a fixture in town for as long as they have, I figured you'd be the perfect candidate.

"The position is full-time and offers medical benefits after six months. Shifts rotate every two weeks—we've got two other dispatchers on staff. Sick days and vacation time are covered by local volunteers. As per an agreement with the state, you'll be paid for forty hours of training—enough to cover certification for medical, fire, and police dispatching. Typically you'd need two years of experience to qualify for long-term employment, but the state is willing to waive the requirement for 'outstanding' experience, and I'll eat my hat if they don't accept you based on your service to our country."

Sinclair was not wearing a hat.

"Funding for emergency services in rural areas is lackin', but we do our best to make sure our men and women are compensated fairly for their time." Sinclair pulled a folder from a previously unseen stack behind his monitor and handed it to Chris. "You won't find a better offer for a hundred miles, at least."

Chris opened the folder and looked at the documentation inside. Amongst the standard paperwork he'd need to fill out for book-keeping purposes was a description of his job duties, expectations, opt-ins, and salary. The figure was on par with what he'd made while in the Army—which wasn't all that much without his bonuses and allowances, but would keep him and Jack going regardless. "The training you mentioned—can I do it here in town?"

Sinclair shook his head. "We'll be shipping you off to Des Moines."

That was a problem. Jack was a tough kid, and under normal circumstances he'd be able to tolerate a week apart, but the last few months had been anything but normal. Worse, Chris would have to lean on Liberty for help while he was away, and that meant leaving Jack with the asshole who lived with her.

He looked at the documents in his hands, then at Sinclair, who was reclined in his chair and watching him from over his mustache. The sheriff was right—if he didn't take this offer, it wasn't likely he'd find another job offering what this one paid, not to mention the medical benefits. Yes, he was worried about Jack, but he'd be a hell of a lot more worried if he turned down the job and Jack broke his leg, or hit his head, or succumbed to his horrible cooking.

"Will I be working at this location?" Chris asked at length.

Sinclair laughed. "In my office? No. But if you join the team, you'll be workin' in this buildin'. All our emergency services are based here—fire and EMT units are in the back with their street-facing entrance over on Grand, but we all share a central common room. There's a dispatch office tucked away between here and there."

"Great." As long as he didn't have to travel to work every day, that was fine. "If I sign on, how soon until I'm expected to go to training?"

"Next week good for ya?"

It'd take a little bit of finesse and a stern word or two with Liberty, but for Jack's sake, Chris figured he could make it work.

8

WARREN

The mini-weasel peered at Warren. Warren peered at the mini-weasel. What he'd done to deserve a child's scrutiny, Warren didn't know. It was going on one in the afternoon during one of the rare times he had a Saturday off, and all he'd been trying to do was enjoy a little peace and quiet in the living room while he snacked on the knockoff Thin Mints Libby had bought for him as reparation for her charge's gluttony.

Actually, scratch that. Clarity dawned on him. He *did* know why Jack was staring him down.

The kid was fiending for his cookies.

Warren removed the box from his lap and put it on the arm of the couch. Jack's eyes followed.

He pushed the box onto the end table. Jack took a small step closer.

To keep the little mint maniac from committing grand theft Thin Mint, Warren adjusted his position so he was seated cross-legged on the couch, his back to the couch's arm to block the cookies from view. Slowly—very slowly—the mini-weasel draped himself over the opposite arm and slithered in Warren's direction.

When he was one seat cushion away, he stopped and looked up at Warren with big, unfairly adorable eyes. "Whatcha thinkin' about?"

What Warren wanted to say was, "Murder"—Libby's, of course, since it'd been her who'd given Chris the okay to park his Thin Mint loving kid here for the week—but that wasn't child-appropriate, so he settled on, "Adult stuff."

"What kinda adult stuff?"

"The most dreaded and feared kind."

Jack scrunched his nose. "Taxes?"

"Worse. Responsibility."

"Gross."

"Yup."

Seemingly placated by the response, Jack continued his slow crawl across the couch and gingerly laid his chin on Warren's knee. Warren stared at him. "You okay, kid?"

"*No.*"

"What's wrong?"

"I'm bored." Jack stuck out his tongue, which he very nearly pressed against Warren's pants. Warren virtually recoiled in horror. "Do you wanna play a game with me?"

If it meant escaping contact with a mini-weasel's germy tongue, Warren was down for just about anything. "What kind of game?"

Jack thrust a tablet in Warren's direction that had seemingly appeared out of nowhere. "It's a game me and my dad play sometimes, but I forget all the rules, so you should message my dad and ask."

Warren narrowed a single eye and looked at the tablet suspiciously. He hadn't forgotten the way Jack had been looking at his Thin Mints. "You're trying to trick me, aren't you?"

"*No!*"

"Are you lying?"

Jack's lips wobbled as he held off a laugh that only just made it into his voice. "*Maybe.*"

"You're a troublemaker." Still, against his better judgment, he took the tablet. Weasel spawn or not, there was no way Jack would be able to sneak off with Warren's cookies in the few seconds it'd take to send Chris a message. Which was weird to think about. *Very* weird. But it wasn't like he was going to make a habit out of it, and besides, Chris would never know it was him. All correspondence would be made through Jack's account, and it would only last long enough for Warren to get a feel for whatever game it was they liked to play.

An app called Messenger Kids was already open on Jack's tablet. As far as Warren could tell, it was exactly like Facebook Messenger, but with fewer sex bots. The top conversation, and the one preselected on the screen, was with an individual nicknamed "Dad" that used Chris's Facebook display picture. The image was small enough that Warren wasn't forced to weather the intensity of his eyes, but his stomach lurched and his heart flipped all the same.

In a bid to distract himself, Warren read the last few messages exchanged between "Dad" and Jack.

Jack: Dad
Jack: Daaaaad
Jack: Dad
Jack: Dad Dad Dad
Dad: What?
Jack: I can't sleep, any tips?
Dad: Maybe stop messaging me, you goob
Jack: But I wasn't messaging you when I was trying to sleep, only after I found out I couldn't
Jack: Do you think I could come sit with you in the living room for a little?
Dad: Okay, but not too long. You've got school tomorrow

"Are you looking through my messages?" Jack piped gleefully two messages from the end of the conversation, like it'd been his plan all along to turn Warren to the dark side with his cuteness. "That's pretty rude, you know."

"No."

"Are you *lying?*"

"*Maybe.*"

Jack burst out laughing, giving Warren time to finish snooping. The last two messages were timestamped from earlier that morning. Jack had sent Chris a sticker of two cartoon cats hugging captioned "love you" above and "miss you" below. Chris had sent a similar sticker back. A heart sticker didn't change Warren's mind about him being evil, but it was nice to see that even douchiweasels could be sweet.

Before his brain could twist that revelation in a ridiculous thought, Warren shot Chris a message. He figured it likely that Chris would be too busy to answer, so he handed the tablet back to Jack only for the device to beep as it received a new message.

Jack handed the tablet right back. "Since you sent the message, you should answer."

"And you *swear* this isn't a trick?" Warren narrowed his eyes. "You're not trying to nab my cookies, are you?"

"No!" The only way Jack could look any more angelic was if he grew wings. It was too bad his halo was propped up with little horns. "I promise I'm not."

"Not what?"

Jack grinned widely. "Nab your cookies."

As a victim of weasels much more skilled than the one he was sharing the couch with, Warren was wise to his tricks. He narrowed his eyes further, making Jack laugh. "Nope. I'm on to you. Say it all together."

"Say what?"

"That you're not trying to nab my cookies."

Jack snickered.

"You can't say it, can you?" Warren set the tablet on his lap and held Jack's gaze, playfully putting him on the spot. A hint of a grin peaked one corner of his lips. Yeah, the kid was trouble, but he was cuter and more innocent than Chris had ever been—probably due to his Owens genes. Warren and Libby were best friends forever for a reason, after all. "I caught you, you lying liar."

"I'm not lying!"

"Then say it."

Jack gave him a shit-eating grin straight out of Chris's playbook. "It."

"No! I mean—"

"I said what you wanted me to say." Jack wiggled an eyebrow and hopped off the couch, no doubt to run his victory lap. It was, admittedly, embarrassing to be bested at mental jousting by an eight-year-old, but Warren wasn't yet down for the count. He snatched the box of cookies and set them in the hollow of his lap, which he covered with Jack's tablet. He'd like to see the kid get them now.

While Jack ran circuits around the couch, Warren returned his attention to the conversation.

Jack: What are the rules to that game we always play?
Dad: What game?

It looked like Chris was equally as baffled. Good to know he wasn't alone. Warren shot him back a message.

Jack: The one we play all the time
Dad: I'm not sure what game you're thinking of
Dad: Are you talking about a video game?

"Your dad wants to know if you're talking about a video game," Warren relayed.

Jack's thudding footsteps slowed. He rounded the couch and came to stand in front of Warren again, his lips scrunched to the side. A section of his hair had fallen across his brow and partially obscured one of his eyes, but he didn't seem to have noticed. "Mm,

55

no, it's not *really* a video game. If you give me the tablet back, maybe I can talk to him and figure it out. It's too hard to explain in person."

"Okay…" Warren handed it over. He still wasn't convinced it wasn't all a ploy to get his cookies. Jack was cute, but he was also cunning. If Warren was going to make it out of this with sweets to spare, he was going to have to stay on his toes. "Couldn't you just have done that in the first place?"

A wicked twinkle in Jack's eyes clipped his wings. He pushed his hair away from his brow and sprang across the room, tablet in hand, to shelter beneath Libby's newest hammock. While he touched base with Papa Weasel, Warren unfurled his legs and contemplated safe places to store what remained of his Thin Mints. Jack was clever enough that the top shelf of the pantry wouldn't cut it—he could knock them down by climbing onto the step stool and swiping at them with a broom. Maybe he could take the sleeve out and hide them in an open box of saltine crackers. Or maybe—

"Wren?" Jack asked, half an inch away from Warren's ear.

Warren almost hit the ceiling. Holy *shit*, the kid was sneaky. Where had he come from? It was no wonder why so many horror movies starred creepy kids—Jack wasn't even possessed and he'd still almost sent Warren into cardiac arrest.

Too spooked to answer right away, Warren turned his head slowly to look at the little hellion bent on ending his life. Jack had folded his hands behind his back and was standing on his toes, like he was waiting not-so-patiently for Warren to give him permission to speak. "Yes?"

"My dad says that the game is too complicated to explain, and that you should send him a message from your phone." Jack summoned a scrap of paper into being, which he whipped out from behind his back and presented to Warren. On it was a string of irregularly crafted digits that fitted a third-grade boy's penmanship. Where the hell had he gotten a pencil from? Maybe the whole possessed kid thing wasn't such a stretch. "This is his phone number. You should text him to say hello."

Oh.

Warren looked at the scrap of paper.

Jack's scheme had never been about the cookies, had it?

He looked from the paper to Jack, whose eyes sparkled with hope, and pushed a slow sigh through his nostrils. But before he could let the kid down, Libby burst out of her office and made a beeline for her nephew.

"Jack!" She stopped running and slid the rest of the way on her socks. Jack whirled around to face her just in time for Libby to give him a noogie. "I just remembered it's Saturday. You know what happens on Saturday?"

"What?"

"*Puppies.*"

Judging by Jack's lack of reaction, Warren wasn't the only one struggling to follow her train of thought.

"At Pick of the Litter Pet Center. It's the pet shop in town. On Saturdays they schedule puppy play dates, which are like, the best thing ever. You wanna go meet some cute puppies?"

Her enthusiasm was contagious enough that Jack seemed to forget all about Warren. "Are there really puppies there?"

"Yup!"

"What about wiener dog puppies?"

Libby somehow managed to shrug while replying with more excitement than ever, "Maybe! Who knows? It's a puppy grab bag. *Mystery* puppies. All puppies all the time. Well, except for the Saturday I tried to bring my raccoon, but that's a story for another time. You wanna go put on your shoes while I put on some normal people clothes?" As usual, Libby was in her work uniform—pajamas. "We don't have that much time before the play date is over, so we've gotta go fast."

"Okay!"

Warren sat perfectly still and watched as both of them flew into action. Libby ran for the stairs, at the top of which she'd find her room and, in it, her normal people clothes, and Jack bolted for the front door and the shoe rack next to it, which he'd kicked his sneakers under. Amongst the ensuing laughter and chaos, Jack dropped the scrap of paper. It fluttered to the living room floor, where it stayed until both Jack and Libby were out the door and well on their way to their puppy play date. Warren was wise enough to know not to interrupt when an Owens was on the move. It was a shame that Jack had his heart set on something that wouldn't happen, Warren thought as he collected the scrap paper and walked it to the recycling bin, but it was better that Warren had nothing to do with Chris. If their friendship had been meant to be, it would've crystallized years ago. The truth was, they were two entirely different people who would never get along, no matter how much a cute kid insisted otherwise.

Nope.

Not happening.

But when he came to a stop in front of the recycling bin, he found it difficult to let go. With information like this, he could...

Well...

He could prank Chris.

Yeah, that was it.

Prank him.

Warren flexed the paper between his fingers and ran the pad of his thumb across its surface. There were tons of websites out there greedy for phone numbers, and he could subscribe Chris to *all* of them. It wasn't like he was looking for an excuse to keep it for himself. This was his best—and maybe only—chance to see that justice was served. Chris would have no way to prove it was him, just like Warren had had no way to prove Chris had been targeting him all those years ago.

But...

Warren sighed.

It wouldn't be right to start harassing Chris now. As much as he hated the guy, it'd been years since Chris had last been an asshat to him. Well, apart from that time last week when he'd opened the door and found Chris on the doorstep, but those had been extenuating circumstances. Warren was mature enough to admit it.

So why didn't he want to throw the phone number away?

Warren traced the digits on the paper with his eyes. The nine that capped the sequence was jagged, and there was a wobble in its tail, like Jack had been in such a rush to finish that he'd yanked the paper away before lifting the pencil. The emotion in his eyes when he'd handed it to Warren... the unencumbered innocence. At a glance, the kid was his father's stunt double, but that was where their similarities ended.

Those eyes.

Those eyes were Chris's, but they didn't belong to him. It was foolish to think that the friendliness there would carry between father and son. Everything was still wrong between them, and if Warren let Jack poison his perception, he'd only make it harder for himself.

He tossed the paper into the bin.

Chris—like most evil beings—was sexy as hell, but Warren's dick wasn't going to win this fight. He had principles. Standards. Morals. Besides, Warren was one of the good guys, and good guys didn't feed anyone's number to robocallers. Not even numbers that belonged to doucheweasels. It was better that he walk away.

Warren abandoned the recycling bin and the number in it to head back to the living room, where his knockoff Thin Mints were waiting. Chocolate would never betray him. With a little cocoa therapy, he'd forget all about Chris, and...

The box was gone.

What. The. Fuck.

Warren dropped to his knees and checked under the couch, scanned the end table with increasing desperation, then finally pulled off all the cushions and pillows, hoping he'd find it wedged in the place where remotes went to die.

Nothing.

Not a single minty crumb.

There was only one rational explanation—the "innocent" mini-weasel who'd been this close to bringing him to the dark side had run off with them all. What was that he'd said about similarities between father and son? Maybe they ran a little deeper than he'd originally thought.

9

CHRIS

Downtown Des Moines sparkled at night. Rows of windows lit up its buildings like the buttons in an elevator, shining white and gold against the inky, starless sky. By day the magnificence of the city was overlooked thanks to busy streets and packed schedules, but at night it was unmistakable. Chris soaked in the sights from his hotel window, from the golden-yellow grandeur of the tallest building on the horizon to the cool blue splendor of a squat high-rise that peeked over a few shorter buildings in between. None of it was short of incredible. It didn't matter how long he spent away from home—at heart he was a small-town boy; the city would always impress him.

His enjoyment was cut short when his phone chimed. His delivery driver had arrived. Chris went to greet him at the door, then carted his food back to the bed and unpacked his meal on the bedside table. Tonight he'd gone for lo mein. The little white box let out a puff of steam when he opened it, so while Chris waited for it to cool, he turned on the television for background noise and checked in on his son.

Chris: Do anything fun today?

Jack: Hi Dad

Chris: Hey champ

Jack: I did a really fun thing today. You'll never guess what it was

With Liberty around, Chris didn't doubt it.

Chris: What?

Jack: Me and Aunt Libby went to see puppies, and I got to pet a lot of them

Jack: Some were really cute

Chris: Yeah?

Jack: Yeah

Jack: When I'm older I'm going to live in a place where I can get a dog, and he'll be my best friend

Ah, the subtle art of a guilt trip. It was a good thing Free had already braced him for it—Chris still remembered the bitching she'd done behind the scenes when taking care of Jack's old hamster, Cheeks, had become her responsibility, and he wasn't about to saddle himself with raising a puppy while adjusting to life as a single dad.

Chris: Okay. When you have a place of your own, you can do that. Just remember that dogs are a lot of work

Jack: I know

Jack: What did you do today?

Chris yawned and settled against the headboard, propping pillows around him to make himself more comfortable.

Chris: I went to class. I need to work hard every day to learn as much as I can so I can graduate and get something called ED-Q certification. That's the only way I'll be able to work at my new job. But now I'm back in my room for the day and getting ready to eat dinner.

Jack: Oh.

Jack: Dinner???

Jack: It's late

Chris: Yup.

Jack: What are you having?

Chris: Lo mein. It's a kind of Chinese food

Jack: Oh

Jack: you know who else likes Chinese food?

Chris did not. Neither Free nor Jack cared for it.

Chris: Who?

Jack: A guy I met that maybe you can be friends with

Jack: I told him you and him would go out for dinner soon

That… wasn't right. Chris squinted, hoping that if he read Jack's last few messages more carefully, he'd figure out the typo, but there was none to be found.

Jack had set him up on a playdate.

Joy.

Chris took a deep breath and tilted his head back, only stopping when it bumped the headboard. Jack was a sensitive kid with a big heart who'd inherited his mother's too-much gene. It wasn't like he'd put Chris in an awkward position on purpose. He'd seen a chance to help Chris make a friend, and he'd taken it.

When Chris looked at his phone again, Jack had added a few messages to their conversation.

Jack: He's really, really nice, I promise. You'll like him.

Jack: Here's his phone number.

The phone number he'd posted looked real, Lethridge area code and all. Whoever it belonged to must have fallen victim to Jack's puppy-dog eyes and complied with his demands to keep from breaking his heart. Not that Chris could blame him. The kid was smart—Jack knew he was cute, and he used it to his advantage.

Jack: Will you go to dinner with him, Dad? That way you'll have a new friend

The truth emerged. Chris pushed a noisy snort through his nose and reached for his lo mein, shoveling a few forkfuls into his face before he replied.

Chris: It was nice of you to help me out like that, champ. I'll take it from here. In the future, I'd really appreciate it if you could trust me to make my own friends. You know how sometimes you don't get along with everyone in class?
Jack: Yeah
Chris: It's like that for adults, too. There are some adults who don't get along. I wouldn't want to go out to dinner with someone I don't get along with
Jack: That makes sense. I'll try not to do that again
Chris: Thank you
Jack: You're welcome!
Jack: Aunt Libby says I have to go get ready for bed now. Night, Dad
Chris: Sweet dreams

The green dot at the bottom of Jack's display picture turned gray. Chris finished off the last of his dinner, then sank into bed and stared at the popcorn ceiling. What was he going to do about the guy Jack had roped into his friendship scheme? If he was a local like his number suggested, it wouldn't be a bad idea to reach out and thank him. In a town as small as theirs, there was a good chance he'd run into him while out one day with Jack. It'd be worth his time to reach out and avoid a potentially awkward situation rather than let it go unchecked and suffer for it later. Besides, it wouldn't take much. A single text would do.

Chris kicked off his socks and ditched his jeans, then, once he was settled, sent the message.

Chris: Hey, this is Chris. You gave your number to my son, Jack, while you were out today. It was kind of you to do. Thanks for being such a good sport, but don't worry—you're off the hook for dinner ;)

The indicator at the bottom of the screen went from sent, to received, to read. It showed the person on the other end was typing, then that they'd stopped. After a tense minute of on again, off again, a short message arrived.

Unknown Name: You're kidding me

That wasn't the kind of reply Chris had been expecting.
He frowned.

Chris: Sorry, I'm not sure what you're getting at. What do you mean?
Unknown Name: Block this number

Tone was hard to convey through text, but Chris couldn't help but get the feeling that the guy he was talking to was pissed.

Chris: Excuse me?
Unknown Name: Oh my god, you're trying to mess with my head again, aren't you?
Unknown Name: I don't know how I can make it any more clear—block this number

Yeah, he was pissed all right.

What the hell was his problem?

Chris's frown pinched in at the corners and he furrowed his brow. Had he been a dick? He scrolled back up to read his original message, but no—there wasn't anything aggressive about it. Chris had even put an emoji, for fuck's sake. An *emoji*. And not the upside-down sarcastic one, either.

Chris: What the hell is your problem? I wasn't anything but nice to you
Unknown Name: Guess now you know how it feels
Unknown Name: Look, I'm not joking. Block. This.
Number.

What kind of an asshole met a little kid, gave him his phone number, then went out of his way to be an asshole when someone dared message him? Adrenaline heated Chris up from the inside.

Fuck this guy.

Fuck him hard.

If this was the way he treated people his own age, how big of an insufferable bastard had he been to Jack?

Chris wasn't going to let it slide.

Chris: Suck my dick, asshole
Unknown Name: Really?
Unknown Name: You really want to go there?
Unknown Name: Fine. You want it so bad, I'll do you one better and show you what a real asshole looks like while I'm doing it. You know any places that sell mirrors your size?
Chris: Fuck off
Unknown Name: No. I'm not going to be quiet anymore.
Unknown Name: You don't scare me.

The same swirling, pulsing heat that filled Chris with the will to fight tinged with irritation. It curled in his stomach and shot into his head, grating at the back of his mind like a mouse gnawing on drywall. Simultaneously, some of that rage plunged south and clenched in Chris's groin. His cock throbbed to the beat of his heart.

If the fucker wanted a fight, he'd get one.

He jabbed the call button at the top of the screen. The call connected, then almost immediately dropped. A text followed a quick second later.

Unknown Name: Don't fucking call me!

Chris: Not scared, huh?

Chris: Guess it's not hard to be brave when you're hiding behind a keyboard.

Unknown Name: You're a psycho

Unknown Name: All I asked was that you block my number and you go off on me? What's brave about that? Thank you for reminding me that you're not any different than you were when we were in school. It sure is good to know that some things never change.

Recognition flashed through Chris hotter than his anger. Determined to see if he was right, he jabbed the call button again. The call connected and was disconnected just as quickly—it seemed an awful lot like the guy on the other end didn't want Chris to hear his prerecorded voicemail message, which meant it was someone Chris had spoken with since coming back to town.

There was only one asshole who fit the bill.

Unknown Name: I said stop calling me!

Chris: Afraid I'll recognize your voice, Warren?

Chris: I'm done with all the bullshit. It's time we finish this like men

WARREN

Chris: You, me, my apartment. One in the afternoon this Thursday.
Chris: If you're not afraid, prove it

An address populated the screen.

Chris wasn't messing around.

Down the hall, Libby and Jack were on their way to the guest bedroom. The bright notes of their voices drew near. As they approached, Warren bolted across his bedroom and made sure the door was locked, then collapsed into bed and did his best to figure out what the hell he was going to do. It wasn't like he could show up at Chris's apartment—that was how people got murdered. But if Warren didn't show up, then what? He'd prove to Chris that he could get away with anything he wanted, up to and including using his son for his twisted narcissistic mind games. It hadn't escaped him that on the exact same day Jack had tried to give Warren his phone number, Chris had mysteriously gotten in touch. It was a little too convenient. Why, all of a sudden, would Jack decide to hand out his dad's phone number? Chris had to have had a hand in it. Like a true weasel, he wasn't happy unless he was causing prob-lems, and Warren was an easy target. The more he thought about it, the clearer the truth became. When he'd failed to reach out through text, Chris had taken it upon himself to track down his number and come up with some bullshit story to establish contact while making himself look innocent. It was the same old song and dance he'd performed when they were in school.

It was too bad Warren wasn't interested in the production.

Curtain call was coming. Warren needed to put an end to Chris's act for good.

What was Chris going to do, anyway? Actually murder him? Pound his face in? Break his bones? Yeah, he was an asshole, but he wasn't stupid. There was no way he'd risk jail time when he had a kid at home. And it wasn't like he'd set up camp in the middle of nowhere. Judging by his address, he lived in the Delmar Apartment Complex. If things got too loud, someone would call the cops and it'd be Chris who'd suffer the consequences.

Warren didn't have anything to be afraid of.

The ball was in his court now—after years of yielding to Chris, it was his turn to decide how they played the game.

The summer of Warren's fourteenth birthday, he'd heard a rumor that someone living in the Delmar Apartment Complex was a mobster in the witness protection program. For the next few weeks, he and Libby had scoped out the three buildings on the lot, analyzing the people who came and went while they tried to find "the one." In the end, they never determined if the rumor was true, but they'd learned enough about the people in the apartments to not really want to come back. For one, they were boring—the majority of them were adults who followed predictable schedules and never did anything out of the ordinary. For two...

Well.

The ones who weren't boring were a little *too* interesting, and after an encounter with a skinny man and something that probably wasn't Pixy Stix, neither Warren nor Libby were inclined to return.

In the sixteen years bridging that time, the Delmar Apartment Complex had further declined. Ivy crept unchecked up the back and sides of one of its buildings, but the neglect didn't end there—a couple of its windows were visibly broken, and the concrete stairs leading to its main entrance had started to chip and crumble. The second building on the lot was likewise in a state of obvious disrepair. Two broken windows, crumbling mortar, and a few very strange stains originating from a top-floor window pocked the facade. The third apartment—the one Chris lived in—was no better off. Its balconies were rusted and worn, cluttered with sun-bleached junk that looked like it'd been left there by the building's very first tenants. The concrete steps had started to settle and become uneven. The door was propped open by a stray brick. If there hadn't been a kid in the equation, Warren would've considered it karma that someone as toxic as Chris had wound up living in a dump, but now all he felt was anger. What the hell was Chris's problem that he'd quit his job and move into a place like this? How selfish did he have to be to rob his son of a better quality of life so he could take it easy in his middle-of-nowhere hometown? That sense of indignation swelled as Warren climbed the stairs to the third floor and smelled something thick, stale, and humid in the air. Mold? Maybe. Whatever it was, the place was a fucking hazard, and no kid deserved to be exposed to it.

By the time Warren arrived at Chris's door, he was pissed.

When he knocked, he was furious.

But when the door opened and Chris dragged him into the apartment by the front of his shirt, then threw him against the door as it slammed shut, Warren's blood boiled.

"You fucking narcissist," he snarled once he'd caught his breath.

71

Chris loomed in front of him, all muscle and goddamn scowls. Thick, dark hair Warren wanted to pull. Coarse stubble. Rough lips. Broad shoulders. "You goddamn arrogant piece of shit, using Jack like a pawn and making him live in a place like this."

"What the fuck are you talking about?"

"Like you don't know?" Warren went to push off the door, but Chris planted a hand in the middle of his chest and held him in place. The second he did, Warren made a grab at Chris's shirt, but Chris caught him by the wrist and squeezed. He stepped forward and forced Warren's arm to the side, pinning it. When Warren struggled, Chris only tightened his grip. Damn, he was strong. Warren's face crumpled with effort as he tried to jerk his arm away, but Chris wouldn't let go. Frustration. Anger. Rage. It sparked and popped inside of him, tightening his stomach and clenching his balls. What he wouldn't give to punch Chris in the face, pull his hair, bite the irritatingly gorgeous line of his jaw... yet simultaneously despised himself for it. This was the man who'd made his life hell, and who was now letting his little boy live in squalor.

Fuck him.

Fuck him hard.

It didn't matter what Warren's dick wanted when his brain knew better.

He balled a fist, wanting to act on his impulses, but before he could so much as twitch, Chris seized him by the wrist and pinned it, just like he had the first. Without his hand on Warren's chest, Warren was able to move, but Chris didn't give him the luxury of freedom for long—he wedged his knee between Warren's legs, one jerk away from sending it crashing into his balls.

Games like these—raw acts of dominance and posturing—always turned Warren on, and this time was no exception. His cock thickened, and he hated himself for it. As angry as he was, he couldn't escape the thought of Chris dragging him by the hair deeper into the apartment, throwing him down, and fucking him hard from behind.

"Listen," Chris growled, leaning in so close that Warren felt the heat of his words against his earlobe. "I'm only going to say this once. If I find out you've said anything hurtful to Jack, *anything*, I will fucking kill you."

"You wouldn't dare."

"Is that a game you really want to play, Reaves?"

A shiver shot down Warren's spine. Chris was a beast. An animal. A wild thing that couldn't be tamed. One wrong move and he'd snap his jaws, yet Warren couldn't help but want it—the power, the devastation, the brutal and unforgiving masculinity. He wanted to feel the scratch of Chris's stubble against his neck, smell the spiced notes of soap that clung close to his skin, know his teeth and their bite.

To be utterly at his mercy.

His heart raced. Sweat began to bead on his brow. He contested Chris's grip and came up short again. In retaliation, Chris slammed his hands into the door and growled in warning like the apex predator he was.

Fuck, was it hot.

Warren drew a shaky breath through his teeth and tried to think of something—anything—else, but with Chris right there on top of him, it was impossible. His mind could object as much as it wanted, but right now his body was running the show.

"All this bullshit needs to stop," Chris uttered, the dull crescents of his nails digging into Warren's skin. Warren clenched his jaw and closed his eyes, but didn't make a sound. He wouldn't give Chris the satisfaction of a groan. "I don't know why you hate me so much, but get the fuck over it. We aren't kids anymore."

"Why I hate you?" Warren snarled. The round of Chris's knee tucked itself closer to his groin, but the promise of pain wouldn't silence him. He'd waited too long for this and wanted it too badly. "You made my life a living hell, and every time you did, you covered your tracks so it'd never look like you did it on purpose. Did you think I wouldn't realize that every time something bad happened to me, it was because of you? You fooled everyone else, but you'll never fool me. You were a bully and an asshole back then, and guess what? Time hasn't changed a thing."

A thick silence wedged itself between them. It weighed on Warren's chest and constricted his lungs, keeping him from taking a satisfying breath. Chaotic energy fizzled in the air and teased the hairs on his arms into standing on end.

"You think I'm a bully?" Chris's voice was the tumbling first pebble preceding a rockslide—a subtle warning of trouble to come. His stubble brushed the edge of Warren's jaw, and when he spoke next, the danger in his voice rushed straight into Warren's ear. "You don't know the first thing about what I could do to you."

It shouldn't have been hot.

It shouldn't have.

But the way Chris's knee pushed into his groin, the aggression in his voice, the scrape of his stubble…

"So I'm going to give you a crash course," Chris continued. "You want me to be a bully? I'll be a fucking bully. Get on your knees, Reaves. You're gonna suck my dick to apologize for what you said about me. And if you don't do it—"

"Fuck you, Chris," Warren spat with as much outrage as he could, but it was hard to snarl when all he wanted to do was whimper.

He wanted this.

Fuck, did he want it.

He wanted Chris to overpower him, own his mouth, and fuck him hard.

"And if you don't," Chris growled, stressing the words. He removed his knee from Warren's groin, grabbed him by the shoulders, and pushed with enough force that Warren's legs buckled. He hit the floor. The dull pain of impact was swallowed by a surge of arousal, and when Chris yanked down his zipper and pulled out his cock, that feeling only grew.

It was happening.

It was really happening.

It wasn't just a dream.

"If you don't," Chris uttered as he grabbed a fistful of Warren's hair, "you'll find out just how nasty I can be."

11

CHRIS

Warren was hard. Chris had felt it the second he'd wedged his knee between his legs, knew it from the way he'd throbbed when Chris had threatened him. He'd shivered when Chris had forced him to kneel, parted his lips when Chris had unzipped his fly, and his eyes... god, his eyes. Black pools of want, both of them, mahogany irises swallowed by blown-out pupils. Warren could gripe all he wanted, but his body said what his mouth wouldn't—that this was what he needed.

And Chris?

Chris would shut Warren up with his cock and get off on seeing him crumple under his command. It was the revenge he never knew he needed.

He wanted to own the bastard who'd sullied his name.

Warren Reaves would choke on his thick, eager cock.

"You want this?" Chris grabbed his dick and ran its head across Warren's cheek, leaving behind a glossy streak of precum. Warren shut his eyes defiantly and attempted to turn his head to the side, but Chris shut that shit down with a tug of his hair and a growl of warning. The moan Warren fed him in reply made him throb.

"Don't pretend you don't," Chris snarled. He introduced his tip to Warren's lips and pushed forward only to be met by clenched teeth. Warren wouldn't let him in.

Fucker.

If he didn't want this, he would be fighting, yelling—hell, he could've bitten Chris's dick. That would've ended things real quick.

But he hadn't.

He wanted this.

But like always, he was being a stubborn ass about it.

"Open your fucking mouth, Reaves. It's time to suck my cock."

Warren didn't listen, but the short, frenetic way he was breathing suggested it wouldn't be long before he gave in. The front of his pants was tented, and Chris was willing to bet that he was harder than ever. Needing to know the truth, he yanked Warren's hair, angling his head back and holding it in place. Like he'd hoped, Warren opened his eyes. His pupils had eclipsed what little color remained, the rings of his irises a memory.

He was getting off on this.

The slut liked it rough.

New wants burned through Chris like jet fuel—Warren choking on his cock; Warren struggling against him only so Chris would fight him that much harder; Warren begging for more when Chris pulled back to let him breathe. It was sick, but he'd never wanted anything more. It didn't matter that he hated Warren. That, if given the chance, he'd do anything to never see him again. Right now, with Warren on his knees and hard for him, Chris wanted between those lips.

Wanted to push past those teeth, knowing they'd never dare bite.

"Tell me you want this," Chris urged, taking a half-step back so his cock parted from Warren's face. Through it all, he kept a grip on his hair, making sure he stayed in place. "Tell me you want me to fuck you."

Nothing.

Warren looked up at Chris, eyes shimmering with lust even as his lips pinched together in contempt.

"Fuck you," Chris rasped, his own breathing ragged in anticipation of what was to come. "Tell me. Tell me you want it. Open your goddamn mouth and let me in, or I won't fucking touch you again."

Irritation sharpened the arousal in Warren's eyes. Chris couldn't look away. Why the hell did he have to look so damn hot when he was angry? Why the hell did he have to look hot at all? Frustrated, Chris snarled and yanked Warren's hair, inadvertently chasing a delirious moan from the man in front of him.

Damn, that moan.

Chris wanted to hear it again.

"Fuck me," Warren begged as his moan faded into nothing. "Fuck me *hard*."

It was what Chris had been waiting for. Cock in hand, he crowded Warren and reintroduced his tip to Warren's bottom lip, and Warren had the gall to look at him with those sex-starved eyes for a fat second before he parted his lips and let Chris in.

Pleasure.

Exquisite, rippling pleasure.

Chris groaned and pushed inward, claiming the tight, wet heat that enveloped him. The urge to fuck grew, then exploded when Warren's tongue pushed into the underside of his cock, narrowing the scope of his mouth. Unable to resist, Chris grabbed fistfuls of his hair and pumped into him, sinking as deep as he could.

"Take it." Even to his own ears, Chris's voice was strained. "Fucking take it, Reaves. Wanna see you choke."

Warren moaned. The sound was sin—dark, forbidden, and eager. It alone made Chris never want to stop, but Warren sweetened the deal by tilting his head back and giving Chris clear passage into his throat. Chris groaned and thrust in, holding Warren's head in place to fuck him properly while Warren coughed and sputtered. Tears streamed down his cheeks and his face began to redden. Chris saw it all—saw the way Warren sucked at his shaft and begged with each gasp for more—and didn't stop. Not now. Not ever.

"You like it, don't you?" Chris thrust harder, and Warren's throat constricted around him. White-hot pleasure tightened his balls. "You like being forced onto your knees and fed cock. How long have you been waiting for this, Reaves? How long have you wanted me to fuck the shit out of you?"

Warren made a desperate noise, but when Chris drew back to let him breathe, he grabbed Chris's ass and forced him back into his throat. Chris gasped, then hissed in satisfaction. His pleasure spiked, and the hiss turned into a moan. Cum rushed through him, the first jet of it spilling down Warren's throat. The rest Chris shot onto his face, painting him so the world would see what a little slut he was.

"Get up," Chris growled when he had nothing left to shoot. Warren was panting for breath and looked dazed, but Chris yanked him up by the hair anyway. There were only a few inches of difference between them, but he used his height to his advantage, looming over Warren while he pushed him back against the door and slotted his knee snug with his groin. The poor baby was still rock hard and wanting. Too bad for him. Chris was going to leave him that way.

"You see what I can do to you?" Chris grabbed Warren by the chin and thumbed a milky streak of cum from his cheek, which he went to smear across Warren's bottom lip. Without being asked, Warren sucked the digit into his mouth and lapped the cum clean. If Chris hadn't just come, he would've ripped Warren's pants off him then and there, thrown him down, and put his hole to work. But he couldn't. Not now. Warren needed to be taught a lesson, and Chris couldn't let himself get distracted. He picked up speaking from where he'd left off. "This is just the start. If I find out you've done anything to hurt Jack or damage his opinion of me, next time I won't be nice. Your ass is mine now, Reaves. You do or say anything against me and I'll make sure you suffer."

Warren moaned and let go of Chris's thumb, but was quick to take it again when Chris pushed more cum from his cheek across his lips.

"You leave me and my boy the fuck alone," Chris warned, leaning in to whisper it into Warren's ear. The heady smell of sex clung to his skin—fresh sweat, musk, and a salty note of semen. "You do what I say and I'll leave you be. You got it?"

"Yeah."

"Good." Chris tucked himself back into his pants, twisted the doorknob, and pushed Warren into the hall. Warren stumbled, but managed to keep his balance. "Now fuck off."

Chris slammed the door shut not because he was angry, but because he was afraid that if he didn't, he might change his mind about letting Warren go. The sight of him out in the hall, blond hair mussed, clothes rumpled, and face streaked with cum was too much. He wanted more. Wanted to punish Warren—to turn the prickly asshole who'd ruined him into a docile kitten of a man who'd do anything for his cock. It was fucked up and he knew it, but it didn't stop him from standing in front of the door, imagining Warren inches away pining for more while Chris was pining for him.

WARREN

Warren: Libby, are you home right now?
Libby: Mm, yeah?
Libby: What's up, big guy? You get locked out again?
Libby: You know that since the Great Tequila Wobble of 2018 I keep the kitchen window unlocked so we can shimmy our drunk asses back into the house, right?

Warren didn't know there had been a Great Tequila Wobble of 2018, but he assumed it was a Libby thing, so he let it slide.

Warren: No, it's not that
Warren: I was hoping you could pick me up. I'm not good to drive right now
Libby: You okay?
Warren: Yeah, just kinda spacey
Libby: "kinda" isn't a typo for Kevin, right?
Warren: Libby
Libby: JUST CHECKING
Libby: Where you at? I'll be there in a sec

Libby was true to her word and arrived in the parking lot of the old strip mall down the street from Chris's apartment not all that long after Warren sent her the address. It was as far as he'd been able to drive before he'd determined he really shouldn't be behind the wheel.

"Hey there, little lady," Libby said in a deep Southern drawl as she leaned on his car door. "Fancy seein' you here. Heard you needed a lift."

The cowboy act had apparently been planned—Libby was dressed in lasso and horseshoe print pajamas. "I didn't realize the cavalry had such a lax dress code."

"What are you, the fun police?"

If only she knew.

"C'mon." Libby slapped the car roof a few times. "What we need right now is less of you being jealous over my amazing life choices and more of you piling into my sweet ride. You okay to stand? You do look pretty out of it."

"I should be okay."

"If you change your mind, just let me know." She stepped back from the car. "I mean, by the time you figure it out you'll probably already be on the ground and I doubt I'll be able to haul you into my car, but let me know anyway. I can probably rig up some kind of macramé net and pulley system that'll take care of it."

"Or you could call Pete?"

Libby trumpeted her lips. "As if. I may not be strong, but I'll have you know that I'm a resourceful and independent woman who doesn't need the help of a dreamy EMT to lift my roommate off the ground. But you know, if you wanna have Pete pick *me* up..." She sighed happily. "Anyway, let's get you home. You can tell me all about what happened on the drive back."

Warren told Libby nothing about what had happened on the drive back, partially because he didn't want her to know, and partially because he was sure that if he did, his dick would straight up explode. He'd always thought that Chris was straight. He'd been going steady with Libby's sister, Freedom, all through their junior and senior years, and everyone back then had known that after they graduated, he was going to marry her. The idea that Chris might like men had never crossed his mind.

But it had obviously crossed Chris's.

What had happened between them... that wasn't something straight guys tended to do.

"What were you doing at that strip mall, anyway?" Libby asked as they crossed the bridge leading to the east bank. "The only businesses left there are that shady real estate place and the termite extermination company. Don't tell me we've got bugs."

Warren fixed Libby with a flat look. "Libby, our house is made of brick."

She shrugged. "Maybe our termites are extra determined."

They rounded a corner. Warren watched the bank disappear in the rearview mirrors and grimaced. If it'd been any other day, he would've quipped back with something witty that would've distracted Libby from the conversation, but every thought he had led back to Chris.

The sight of him.

The smell of him.

The *taste* of him. It lingered on the back of Warren's tongue, a reminder of what they'd done. Warren had sucked cock before, but never like that. Never in a way that'd pushed him to his limits and satisfied the part of himself that wanted to be used. Even the guys he'd begged to be rough with him had never managed to be half as hot as that.

"Okay, I'm officially spooked," Libby said in a far more serious tone of voice. "Warren, what's wrong? You're not acting like yourself."

"I'm fine," Warren replied, and it was the truth. The problem

85

wasn't that he'd lost himself, but that he'd found everything he wanted with the wrong guy.

The day dragged by. By that evening, Warren had resorted to pacing in order to pass the time. Libby was busy with work, Jack was home with his dad, and Pete—Warren's EMT partner—wasn't answering his texts. It was torture. No matter what he did, thoughts of Chris wouldn't leave him alone.

It was just a dick, Warren reasoned with himself as he passed the pantry door. *You've sucked dick before. Bigger dicks. Dicks that belonged to guys who aren't dicks themselves.*

But Chris's dick was perfection—big enough to choke him, wide enough to satisfy, but not so large that it'd broken his jaw. It was cut and curved and veined. If a dick like that fucked his ass, it would be total bliss. The stretch. The fullness.

Warren bit his lip.

Fuck.

A dick like that would twitch in his ass as it unloaded—would pump him full—and balls as heavy as those would make sure he felt every drop.

Too flustered to continue pacing the house and embarrassed over the #TeamSeriouslyMisguided boner tenting his pajama pants, Warren came to a stop and took a deep, grounding breath. If Libby saw him like this, she'd have questions. Questions he didn't want to answer. What he needed was to get his head on straight and forget about Chris. Angry, rage-filled sex wasn't worth the price of admission. Besides, there was no guarantee the ride was still open. Yeah, Warren had been out-of-his-mind horny, but he was pretty sure he'd heard Chris tell him to "leave him and his son the fuck alone."

An invitation for future dickings that was not, and that was a good thing. Warren had principles. Doucheweasels weren't to be

86

fucked with. His indiscretion was a fluke, and it wouldn't happen again. All he needed to get Chris's dick off his mind was a new dick to obsess over. The next time he had a short work week, he'd organize a trip to Des Moines and hook up with someone else, thereby banishing their romp to the shadowlands of his memory.

It'd worked before. There was no reason it wouldn't work again.

"Warren?" Libby asked hesitantly from the kitchen doorway, startling him from his thoughts. "You okay there, bud? You're just... staring... at the recycling bin."

Warren blinked back into focus. Libby wasn't wrong. He'd ended his pacing, of all places, in front of the recycling bin and had been *Blair Witch*ing at it. Hard. A pang of nameless emotion struck as he realized what it was he'd been fixated on—a scrap of paper poking out from beneath several days' worth of flattened cardboard boxes. A scrap of paper inscribed with a jagged nine.

Warren wrenched his gaze from the paper and spun on his heel to face Libby, who squinted at him like she suspected he was a particularly vacuous pod person. At this point, Warren wasn't sure she was wrong. Being body snatched *would* explain why the hell everything in his life was so fucking weird right now. But Libby didn't just scrutinize his face—her gaze dipped lower, and she gasped. "Oh my *god*, Wren. Are you... are you hot for the Quaker Oats guy?"

"*What?*"

"Your dick." Libby covered her eyes, but by then it was too late. The snickering had already begun. "Oh my god. Oh, my *god*. I cannot believe you got a stiffy from staring at my box of oatmeal. Wren, I know it's been a while since you got laid, but *really?*"

"I..." Warren glanced over his shoulder at the top box in the bin. The Quaker Oats man stared back at him, smiling like he was into it. "*Oh my god.*"

That only made Libby laugh harder.

"Libby, I'm not—"

"Not into Oaty Daddies?"

"The Quaker Oats guy is *NOT* my Oaty Daddy."

"I wish I was recording this," Libby gasped through fits of laughter. "Oh my god, Wren. You weirdo. I love you." She wilted onto the doorway, laughing into her hands. "I'm sorry for laughing, but I—" Apologies were apparently hilarious, because she burst out laughing anew. Tears pearled the corners of her eyes. With a wave of her hand and several gasped breaths, she worked herself down from her high and brushed away her tears. "Oh. Oh god. Okay, okay, I've got this. I'm good. No more laughing. It was a total dick move. This is supposed to be a no-judgment-except-for-on-raccoon-based-decisions household, and it was wrong of me to shame you for being attracted to the nice cereal man."

Warren groaned.

He was never going to live this down.

"I just want you to know," Libby continued, barely managing to contain snorts of laughter, "I fully support you dating someone who keeps you regular. I'll leave you and your honey bunches alone."

Whatever she'd been coming into the kitchen to get must not have been all that important, because Libby all but flew out of the room. The sound of a door closing followed not long after—she'd shut herself in her office.

"Oaty Daddy," Warren muttered in disbelief. He turned to glare at his whole-grain lover, whose cheerful smile promised Warren that he understood, and that no matter how long it took Warren to come around, he'd wait. Disturbed, Warren flipped the box over. It really had been too long since he'd gotten laid. There was no world in which "steel cut" should've resonated with him like *that*.

When his newest embarrassment had been laid to rest, there was nothing left in the kitchen for him to do. A wiser, adultier version of himself would've taken the chance to leave the room while Libby was still shut up in her office, but Warren hadn't been firing on all cylinders since his run-in with Chris that afternoon, and he spent a while longer looking at the jagged nine peeking out from beneath his potential love interest than he cared to admit.

You should text him, the same part of his lizard brain responsible for the *Zoolander* dream debacle insisted. *So what if he's literal human garbage? You don't have to like him to suck his cock.*

That was true.

Problematic, but true.

It'll be even better if you hate him while you suck it. You know you like it rough. Maybe if you're bad enough, he'll get fed up and fuck your ass.

Most people had a shoulder demon and a shoulder angel, but Warren? Warren had a one-eyed monster who couldn't leave well enough alone.

Before the Quaker Oats man could catch on to what a pervert he was, Warren fled the kitchen and headed up to bed, where he stared at his phone while it charged on his bedside table like it was a cobra ready to strike. What was that he'd said about principles? Something something fuck with douchcweasels? It was hard to remember when all he could think about was the dull pain as his knees hit the floor and the pleasure that had followed.

Hands in his hair.

A cocky smirk.

A punchable face.

Being totally, utterly helpless.

Warren's fingers curled.

It wasn't like Chris would've whipped out his cock on a whim. Straight guys didn't get mad at someone and, *whoops!* Blowjob. This was something Chris had wanted—even if subconsciously—and when given the chance to act on his desires, he'd gone for it.

Which meant that there was a chance he'd want to do it again.

Warren's cock throbbed, this time definitely not because of an Oaty Daddy. He reached for his phone. Chris wasn't the kind of guy he wanted to date, but he was exactly the kind of guy Warren wanted to fuck, and as long as Chris kept being rough and taking what he wanted by force, Warren would keep crawling back. It made sense. Kind of. He hated Chris, and Chris hated him. The lack of respect meant they could feel good about doing all kinds of filthy things to each other that most people wouldn't dream of doing.

So, hoping for the best but expecting the worst, Warren sent Chris another text.

Warren: Let me suck it one more time

CHRIS

Unknown Name: Let me suck it one more time

Chris nearly dropped his phone. He'd been stationed in Jack's room, waiting for him to finish brushing his teeth so he could put him to bed, when it'd arrived.

Chris: No
Unknown Name: Fuck you
Chris: You wish
Chris: Why the hell are you texting me anyway? I thought you wanted me to block this number
Unknown Name: Screw you. Don't try to deflect and put the blame on me. If you didn't want to hear from me, YOU would've blocked ME

Chris clenched his jaw. Fucking Reaves. What the hell was his problem?

Chris: That's bullshit and you know—

"Dad?" Jack asked in a small voice from the doorway, bringing Chris's furious typing to a sudden stop. "Are you okay? You look mad."

Chris tamped down the urge to hurl his phone out the nearest window and slid it into his pocket instead. The conversation could wait. Jack was more important. "I'm fine, champ. You finished your bathroom routine already? That was fast."

"Was it?"

"Yeah. Sure was." Only Chris wasn't sure at all. He'd been a little too distracted by the asshole in his pocket to keep track of how much time had passed.

Jack came to sit with him on the bedside, folding his legs beneath him. The Minecraft pajama bottoms he had on were starting to wear thin, and he was half a growth spurt away from being too tall for them. When Chris's first paycheck came in, they'd go out to get him some new clothes, but until then, he had to hope that Jack stayed little long enough to keep wearing what he'd brought from Fort Hood.

"Dad?" Jack asked again. He yawned and tucked himself against Chris's side, so Chris wrapped an arm around him and held him close. "I'm sorry I asked that guy to have dinner with you. I didn't mean to make you upset. I just thought maybe you could be friends."

Chris's phone buzzed angrily.

"I know. But we talked it out and it won't happen again, right? So you don't need to feel bad."

Another angry buzz.

"Mmhm," Jack murmured. "When's Mom coming home?"

"Not for a while."

"Will she be gone as long as you were gone when you were on deployment?"

"Maybe." Chris ruffled Jack's dark mop of hair in an effort to keep the conversation upbeat. "It's hard to say."

"I'm gonna call her tomorrow," Jack declared, then wormed out from under Chris's arm and crawled across the bed. He plopped down so his head was resting on the pillows and kicked his legs out. "I hope she'll come back home to our new house here and not to the old house. That would be bad."

Chris could think of worse things.

"Aunt Libby says that she's really busy during the day, and that's why she hasn't been able to answer the phone all that much. It made me think that if I tried to call her early in the morning, she might be less busy and able to talk. I'm gonna try to get up before you come wake me up for school so I can call her, so if you see me awake, don't get freaked out, okay?"

"Okay."

Chris rose from the bedside and wrangled the covers out from beneath his son. Like he did every night, he tucked Jack in and kissed his forehead. "Night. Love you."

"Love you, too."

Most nights once Jack was down for the count, Chris would head into the living room and either space out in front of the television or comb online resources for nearby jobs, but with a new career under his belt and a buzzing phone in his pocket, he made a detour into his bedroom. Once the door was locked, he sat on the bedside and checked on the insanity no doubt waiting for him behind his lock screen.

Unknown Name: You're quiet all of a sudden. Did I strike a nerve?
Unknown Name: You can't tell me you didn't want this to happen
Unknown Name: No guy gets so angry with another guy that he forces him to suck his cock. You wanted this

The smart move would've been to block Warren's number. There was no reason for the conversation to continue. Chris didn't need to explain himself, his choices, or his sexuality to anybody, let alone someone so vile, but a twinge of irritation prickled the back of his mind and a corresponding ripple of arousal spread deep in his gut. What he wanted more than silence was to shut Warren up. To come out on top. To know that after the wrongs he'd suffered, Warren would finally learn his place. It wasn't about being the bigger man—it was about assuming control.

Chris: That's bullshit and you know it
Unknown Name: Yeah?
Unknown Name: Then why are we having this conversation?
Chris: You messaged me, I told you no, and now you're attacking me to try to get your way. Fuck off
Chris: You aren't good enough for my cock
Unknown Name: The way you came all over my face suggests otherwise

A memory of a sex-drunk Warren, face glistening with lines of milky cum, popped into Chris's mind. Those dark eyes. Those swollen lips. Blond hair all askew.

Chris shifted his hips. The more he thought about it, the harder he got. Hating himself for it just a little, Chris thumbed open the button of his jeans and undid his fly, then kneaded his cock through his boxers as new fantasies sprang into being.

The pink tip of Warren's tongue teasing his slit.

A tiny, wanton whimper as Chris rubbed his cock along Warren's bottom lip.

Tight, slick heat as Chris fucked his face and reminded him exactly who he belonged to…

Chris stifled a moan and sank into bed. The kid who'd blighted his name would become the man who paid for it.

Chris: You really think you can handle this?

Chris tugged down his boxers and snapped a picture of his cock.

Chris: I held back last time. If you want it again, I'm not gonna be so nice

Unknown Name: Fuck…

Unknown Name: I want you to choke me with it

Unknown Name: Pound it down my throat and don't fucking stop

A silent moan strained its way through Chris's clenched teeth. The next one promised not to be so quiet. Chris rolled onto his side as he pumped himself and pushed his face into his pillow, muffling a string of throaty noises he couldn't help but make.

Fuck Warren.

Fuck him figuratively. Fuck him literally. Just *fuck* him.

It was a while before Chris composed himself enough to send another message.

Chris: The next time I see you, I'm going to make you suffer

Unknown Name: Do it

Unknown Name: You already made me yours. Now prove it.

Fuck.

Chris squeezed his eyes shut and bucked his hips, rutting into his clenched fist. If he hadn't needed to be there for Jack, he would've already been on his way over to Warren's to do exactly that. Warren needed to be taught humility. Under the guidance of Chris's firm hand, he could… could…

The strained cry of pleasure Chris made was muffled by his pillows, and the sudden flow of his spend was caught in his palm. Orgasm hit fast and hard and left him panting for breath.

Chris: Is this what you want?

Chris took a few pictures of the pool of cum in his hand, but most of them were blurred—he was shaking. The one picture taken in focus he sent to Warren.

Unknown Name: God yes
Unknown Name: I want all of it inside me
Chris: Next time I see you, next time I have a chance, I'm gonna make you choke on it
Unknown Name: You can try, but know I'm gonna put up a fight
Chris: Good. I want you to
Unknown Name: I fucking hate you for making me want this so bad
Chris: Don't worry. I hate you for it, too

WARREN

Friday morning at the station started the way it always did—with Warren's EMT partner, Pete, ambushing him from the back of the ambulance during rig check. Fortunately, Warren was used to almost two hundred pounds of muscle hurtling at him out of nowhere in the wee hours of the morning, so he was able to step aside before the blur of ginger mischief could turn him into a pancake.

"Fuck!" Pete said, laughing as he hit the ground. Momentum pushed him onward, and to keep from falling he jogged a few feet. Once he was able, he turned around and fixed Warren with a sunny smile. "Morning, Wren."

"Morning, Pete."

"You look dapper today." Pete arched a brow, grin sharpening. "Too dapper. We lookin' at a Code Three?"

"Priority One."

"Ouch." Pete winced. "You look too in love for a DOA. What gives?"

At the mention of love, Warren's upper lip peeled back in disgust.

Pete laughed. "That bad?"

"Worse." Hoping to avoid a conversation about Warren's very bad, lizard-brained choices from the day before, he stepped up into the cabin of the ambulance. "I'd rather not talk about it. It's not worth the time or the mental bandwidth."

The soles of Pete's boots thudded on the metal step as he followed Warren in. "You sure?"

"Positive. Now, did you get a head start on rig check, or did you dick around waiting for me to get here?"

"You know I'm all dicks all the time, baby." The lascivious note in Pete's voice made room for a modicum of professionalism. "I did get the 411 from Mikey, though. We finally got a new battery for the heart monitor. I never pegged myself for the kind of guy who'd be excited over lithium ion, but here we are. Life, right? I mean, look at how shiny it is."

The battery *was* pretty shiny. Warren admired it for a minute while Pete stood proudly at his side.

"It's pure, Wren," Pete whispered, professionalism gone. "This sweet, innocent battery isn't fed up with our bullshit yet. It must be protected at all costs. *All* costs."

It was Warren's turn to grin. "Guess that means no more naked pillow fights, huh?"

"Fuck that!" Pete laughed and checked him playfully with his shoulder. "Everyone's gotta grow up some time, even this battery. What better way to do it than by witnessing the horror that is our floppy dicks? But... let's lay off for a week. It's only fair. Besides, there's no telling what kind of dick-inspired shenanigans Mikey and Jay will get up to in front of it when we're not around."

That was true. Warren had seen things during his daily rig checks that'd made him question what those two got up to in the privacy of the truck on dead, lonely nights, but he did his best not to linger on it. If he did, he'd have to confront the reality that the mess he'd found that one time wasn't really spilled Surgilube, and that... that was a thought he could live without.

"Anything else Mikey clued you in to?" he asked.

98

"Nah. They had a quiet shift. It'll probably be busier for us with the weekend on the way, but if we're lucky we'll have enough time to think of a name for the new little lady on board." Pete lovingly patted the battery on her casing. "I'm thinking Carmen. Like of the Electra variety. What do you think?"

"Remind me why I ride with you again?"

Pete flashed him the biggest grin, all sparkling white teeth and trouble. "Because it's you and me 'til the end, baby. Assigned to each other by chance, but united as a team by *love*. Plus, what other partner'll rub your feetsies when they're all tuckered out?" Warren opened his mouth to state that not *once* had Pete ever "rubbed his feetsies," but Pete beat him to the punch. "I mean, not me, but if you find him you absolutely have my permission to dump my ass and never, ever let him go."

Pete clapped him on the shoulder, grin ever-present. "Now, let's get rig check going, huh? It's not like we have all day."

After years spent working in emergency services, rig check was second nature. At the start of every shift, Warren assessed the functionality and cleanliness of the ambulance, then checked on and tuned the equipment. Batteries needed to be kept charged, stretchers needed to be wiped down and disinfected, and the pressure level of the portable oxygen tank needed to be recorded. Other odds and ends were checked on as well—there were PPE supplies to be replenished, clean linens to be stored, and miscellaneous medical supplies to stock. Provided they weren't dispatched while it was in progress, rig check ate up anywhere from half an hour to three hours of their day.

It was also when Pete tended to be the most talkative.

"I mean, it's not that I don't like dogs," he explained to Warren on that particular morning as he disinfected the interior door handles. "But I mean, I'm pretty sure someone scammed that girl out of her money. There's no way you'll convince me that thing wasn't a giant rat."

Warren looked up from the trauma kit he'd been doing inventory on. "A rat?"

"A *giant* rat. We're talking full-on hairless tail and a long nose. Yeah, the thing had floppy ears, but it was *not* a dog. It was a rat. A rat in disguise. A *giant* rat in disguise. I'm lucky I made it out of there without that thing eating my soul."

"Is that what giant rats do?"

"I don't know, but I wasn't going to stick around to find out." Pete tossed the disinfecting wipe onto the garage floor and went to get a fresh one. "That thing was a deal breaker."

"So I take it to mean there's not going to be a second date?"

"Oh, hell no." New wipe acquired, Pete went to clean the stretcher. "Can you imagine waking up one morning to find that thing licking your face? I can't. The girl was nice enough, but there wasn't a spark, and I'm not going to risk having my soul gobbled up by some alien in rat-dog clothing on the assumption of a great lay."

Warren frowned and furrowed his brow, a bottle of irrigation solution in hand. "Wait... when did the giant rat in disguise become an alien?"

Pete waved a hand dismissively. "Not important. What matters is that I'm no longer at risk of death. You're looking at a free agent. The curse has yet to be lifted, but you know what? I'm okay with that."

The curse Pete was referring to was his chronic singledom. Warren couldn't remember the last time Pete had gone on a second date. But, despite his continual failure to land the girl of his dreams, Pete kept trying. And trying. Apart from Libby, it seemed there wasn't a woman within ten years of Pete's age in all of Iowa he hadn't gone out with. Which was a shame, because Warren was pretty sure that if Pete and Libby got together, they'd stay that way.

"So... you're free next weekend?" Warren put the bottle back in the trauma kit. Like every other time he'd checked, it was unexpired.

Pete stopped what he was doing to bat his eyelashes at Warren. "You know I'm always free for you, sugar lump."

Warren rolled his eyes.

"But to honestly answer your question, no. There's a girl in Lyle I'll be heading over to spend some time with. Seems nice. Hoping she's rat-dog free."

"How the hell do you always have a date lined up?"

Pete finished with the stretcher, chucked his wipe through the open doors and into the garage, and winked at Warren. "When you look this good"—he ran both hands down his chest to his groin suggestively—"there ain't no stopping it. I may not have any milk to shake, but I've found the promise of cream brings ladies to my yard all the same."

Warren gagged. Pete laughed.

"You sure you don't want to talk about your Code Three, Wren?" He wiggled an eyebrow. "The best way to get me to shut up is to distract me."

Warren chucked a six-pack of hemostatic dressing at him. Pete karate chopped it out of the air.

"I'll take that as a no."

"It really isn't worth talking about."

"Well, suit yourself." Pete hopped down from the back of the ambulance and collected the wipes he'd thrown away. "I'm gonna toss these and see if Kathleen's already brewed coffee. If the pot's fresh, you want some?"

"Yeah, thanks. One sugar."

Pete smirked. "Any cream?"

Like a swordsman drawing his blade, Warren busted out a tube of Surgilube and brandished it at Pete. "I will literally pour this entire thing down your throat."

The garage echoed with Pete's laughter and the gleeful cry of, "Wrong hole! Wrong hole!" as he fled for the safety of the station.

Fifteen minutes later, Pete hadn't returned from his coffee run. In his absence, Warren finished checking their rig. Then, with nothing else to do, he made finding his missing partner his top priority.

It didn't take long.

The door leading from the garage into the station admitted into a common room shared by all of Howard County's emergency service providers. It was stocked with old couches, secondhand armchairs, a television that was permanently tinted a sickly green, and a kitchenette with a shared fridge that had been ground zero for more interdepartmental wars than Warren could remember. While it wasn't unusual to find some of the guys loitering in the common room while they waited to be dispatched, today it looked like every man and woman on duty was there, and they'd all clustered into the same corner of the room.

Something was up.

Warren squinted from where he stood, trying to get a look at what they were doing, but Meatball from fire services was blocking his line of sight with his big beefy body.

"What was Texas like?" That came from Melody, also from fire services, who was the brain to Meatball's brawn.

There came a chuckle, and then a voice that made the hairs on Warren's arms stand on end. "It's pretty much like how they say it is—big."

"Do you miss it?" asked that traitor, Pete.

"No."

Warren remained frozen on the spot. There was no mistaking it.

He knew that voice.

Had dreamed about that voice.

And now...

"Wren!" Pete exclaimed, the top of his head appearing from around Meatball's broad frame. "There you are. I was just about to get you. Come meet Chris! He's gonna be working dispatch."

15

CHRIS

Warren Reaves.

Warren fucking Reaves.

A flurry of emotion hit Chris all at once, not all of it pleasant. Surprise. Disgust. Anger.

Arousal.

The last impacted hard and left him reeling.

It'd only been one time, but the thoughts in Chris's head wouldn't leave him alone—full lips wrapped around his cock. Blond hair jutting from between the gaps of his clenched fist. Brown eyes eclipsed with desperate need...

The man who stood before him now was the same one who'd sucked Chris's thumb into his mouth to clean it of cum. Who'd let Chris own his throat. Yeah, the midnight blues of his medic's uniform made him look respectable, but they didn't change the fact that this was the man who'd texted him last night begging for more. And if the stunned, lust-darkened look in Warren's eyes was to be believed, those messages hadn't just been for show.

"So, uh, you two know each other?" Meatball asked awkwardly, snapping Chris back to the present. A long, uncomfortable silence had descended upon the room, and it seemed like everyone had picked up on the manic energy thickening the air. Even Melody, the vivacious brunette firefighter who'd been sidling up to Chris since they'd been introduced, had backed off a few steps to give him some space.

"Yeah," Chris said before another silence could take hold. He tucked his hands into his pockets and relaxed his shoulders in an attempt to look casual, but the truth was anything but. If the sexual tension didn't kill him, the hot-as-hell glossy look in Warren's eyes would. "More or less. We went to school together."

"Great!" Meatball slapped him on the back, which would've sent Chris straight through the nearest wall if he'd been any less sturdy. Meatball, he assumed, was an aural autocorrect for meat wall—the man was huge. "Bet you had no idea when you woke up this morning that when you came into work, you'd... uh..." His hand dropped. "I forgot what I was saying. But welcome to the family! You're going to fit right in."

A glint of something lustful shone in Warren's eyes at that last part, triggering a surge of arousal in Chris that sweetened into something dark and forbidden he didn't want to acknowledge— something rich and heavy that nuanced the feeling in the air.

Did Warren feel it, too?

Desire prickled its way through Chris until no part of him was left untouched. The explosive chemistry between them—the raw need to tear each other apart only to stroke and shape each other back into something whole—couldn't be one-sided. Chris refused to believe it. Warren had a good poker face, but Chris was catching on to his tells.

Even here, Warren wanted him... and god, the things that made him feel.

"Wren's a paramedic," Melody supplied as wicked thoughts burned their way through Chris's brain. "He's partnered with Pete. They're the only ones in the area certified to conduct medical air transport. Fancy, right? When shit really hits the fan, they're the ones you'll be calling on. Him and Pete are on call twenty-four seven for accidents that require medivac here and in neighboring counties, so you might have the chance to bug 'em even when they're not on duty. Wren's probably saved more lives than any of the paramedics in all the surrounding counties combined. Isn't that right, Wren?"

Warren startled. His eyes lost their softness. "What?"

"She's braggin' on your un-kill count... again." Meatball slapped Chris's back one last time then brushed by him to go stand by Warren, who'd gone from looking like he wanted to climb Chris's bones to wishing he could crawl into a hole. "Talkin' you up to the new guy."

"It's not really that impressive," Warren mumbled. His gaze met Chris's for a second, and like a flint striking steel, the spark of what had once been returned. It blazed bright for the short time their eyes were locked, but was extinguished the moment Warren looked away. "Anyone know if we're good on coffee?"

"Hell yeah, we are," the redhead—Pete—announced as he left the crowd around Chris to press a coffee mug into Warren's hand. "One sugar, *all* the cream—just the way you like it."

All cream, huh?

Somehow, that wasn't surprising.

The Howard County dispatch office was only a little bigger than the closet Sheriff Sinclair worked in. Under ordinary circumstances the lack of space wouldn't have been all that bad, but with Chris and his field training officer, Erika, sharing the same desk, it was a bit of a tight fit. Especially because Erika was all elbows.

"Now," Erika said as her cardigan-clad elbow threatened to decimate Chris's solar plexus. "All that stuff you learned while getting certified? Only some of it is going to be useful out here in a rural office. Our call volume is typically low, but if you get a spike you don't have a pod to pick up the slack, so it's all on you. The key is getting into the habit of being as efficient but as thorough as you can with each call. Don't get used to resting on your laurels just because most days are slow."

Chris nodded, then flattened himself against the back of his chair as Erika's elbow went in for the kill. Thanks to his quick reflexes, it barely brushed his chest. Erika didn't seem to notice— her eyes were glued to the computer monitor situated at the back center of the desk.

"You'll have to get used to the radio, too," she revealed, gesturing at what appeared to be an ancient box alarm clock hooked up to an old-fashioned mic. "Our crews don't spend too much time out of the station unless on call, but once they've been dispatched, the radio's the only surefire way to get in touch and provide updates and support. Most corners of Howard County don't have strong cell service, and due to the nature of our profession, we can't afford dropped calls or missed connections."

She wheeled away from Chris, temporarily ending the olecra-nonular onslaught.

"But I think one of the hardest parts of the job that no one tells you to expect is... well... in small towns like this, everyone knows each other." Erika slid a drawer open and took from it a faded paper folder—the kind Jack used at school. It was stuffed so full of docu-ments that it gaped open. The joints of the inner pockets had started to stretch thin. She laid it reverently on the desk and opened it up, revealing a motley collection of greeting cards, children's drawings, and handwritten letters. "The people you talk with day in and day out will be people you recognize—the mail lady, your next-door neighbor, maybe even a member of your family. When they call, it's up to you to keep a level head and talk them through what very well might be the worst day of their life... and maybe yours. For most dispatchers, that's where their connection to the caller ends, but for us, it's not that clear cut. Our callers know us as well as we know them, and they'll remember the kindness and compassion we show them when their world is falling apart."

Erika eased one of the drawings out of the folder. In it, a younger version of Erika was smiling and holding hands with a little girl—presumably the artist. Time had smudged the coloring and line work a little, and the corner of the paper it'd been drawn on had started to curl. Erika smoothed the curl in the opposite direction, the tips of her long nails brushing its surface.

"One day," she revealed as she slotted the drawing back into place, "if you stick with this job long enough, you'll have a folder like this, too. The woman who worked here before me had one, and so do the other dispatchers who work in this office. Howard County isn't that big, and yeah, you might get calls from Chester or Cresco or even Vernon Springs, but whether it's a week, a month, or a year from now, you'll be dispatching for Lethridge eventually. Trust me when I say the people here will remember the kindness you show them."

She gestured at the drawer. "Since I'll be leaving once you've acclimated, I surrender my folder spot to you. You can use it to keep a record of all the lives you'll touch while on the job. On hard days —when work hits a little too close to home—it might be the only thing that'll help see you through."

Chris spent a long moment studying the contents of Erika's folder, then turned his attention to the woman it belonged to. Erika didn't look all that old. Streaks of silver ran through her graying hair, and her hands showed early signs of wrinkles, but she didn't have any of the other hallmarks of old age. With the way she talked about the job, it struck him as strange that she'd leave it. "It sounds like you enjoy working here. Why are you leaving?"

"Oh." Erika smiled and closed the folder. "My husband is retiring and we're uprooting to his hometown in Colorado. I wouldn't leave if we weren't. It's a tough job, but it's rewarding like nothing else I've ever done. I think once you're a couple years in, you'll under-stand what I mean."

Erika wheeled back so she was in front of the computer and said brightly, "Now, about our emergency OS..." She yanked the keyboard forward and slammed her elbow into Chris's chest. The air left his lungs for safer, elbow-free grounds. Without a sound, he folded onto the desk and let out a rattling wheeze.

"Hey! No sleeping." Erika poked him in the shoulder. "What did I say about resting on your laurels?"

"Got it," Chris choked, and wrenched himself back up.

That cinched it—if he survived two weeks with Erika's elbows, the first thank-you note in his folder would be from himself.

16

CHRIS

At the end of an elbow-plagued shift, Chris sank into the worn leather driver's seat of his old Acura and closed his eyes. Training in Des Moines had familiarized him with the core concepts he needed to be an effective dispatcher, but the demands of the job would take some getting used to. It was a damn good thing Erika was sticking around long enough to teach him the ins and outs of their station, because without her, the job would've knocked him flat on his ass.

After a quiet moment spent decompressing, he took his phone from his pocket—Jack was waiting for him over at Liberty's, and they needed to know he was done and on his way. A few messages were waiting, so Chris checked them first to make sure they weren't from Liberty.

They weren't.

All of them were from Warren.

Unknown Name: So now you're a bully and a stalker?
Unknown Name: I'm not buying that this was all some coincidence. First Jack, now this? No way. You're doing it on purpose

Unknown Name: If this is some scheme to ruin my life by getting me fired, quit now before you get someone seriously hurt. This isn't high school—it's my job to save lives, and I'm not going to let you hurt other people just so you can get at me

Chris strained a sigh through his teeth.

Chris: I'm on to you, Reaves. Don't try that shit with me

There was no immediate reply, so Chris sent a quick message to Liberty to let her know he was heading out, then cast his phone onto the passenger seat and got going. Warren could wait for his explanation. After all the shit he'd pulled, he deserved to squirm.

Before the car came to a complete stop, the front door of Liberty's house burst open and out came Jack, who barreled down the steps and across the lawn with the speed of someone who'd committed a crime and wasn't sure he was getting away with it. As he wrenched open the rear door and clambered into the vehicle, Chris figured out why—there was a tub of cookies tucked under his arm and a very messy Liberty on the doorstep. It looked like she'd gone head to head with a mountain of all-purpose flour and lost.

Chris looked at his son, who was as clean as an eight-year-old could be, then at his ex-sister-in-law, who smiled and waved. When she dropped her arm, a powder-white cloud puffed into the air and floated away.

"You, uh, had fun baking today, champ?" Chris asked cautiously.

Jack finished strapping himself in and set the tub of cookies on his lap. "Yep."

"What happened to Aunt Liberty?"

"Oh." Jack rolled down the window and leaned out of it to shout, "It's a little worse than I thought, Aunt Libby! You're probably gonna wanna shower."

"Will do, buckaroo!" Liberty shouted back. "See you Monday!"

"See you Monday! Bye!"

Liberty went back inside and Jack rolled up the window. When it was all the way in place, he turned and smiled hugely at Chris. "Aunt Libby and I made cookies today, and while she was melting butter in the microwave I hid a fake spider in the flour. When she went to get some she saw it and got scared and dropped the whole bag. It got *everywhere.*"

"Except for on you."

"Yup!"

Chris pointed at the tub. "Yet she still let you take all those cookies home even after you pulled a stunt like that?"

"Yup!"

"She's nicer than your old man." Chris reached back and ruffled Jack's hair. "Pranks can be fun, but make sure they don't become a habit, okay? If you do it too much, other people might think that you're mean."

"Okay, Dad." Jack swatted playfully at his hand. "But only if you stop, too. You're gonna mess up my hair!"

Chris smirked. "You got someone you're trying to impress?"

"*No!*" Jack declared a little too forcefully.

Funny how, later that night, the "Billy" he asked permission to video chat with was of the "ie" variety. Chris didn't mind. She seemed like a nice girl, and, more importantly, she distracted Jack enough that Chris could devote his attention to the shitshow that was the texts waiting for him on his phone.

Unknown Name: What the hell are you talking about?

Unknown Name: You can't gaslight me into believing I'm the problem
Unknown Name: If you think that's going to work, you can fuck directly off.

Oh, how *prickly*.

Chris tilted his kitchen chair so it was on two legs. Its back nestled the wall. From there, he could keep an eye on what Jack was up to without invading his privacy or running the risk of over-the-shoulder text reading should he walk by. For now there wasn't any risk of that happening, since he and Billie were playing Minecraft, but there was no telling when that might change.

Chris: This is starting to get boring
Chris: Either find a fresh approach or let it die. You're better than this, Reaves
Unknown Name: Better than what?
Unknown Name: I'm dying to hear how you're going to spin this one

Jack gasped. Chris lifted his eyes from the screen, panicked that somehow he'd figured out what was going on, just in time to see a creeper blow a hole in the side of Jack's base.

"Creepers are so annoying," Jack grumbled. "Are you okay, Billie? He didn't get you, did he?"

"I'm okay," came the reply. Billie's flower-crown-wearing avatar hopped into view and started patching the wall with the cobble-stone block in her hand. "When we get this fixed, do you wanna go mining?"

"Yeah!"

While they fixed the damage done, Chris shifted his focus to his own creeper—Warren.

Chris: Don't even start with that reframing horseshit
Chris: You did this last time, too. I see right through you.
Chris: Riling me up is your MO.
Unknown Name: Oh my god
Unknown Name: Please, explain how you doing everything
in your power to make my life harder is my fault.

Oh, he was good. Chris took a slow, steady breath through his
nose to defuse the rage set to blow inside of him and dismissed the
urge to smash—or maybe fuck—Warren's face on the exhale. If he
got angry, Warren would win, and there was no way in fuck he was
going to let that happen.

Chris: Sure
Chris: Here's everything you're doing and why.
Unknown Name: Oh, this should be good.
Chris: Stage one: getting me angry
Chris: You hurl insults and accusations so I'll retaliate and
defend myself. When I do, you only attack me more, perpetu-
ating the cycle so I'll get angrier and more careless

Jack and Billie had found an underground cavern crawling with
monsters. While Jack planted torches to keep more from spawning,
Billie fended off a zombie with frantic swipes of her sword. No
matter how many blows she landed, the zombie never gave up. It
died snarling.

Chris: Stage two: baiting me into doing your bidding
Chris: Once I'm so angry I can't think, you take advantage to
get whatever it is you want—which I'm pretty sure is
my cock
Unknown Name: That's bullshit!

A skeleton archer fell to Billie's sword, dropping some of its bones as spoils. Jack finished lighting up the area and raced in to help her fight off the forces of evil.

Chris: You know, I thought it was bullshit too until I saw the way you looked at me when I pushed you onto your knees. You know what a man who hadn't anticipated giving a blowjob would've done? He would've fucking decked me in the jaw. But you... you took it and wanted more
Chris: And how are you gonna get it? By baiting me into shutting you up just like I did before
Chris: You like it rough. You can't hide it. All of this acting out is your attempt at getting laid

There was no response. At least Warren was man enough not to argue with the truth.

Chris: I don't know how you knew I was bi, but it doesn't really matter. I know what you're doing, and I'm not gonna let you get under my skin

Warren started typing. He was either composing the next great American novel, or he was floundering for what to say, because the icon that showed he was typing kept flickering in and out of existence. While Chris waited for a reply, he hooked his foot around the leg of Jack's kitchen chair and tugged it closer so he could use it as a footrest. The scrape of wood on tile distracted Jack from his game, and he climbed onto his knees to check out what Chris was doing. Chris lifted a hand to silently acknowledge him and Jack went back to his game.

Unknown Name: You think all I want is sex?
Chris: Yup

Chris ran his tongue over his teeth and arched a brow.

Chris: In fact, I'm starting to think maybe that's why you
were such a dick to me when we were kids
Chris: Any attention is better than no attention, right? And if
you liked it rough back then, too…
Unknown Name: Christ

There was no indication that Warren was going to add on to
what he'd said, but Chris was in no hurry. The silence trick he'd
used with Jack wasn't only effective on kids—if he waited long
enough, Warren would fill the silence. He placed his phone on the
table and used his downtime to check back in with what Jack and
Billie were up to. It seemed their mining expedition had gone well—
they'd followed the stream of an underground waterfall and discovered an intersecting river of magma. A cluster of diamonds was
centered over the thickest part, and they were in talks about how to
harvest them without dying.

Chris checked his phone. A few new messages were waiting.
Funny how that worked.

Unknown Name: I hated you in high school, just so
you know
Unknown Name: I only wrote the doucheweasel thing
because you pushed me into doing it. What did you expect
after treating me like shit year after year?
Unknown Name: Me being fucking furious with you has
nothing to do with me having "feelings" for you. The only
thing I feel for you is resentment
Unknown Name: You're hot and I was horny. That's all
Chris: If that's true, why are you being such an asshole to me
right now?
Chris: We haven't seen each other in over a decade. Are you
really gonna tell me that you're still trying to rip my throat

out over things you think I did to you when we were kids? I don't buy that for a second. Yeah, you hate me, but you lashing out at me like this has nothing to do with our past. All you want is to goad me into fucking you into submission
Unknown Name: I fucking hate you right now
Chris: Only because you know I'm right

Pinpricks of pleasure crept southbound through Chris's chest. It'd taken a while, but he'd figured out Warren's game, and now that he had, he could put a stop to it.

Chris: So here's how it's gonna be
Chris: You can hate me all you want
Chris: You can resent me
Chris: You can throw darts at a printout of my face... I don't care
Chris: But this bullshit you're pulling, running hot and running cold, fighting with me one second and looking at me with bedroom eyes the next... it's gonna stop. And it's gonna stop because I hate you, too, Warren. I hate that when potential employers google my name, the first thing that pops up is your fucking doucheweasel bullshit. I hate how one day, Jack is gonna come to me in tears because some punk-ass kid googled his dad and found that fucking entry. I hate how what you did to me will haunt me for the rest of my life. And I'm gonna show you how much I hate you by fucking your face whenever I want, as hard as I want.

Warren started to type, but gave up almost as quickly, which was good, because Chris wasn't done.

Chris: I told you you were mine
Chris: You could have backed down and told me no, but you didn't, did you?

Chris: This is what you wanted
Chris: So get ready, because I'm done putting up with your bullshit
Chris: You want it rough? I'll give it to you rough
Chris: It's time you paid for what you've done

1 7

WARREN

Warren launched out of the common room's best armchair and bolted for the bathroom. Up until then he'd been casually browsing his phone and guarding his spot from Pete and Meatball, who were midway through their annual *Golden Girls* marathon and hungry for the best seat in the station. Case in point, the moment he moved both of them shot up from the couch and lunged.

It was chaos.

Wild, inarticulate shouting.

Grabbing hands.

Flying elbows.

Warren yelped and dodged the worst of it by ducking under Meatball's arm a second before Meatball grappled Pete to try to keep him away. Warren didn't see the ensuing tussle, but he did hear it—squeaking shoes, grunts of exertion, squeaking chair springs and all.

"It's mine!" Pete crowed as Warren made it to the bathroom door. "You can squish me as flat as you want, but you'll never claim the throne!"

"You wanna bet?"

Warren didn't stick around to find out who won. He shut the

119

bathroom door, found the presence of mind to lock it, then planted his back against it and let out a shaky breath. If the guys saw that he was getting hot and bothered, he wouldn't hear the end of it. It'd be Oaty Daddy all over again, but *worse*. And if they found out about what had happened with Chris...

God, what a mess that'd be.

After a few grounding breaths, Warren sent a reply.

Warren: You wouldn't dare

Chris: I wouldn't dare what? Fuck your mouth?

Chris: I'm pretty sure I already did

Chris: You know you could end this, right?

Chris: All you have to say is that you want me to stop

Chris: But you're not going to, are you? You like the way fighting with me makes you feel

Fuck.

Fuck fuck *fuck.*

Warren squeezed his eyes shut and opened his mouth in a silent moan. It wasn't supposed to be like this. Chris was the *enemy*. If only the white flag rising behind his fly would agree. Cheeks flushed with heat, he laid his phone on the lid of the toilet tank, tugged open his belt, and yanked down his pants. With one hand braced on the wall behind the toilet and the other wrapped around his aching cock, he started to stroke.

Fuck Chris.

Fuck him for being so damn hot. For giving Warren what he wanted without even trying. For wanting more.

Warren's grip tightened. He went harder. In his mind Chris was behind him, erection pushing against Warren's ass while he worked Warren toward orgasm.

"Tell the truth," the Chris in his mind demanded in a sultry whisper against the back of Warren's ear. "You do what you do on purpose because you want this. You want *me*."

He was right.

It was true.

After what they'd done, how could Warren want anyone else?

A new message arrived, then another.

Chris: So here's how this is going to work

Chris: The next time you have a shift, I'm gonna park at the back of the lot. When I'm done for the day, I'm gonna wait in my car until Erika's gone, then I'm gonna send you a text. When you get it, you're gonna come find me, and I'm going to fuck your face

Oh, *fuck.*

Warren closed his eyes and sucked in a breath, hand working harder than ever. He imagined Chris behind the wheel, seat pushed back to its limits, legs spread, one arm over the passenger seat. His t-shirt stretched over his broad chest, his blue jeans straining to hold back his erection. Warren would climb in and Chris would lift his head just enough to look at him from beneath his lashes, cocky as fuck and with every reason to be.

He owned Warren, and he knew it.

Chris: Will anyone see you? Who knows. But your best bet is to give me what I want, because the longer it takes you to get me off, the longer you're gonna be out there sucking

Chris: And you're gonna need to hurry, because that's not all I'm gonna make you do

Chris: After I come, you're gonna clean my cock with your tongue. You'll suck it until there's no mess left. Only then will you go back to work and act like nothing ever happened

Chris: Got it?

Warren's breath hitched. He bucked forward and shot into the bowl, knees knocking so badly he was barely able to keep himself standing. His orgasm was dark and sweet and succulent, an indulgence Chris had allowed him. It wasn't fair. Wasn't fair how good it felt, or how much he needed it.

If this was what being with Chris felt like, he would never tell Chris no.

Trembling, he picked up his phone to reply.

Warren: Got it
Chris: Good.
Chris: I'll see you next time you're at work, Reaves
Chris: Sweet dreams.

18

CHRIS

Howard County Sheriff's Department offered curbside parking for what few residents visited each day and a small, employees-only parking lot for its staff. The lot was boxed in on one side by the garage and on the others by a stone fence that partially shielded it from its quiet access street. It had no gate or other barriers to keep the public out—if someone were to ignore the employees-only signage, they'd be free to drive right in.

Coming here was a risk, but one Chris was willing to take.

Chris said goodbye to Erika in the parking lot and headed to his car. He made a show of searching the back seat for nothing in particular to make himself look busy, then took a seat behind the wheel when she was gone. So far, so good. All he had to do now was let Warren know everything was going according to plan.

Chris: Clear

The message went from received to read, and a few minutes later Chris noticed movement in his side-view mirror. Warren, blond and handsome and surprisingly nonchalant, followed the lot wall as far as he could before cutting over to Chris's car. The door opened, his leather seat groaned, and there was Warren, hot as hell and frustrating as fuck, seated right there beside him.

Chris had spent some time over the last few days picturing how today would go. He'd jerked himself off to thoughts of a mouthy, obstinate Warren who'd give him shit from the second the car door opened until the moment Chris put his lips to work. In his fantasies, Warren always mellowed over time, arguing less as he craved sex more, until eventually he was Chris's perfect plaything—tender and sweet, obsessed with his cock. But the Warren sitting beside him now was better than anything Chris had imagined, and Chris couldn't put his finger on why.

All he knew was that he wanted him, and for now, that was enough.

"All right," Warren muttered once the door was closed. "I'm here, so—"

Chris didn't give him a chance to finish—he grabbed a fistful of Warren's hair and dragged him forward, crushing their lips together.

The kiss hadn't been planned, but damn if it didn't feel right. Warren was rugged in all the ways he needed to be—firm lips, coarse stubble, and stubborn opposition. He jerked back instinctively and snarled into Chris's mouth, but his rage sweetened once his brain caught on to what was happening, and he fed Chris a moan that made his cock throb.

It was strange to want something so badly. To be entirely infuriated by it, but to want to possess it all the same. Desire burned its way through Chris, growing hotter when Warren grabbed fistfuls of his shirt in retaliation and pulled himself close, returning Chris's kiss with savage ferocity. As he did, Chris fumbled for the lever of the recliner mechanism. He found it as Warren climbed onto his lap, and they tumbled down together as it activated. No sooner had they fallen than Warren began to work his hips, grinding his covered cock against Chris's. The friction was maddening. Half-wild with need, Chris grabbed Warren's ass and pushed them closer together.

"*Fuck,*" Warren growled as he rubbed their groins together. "Fucking hate you so damned much."

"Then leave."

Warren snarled and redoubled his efforts, just like Chris had hoped.

Nothing changed for a while. Chris was too enraptured by Warren's fierce mouth and the selfish way they grabbed at each other. They seduced each other one fistful of taut shirt or pulled hair at a time, never hesitating to grope or pinch or touch whatever the hell they wanted. If Warren had kept it up, Chris would have come in his jeans, but before that happened, Warren pulled away and scrambled back into the passenger seat, lust darkening his eyes.

It didn't take much to figure out what he wanted.

Lucky for him, Chris wanted it, too.

Chris yanked down his fly, then grabbed Warren by the hair and dragged him toward his cock. Warren struggled, but it was for show —the strength of Warren's grip when he'd pulled himself onto Chris's lap betrayed him. If Warren wanted to, he could break away.

"Suck my fucking dick, Reaves," he growled, pushing Warren down so his nose brushed Chris's shaft. "You're not going anywhere until you do."

"Fuck you!"

"That's the idea." Chris lifted his hips, rubbing himself over Warren's mouth. "Now, are you gonna play nice, or are we gonna play dirty?"

Warren shivered, and it was all the answer Chris needed.

"Fine. Dirty it is."

He grabbed the front of Warren's face and pinched his cheeks until his jaw opened enough that he could slip his thumb inside. If Warren had a change of heart, there was nothing stopping him from biting, but all he did was make a muffled sound of annoyance that grew angrier the more Chris wedged his teeth apart.

"Why fight it?" Chris asked while guiding Warren's open mouth to his tip. "You know it's going to happen. Give in. Suck me."

Warren made an indignant noise.

"All right. You've made your choice."

No more waiting.

He shoved Warren onto his cock.

Tight, wet heat surrounded him. Warren cried out in protest, but at the same time locked his lips around Chris's shaft and hollowed his cheeks as he sucked. From his reclined position, Chris saw it all —the blissed-out look on Warren's face, the veneration he showed to Chris's cock, the hunger in the way he moved—and it made him want more.

"Oh, fuck yeah... take it." He closed his eyes and rolled his head back, but not even his fantasies could compete with the scene playing out on his lap. When he opened his eyes again, it was just in time to see Warren clutch at the side of the seat, knuckles white, while he strained to sink down to Chris's base. "*Fuck.* Take all of it. Wanna see you choke."

The sex-addled sound Warren made was the stuff of wet dreams, and the way his mouth felt? God. Perfection. Chris anchored both hands in his hair and pushed, not holding back. Warren coughed and sputtered, but not once did he try to pull back. Even as his throat convulsed around Chris's cock, he stayed locked around Chris's hilt. It was like he'd been born to do this—born to swallow other men whole.

No.

No, that wasn't right.

Warren wasn't made for other men. His throat was Chris's. Mouth, Chris's. Lips...

Chris moaned.

Before it became too much for either of them, he yanked Warren off his dick and let him breathe, then forced him down again. And again. Warren was quick to adjust to Chris's rhythm, but his body never learned to brace for penetration. Every time Chris slammed him down, Warren's throat tightened around his shaft. It was primal. Ruthless. Needed. After the shit that'd gone down with Free, he had an outlet. And Warren... Warren had him. The look in his eyes, the sounds he made, the enthusiasm with which he moved— everything he did signaled that he needed this badly. It was fucked-up perfection. A wrong Chris both hoped and dreaded was right. They were as awful as they were wonderful for each other, and there was no one else Chris wanted more.

Chris's balls tightened suddenly, and crashing pleasure soon followed. Toes curling, he wrenched Warren's head back as he came, but not fast enough to spill his load entirely on his face. Warren sucked greedily as he shot, swallowing what Chris offered until Chris couldn't take it anymore and pulled out to shoot the rest on his face. One spurt striped his cheek, the other cutting down from his eyebrow across the bridge of his nose.

"Look at you," Chris murmured as Warren caught his breath. "Fuck... look at you..."

A feeling swelled inside him, not lust or any of its cousins, but something that gripped Chris just as deep. Warren's cheeks were pink and his hair was pushed in all directions. Cum glistened on his handsome face, made bright by what little daylight they had left. But of everything Chris saw, the look in his eyes was the best of them all. Soft. Affectionate. Satisfied.

Chris had done that to him.

Chris had made him feel that way.

Heart aching, he pulled Warren back onto his lap and kissed him hard, but the ferocity between them was gone. No more teeth. No more hair pulling. No more fighting. Warren parted his lips, and Chris reverently licked his way inside. Warren tasted good, minty traces of mouthwash meeting the flat, salty notes of Chris's own spend. Chris wanted more—wanted to taste himself in Warren's mouth every time they kissed. Wanted to know that the lips he kissed belonged to him.

He squeezed Warren's ass gently, and Warren whimpered into

his mouth. If only he could get his pants off. If only they had more time...

"Needta... needta get back to work," Warren mumbled against his lips when Chris's hands slid up and along the strap of Warren's belt toward the buckle. "They'll notice I'm gone."

"Fuck them."

"No." Warren kissed him sweetly, and just like that, Chris was his. One word was all it took. A single no and he'd stop, no questions asked. Instead of pulling Warren's belt open, he cradled and squeezed his ass, kissing him back just as sweetly. It was a long while before that kiss broke, and even when it did, Warren didn't stray far—he concluded his train of thought against Chris's lips. "Only fuck me. I'm yours."

"All mine."

Warren tilted his head and brushed their lips together and the kiss started again. Chris was hard. It seemed impossible after having come not all that long ago, but with the way Warren made him feel, it wasn't all that surprising.

"I... I really need to go," Warren said when they next found the strength to part from each other. He untangled himself from Chris's arms and escaped to the passenger seat, where he flipped the visor down and used its mirror to wipe the cum from his face.

"You don't want me to finish you off?"

"No. I'll do it myself back inside." Warren tilted his jaw, no doubt attempting to see if he'd gotten everything. He hadn't. Chris brushed the last of it away with a swipe of his thumb that melted Warren like butter. Like a kitten eager to be petted, he pushed his cheek into Chris's palm and closed his eyes.

"I want you back here tomorrow," he told Warren as the man resolidified. "I want your mouth again."

Warren nuzzled Chris's palm. He nodded.

"Now get going." Chris broke contact before he gave in to temptation. "Make sure you don't let anyone see how hard you are when you head back inside."

"I know." Warren gripped the door handle, but paused before getting out. He looked Chris over curiously—almost fondly—and said without any hint that he meant it, "I hate you, Chris."

A smile raised the corner of Chris's lips. "I know. I hate you, too."

19

WARREN

Warren: Hypothetically speaking, if you start to suspect a person isn't who you thought she is… what do you do?
Libby: SHE?
Libby: Who is the other woman, Wren?
Libby: I THOUGHT WE WERE GOING FRIENDSHIP STEADY
Warren: Don't worry, your position as pajama-wearing zany best friend isn't being contested. I'm just doing some thinking about life stuff is all

Life stuff being the mind-blowing sex and the ensuing make-out session he'd had with Chris two hours ago. The "she" had been a typo, but one Warren was grateful for—if Libby was focused on snooping out "the other woman" in his life, she wouldn't think to look too closely at what was going on between him and a certain doucheweasel.

Libby: … Okay.
Libby: But just so you know, you've made me SUPER curious

Warren: Curiosity aside, do you have any input re: my question?

Libby: Oh, yeah

Libby: You know, I was just talking to CD about this not all that long ago. People change. I don't know how long you've known this particular girl, but if it's been a couple years, maybe she's different now. I don't think it's wrong to reevaluate hard feelings every couple of years depending on how severe the source of those hard feelings is

Warren: That makes sense

Libby: Take, for example, my sister, who used to be a tolerable jerk, but who I now hope I'll never have to talk to again

Warren: What happened? You never told me

Libby: It's not text message conversation. Grab me the next time you're home and we'll have a panty talk

Warren: Hard pass

Libby: What?

Libby: OMG

Libby: *PANTRY

Libby: I MEANT PANTRY TALK

Warren snorted and set his phone on his chest. It'd been a quiet day. He and Pete had yet to be dispatched and the phones were pretty much dead, so he'd retired to the small EMS bunk room he and Pete slept in to sort out what he was feeling.

And jack off.

But mostly the feeling thing.

Chris had kissed him. Worse, Warren had liked it. The ghost of Chris's lips lingered on his skin, and the memory of his firm grip still sent shivers down his spine.

What they'd shared in the parking lot had been better than the sex they'd had at Chris's place. Usually, an uptick in the quality of a lay was a rare and cherished thing Warren celebrated. All too often the guys he hooked up with got lazy or lost interest. But this... this was unusual in the extreme, and Warren wasn't sure what to make of it.

His phone buzzed. He picked it back up to find Libby had sent another text.

Libby: Typos aside, are you doing okay? That's a weird text to send from work. Must be a slow day?

Warren: Yeah, we're slow. It's giving me time to get lost in my head

Libby: I mean, if that's a BAD thing, you could use your free time to be my wingman ;)

Warren: Believe me, I've been trying. Apparently things fell through with the Lyle girl, but Pete already has his next date lined up. I'm about to ask where interested candidates can take a number, because this is ridiculous

Libby: BOO

Libby: Maybe one day he'll notice me

Libby: Do you think changing out of my pajamas would help?

Warren laughed.

Warren: Yeah, maybe

Libby: Hmm. Guess I'll have to go shopping. What do hot girls wear these days?

Warren: Libby, I love you, but you're asking the wrong guy

Libby replied with an emoji sticking its tongue out. From there, the conversation died and Warren returned his phone to his chest. His thoughts strayed back to Chris. Was it morally reprehensible to keep hooking up with a guy he hated? Probably. If he had even a modicum of self-respect, he'd block Chris's number and be done with it.

Only Warren didn't want to.

Not after that kiss.

He closed his eyes and held his lips between his teeth, biting down on them gently to hold them in place. It wasn't like being kissed was an uncommon thing. Humans had lips, and they liked to use them. It was as simple as that.

But Chris's lips were different.

Or... *Chris* was different, Warren supposed, because even if Chris could swap out parts of his anatomy like a Mr. Potato Head, it wouldn't change how hung up Warren was on him.

Stupid lips.

Stupid Chris.

Stupid super-hot sex that'd made him *feel*.

Warren groaned and rolled over, knocking his phone from his chest. It became sandwiched between him and his bunk's thin mattress, where it promptly buzzed. Either it was getting angry that he was crushing it, or Libby was back—maybe with a theory about the woman in his life. Warren fished it out and went to check the message, only it wasn't from Libby.

It was from Chris.

Chris: When are you off next?

Apparently a little kissing was all it took for him to regress into a teenager, because Warren's pulse skyrocketed. Reading Chris's text made him feel exactly the way he had at sixteen when Zach Collins had found out he was gay and messaged him to come over for "movies or something." Which was ridiculous, because he and Chris had already done way more than "something," but that jittery sense of excitement was not to be reasoned with.

Warren: Saturday, why?
Chris: And you're on two days, off four, right?
Warren: ... Yes
Chris: Good.

Chris: You said you wanted me to fuck you and you alone, so now you're gonna prove it

Chris: Meet me at my apartment on Monday at five. Come prepared.

Chris: I'm not going to use a condom

Warren didn't reply, but he did stare at the screen for a long time while his heart used his ribcage like a xylophone.

Him.

Chris.

The apartment at five.

Forget fumbling romps in a basement rec room—Zach Collins had nothing on this.

20

WARREN

On Monday at ten minutes to five, Warren crossed the leaf-littered grounds of the Delmar Apartment Complex to Chris's building. Up the uneven steps he went, through the brick-propped door, and into the lobby. Unlike before, when he'd gone straight for the stairwell in a blind fit of rage, today he stopped to compose himself. It wouldn't do him any good to get to Chris's with his heart in his throat—he needed it available for other things.

Phallic things.

His throat, he meant. Not his heart. Although it wasn't like Chris hadn't filled it, too.

Just not with his dick.

Warren pushed the thought aside. Going down that rabbit hole was only going to make things worse. Whatever happened upstairs would happen upstairs. That was it. Just because Chris had told him to come prepared didn't mean he was going to drag Warren into his apartment—preferably by the hair, but Warren would settle for by the front of his shirt—throw him over the nearest waist-height surface, and fuck him within an inch of his life. Raw. Like the beast he was. No one had ever done it before, not even when he'd asked.

The likelihood that Chris would be the one to step up to the plate was so small, it was laughable. Would they have good sex? Probably. But the kind of rough sex Warren wanted was the stuff of myth.

No average man would be able to stick his sword into Warren's stone, least of all a bastard.

Somewhat soothed by probability, Warren cut across the lobby's tiled floor and headed into the stairwell. The smell of industrial cleaner was strong here, but even bleach couldn't tamp down the dank, humid musk that hung in the air and caught in Warren's lungs. He ignored it and started his ascent to the third floor, echoing footsteps marking his passage.

The third-floor landing was in no better repair than the rest of the stairwell—a dark splotch stained the concrete to the left of the door and the door handle was tarnished and had lost its shine. Warren pushed it down with his elbow to keep his hands clean. There was a chance he'd need them to touch a better kind of filthy thing. Even if Chris wasn't going to be the man who fulfilled his ultimate fantasy, something was going down today, and while Warren liked to go hard, he wasn't into being fucked by dirty dicks.

Down the dimly lit hallway was apartment 304—his destination. Warren came to a stop in front of it. Like the landing handle, the gold numbers screwed to Chris's door were bronzed from neglect. The three hung crookedly, a screw missing. There was a hole in the wood where it had been. Warren peered at it, wondering if he could see straight through into the apartment, but was met with darkness.

He waited.

The door, unsurprisingly, stayed closed.

You have to knock, Warren told himself, though rational thoughts did little to soothe his pounding heart. *He won't know you're here if you don't make yourself heard. Knock on the door. If you don't, he'll think you ghosted him.*

While it was true, it didn't make it any easier. Warren swallowed and lifted his fist, but didn't follow through. Why the hell was he having so much trouble knocking on the door? It was a booty call.

Nothing more. He'd driven over two hours to have sex with a total stranger and hadn't regretted it in the least, so why was it different now?

Rough hands.

Crude words.

A low, guttural growl that'd coiled in Warren's gut.

A shiver ran down his spine.

Maybe the why wasn't such a mystery.

At last, Warren knocked. There was movement behind the door —the scuff of fabric, the scrape of wood, and the clack of metal striking metal. The doorknob turned and there was Chris. Warren could only stare. It wasn't that there was anything different about him, physically, at least. Chris was dressed like he normally was—in blue jeans that fit in the hips and were comfortably loose around the legs and a soft cotton t-shirt that showed off the muscles of his arms and chest. But the story in his eyes and the unending want he found in it... Warren didn't have to read between the lines to know how it would end.

Without a word, Chris took him by the wrist and pulled him across the threshold. The door shut, then latched. When it was secured, Chris curled his free hand in Warren's and pushed him against the door, where he captured his lips in a scorching kiss. It wasn't the ruthless domination Warren had been hoping for, but somehow it was better. Fuller. More satisfying. He moaned into Chris's mouth, and Chris rewarded him by pulling his hair and digging his nails into Warren's wrist. The pain was crisp and carried by notes of heavy, unending pleasure. It was like Chris understood him. Warren never wanted it to end.

But then, a tug.

Warren's eyes flew open.

The kiss was over, but Chris... Chris's grip on his hair had tightened, and he was using it to pull Warren off the door and down the hall.

Warren's feet failed him, and he came close to tripping more

139

than once as Chris dragged him into the living room. Pain prickled across his scalp, but transformed into pleasure before it registered.

Chris wasn't…

He couldn't…

But when they reached the living room and Chris threw Warren down over the arm of the couch, it looked more and more like he would.

Warren's palms met old upholstery. His chest struck the couch's wooden frame. His ass was given a different treatment—one of Chris's broad palms grasped it while his other hand snaked around to undo Warren's fly.

"Look at you," Chris uttered against the back of Warren's ear as Warren panted with growing need. "Back here again, helpless, silently begging for what you know I can give you. You really can't help yourself, can you?"

Warren's fly fell to the persistence of Chris's hand, and no sooner had it than Chris slipped inside and clasped Warren's swollen cock.

Chris chuckled darkly. "Mm, and what do we have here?"

Warren groaned and pushed into his hand, eager to let Chris feel how hard he was. Anything to keep him there. Anything to keep going.

"Filthy," Chris praised—and god, did it turn Warren on. The husky timbre of his voice was a reward unto itself. "No underwear? Reaves, you really did come prepared. Let's see what else you've done for me, hmm?"

Chris's fingers curled beneath the waistline of his jeans and down they went, only stopping when they were around Warren's thighs. Cool air kissed Warren's skin and chilled the slick between his cheeks.

"Beautiful," Chris muttered, letting Warren hear his smirk. Without warning, the tip of his finger met the lubricated skin of Warren's taint, then traced upward until it was forced to part from

Warren's body. Chris made a low sound of delight. "What's this? You *are* filthy, aren't you?"

Warren closed his eyes, all too aware of the way he was trembling. Every muscle in his body was loose, but knowing what Chris was seeing sent shivers through him all the same. With his ass bared, there was no hiding the head of the plug he'd inserted after cleaning and prepping earlier that day. Chris had to be toying with it now—tracing his fingertips over it in the same way he'd teased Warren's ass. The anticipation was electric.

Then, all at once, the plug in Warren's ass strained against his opening. Warren gasped and buried his face against the couch cushion, struggling to hold it in while Chris slid it back and forth. The sensation of slick silicone as it slid inside him made Warren clench around the plug, and as distracted as he was, he didn't remember Chris's hand was around his cock until he started to stroke. The dichotomy left him breathless. Penetrated from one end and penetrating from the other, he moaned into the couch and worked his hips erratically to chase pleasure. Then Chris pulled the plug until the thickest part of its bulb stretched Warren's tight ring, and all Warren wanted was more.

"*Fuck*," he gasped, digging his blunt nails into the padding beneath him. "Oh, *fuck!*"

"What's the matter?" Chris's question was followed by a *zip* and the shuffle of moving denim. "Is it too much for you?"

Never.

Chris could stretch him all day—could fill him with bigger and bigger plugs—and Warren would take them all. Anything to keep feeling like this.

"That's a shame," Chris said when Warren didn't commit to an answer. He let go of Warren's cock, but even being robbed of that pleasure wasn't enough to send Warren crashing down. "I thought you'd be able to take more. Guess you'll just have to suffer through this next part."

Next part?

Warren lifted his head, but before he could make sense of anything, the plug had left his body and something else had taken its place—Chris. The cock he'd taken down his throat sank all the way to its hilt inside of him in one brutal thrust, taking Warren from empty to achingly full. Warren cried out at the same time that Chris did and clutched at the couch to keep his balance, but Chris was moving fast now, slamming into him, forcing him to take more, and more, and more. The force Chris used pushed him at an angle toward the edge of the couch's arm until Warren couldn't hold on anymore. He crashed onto the floor with a gasp. Chris followed him down and shoved his way back inside, then humped Warren into the floor.

"You think it'd be so easy?" He growled as Warren's eyes rolled back in his head and he squirmed to meet Chris's relentless thrusts. "You're mine, Reaves. *Mine.* Until you tell me to stop, I'm gonna take what I want from you. Gonna take it all."

Warren clawed at the floor, desperate to get a hold on something —anything—that would keep him grounded, but there was nothing there. The thick, solid mass of Chris's cock pounded into him and detonated urgency in his gut. As they fucked, Warren came.

"*Fuck.*" Chris strained the word through a grunt. "The way you just clenched… gonna make me come."

But he didn't stop thrusting. Didn't slow down. As Warren shot, spilling onto the floor, Chris pumped into him from behind. It was feral. It was greedy. It was perfect. And when Chris's thrusts grew tellingly deep and desperate, it became everything Warren had ever dreamed. Chris came inside of him, breathing hard against the back of Warren's ear while his cock twitched and pulsed. Warren felt it all, heard it all, and still wanted more.

It was a minute or two before Chris withdrew, but Warren wished it'd been longer. He remained boneless on the floor while Chris stood and hiked up his pants, then zipped them back up. "I've gotta go get Jack," he said, fastening the button of his fly. "We need to clean up and get you out of here."

Cleanup wouldn't be bad—Warren's mess was confined to the space beneath him, and upon further investigation, he found the plug on the floor not all that far away. A few swipes with a paper towel and some cleaner would do.

Warren's ass, on the other hand, was a different matter.

"We agreed that you could come in me—not that you could turn my ass into a flood zone," he grumbled, not because he was upset about it, but because if causing trouble got him fucked like this on the regular, he was going to keep doing it. "Bastard."

"Get the fuck off my floor, cum rag," Chris bit back toothlessly.

Warren smiled. "Asshole."

"Dickhead."

"Bed sore."

"Idiot."

Warren stood on shaking legs and rolled his eyes, yanking his pants back into place. "Yeah, I'm gonna have to call bullshit on that one. While you were off shooting guns and making babies, I was in school. And speaking of idiot, who's the jerk who copied off my biology final? Oh yeah. That's right. It was *you.*"

It was all fun and games until Chris grabbed him by the wrist and spun him around. They were close, almost nose to nose, and Chris showed no sign he was interested in changing that—he kept a firm grip on Warren, never letting go.

"I'll have you know," he warned forebodingly, "that I didn't copy off your biology final. I never copied off you at all. I don't know who put that thought in your head, but whoever did, they were wrong. Yeah, I slacked off in high school, but I put in the work and aced that test fair and square. Go track down Mr. Waterford if you don't believe me. He'll tell you that I was in his classroom every day at lunch two weeks before, and that I stuck around after school to study with him so I'd pass."

It was an uncomfortable feeling to be turned on and gutted in the same breath. Warren stood still and silent, searching Chris's eyes for deception that wasn't there.

Chris released his wrist, but guilt kept its grip on Warren's heart. "Go get your plug, Warren. I need to go pick up Jack."

2 1

CHRIS

After Warren collected his plug, Chris showed him the door. Enough time had passed since Warren had arrived that a bar of dusky sunlight beaming in from between the curtains of the living room window spilled across it, a surefire sign that the sun was setting and night was on the way. That same light rehomed itself in Warren's tawny hair when he stepped forward to open the door. It stretched down the planes of his back and made itself comfortable in the cotton weave of his shirt, where it reflected off something that shouldn't have been visible—a tag. Warren had been so out of it he'd put his shirt on inside out.

Cute.

From the tag, Chris followed the hem along Warren's sturdy shoulder down his arm, and from there to his hip. He hadn't meant to, but his gaze wandered from there inward to Warren's ass. He told himself it was only to double-check that Warren had put his pants on right side out, but it was such a terrible lie that not even he believed it.

The truth was, he wanted to see Warren.

To remember the way his skin had dimpled beneath his fingers when he'd grabbed him by the hips.

145

Even clothed, the sight of his ass made him want to hook an arm around Warren's waist, tug him close, and own the curve of Warren's cheeks with the palm of his hand until Warren was panting with need. It was as tempting as it was infuriating. Chris didn't like to think of himself as a slave to his own impulses, but Warren made it so fucking hard to resist.

"It won't open." Warren rattled the doorknob, the sound bursting Chris's daydream like a pin pricking a balloon. "I turned the latch. Did I lock it?"

"Yeah, you locked it." Chris reached around him and grasped the thumbturn, but didn't follow through with unlocking the door. He kept close to Warren instead, taking pleasure in the tantalizing smell of fresh sweat on his skin and the way sex amplified whatever scents played into making him so distinctly himself. It hadn't been all that long since he'd come, but Chris was stirred by it. Did they have time to fuck again? If he sent Liberty a text to let her know he'd gotten caught up at work...

"Uh," Warren said flatly. "You gonna unlock it, or?"

Chris squeezed his eyes shut. What the hell was wrong with him? Now was not the time. He unlocked the door and dropped his arm, giving Warren some space. "Should open now."

"Great."

The door did open. Warren stepped into the hall. Chris watched him, not sure if he should speak or let Warren go without a word. Free had been his high school sweetheart and he'd never been with anyone else, so hookup etiquette didn't come naturally.

But was what they had a hookup?

Chris eyed Warren, who lingered in the hall with his chin angled to his shoulder and his gaze lowered. His cheeks were rosy, still flushed from sex, and his hair was a mess that a quick swipe or two with his hand had failed to tame. Yeah, there was bad blood between them, but damn if Warren wasn't handsome. Chris could overlook some of his rougher edges if it meant Warren would warm his bed from time to time.

A tense moment passed during which neither of them said anything. It was broken by Warren, who lifted his head and looked Chris in the eyes. "Look, Chris, I... I know it's probably not much consolation, but I really regret the whole Urban Dictionary thing."

"Yeah? That so?"

It seemed the stiffness in his voice set Warren off, because the uncertainty in his eyes sharpened into anger. "Yeah, it is. I should've been the bigger man and not engaged, but the biology thing pushed me over the edge. For what it's worth, it was dumb and I regretted it pretty much right away. If I could, I would've deleted it, but the site doesn't work like that."

Chris frowned. "Edge? What edge? I had absolutely nothing to do with you before your definition went viral."

"Are you being serious right now?" The anger in Warren's eyes spread across his face. He scowled. "I'm trying to apologize. If you're not going to drop the act, the least you could do is keep quiet."

Oh, fuck that. Warren was *not* going to start an argument in the hall where all his neighbors could hear it. Chris stormed forward and grabbed him by the wrist, but no sooner had he then Warren yanked back his hand.

"Fucking stop," Warren seethed. He spoke in hushed tones—thank god—but Chris worried the edge in his voice would cut through the nearby walls. "Don't touch me."

"Someone will hear you," Chris said in an equally stiff voice. "If you want to fight, get the fuck back inside."

"Why the hell would I do that when you're straight-up lying to my face?"

"*Warren.*"

Warren's lip twitched. "Libby said that you'd changed, but I don't think I believe her. You're the same asshole you were when we were kids. You'll never take responsibility for what you've done, will you? You went out of your way for *years* to make my life miserable, and now you're..." A flicker of regret troubled his expression. "Whatever. It doesn't matter. The takeaway is that you're not man enough to own up to your shitty behavior."

Christ, did Warren know how to get under his skin. Chris grabbed a fistful of his shirt and yanked it to knock him off balance. When he stumbled, Chris dragged him back into the apartment and kicked the door shut.

"Fuck you!" Warren snarled. He made a mad grab at Chris, but Chris was done with his bullshit and shoved Warren into the wall before he could make contact. Warren landed harder than he'd hoped, and Chris felt a twinge of regret, but he'd be damned if he let a man poison his reputation here. He'd worked too hard for this, and given up too much. Jack deserved stability. Warren wasn't going to take that from him.

"What the hell were you thinking out there, Reaves?" Chris barred his arm across Warren's chest, not quite locking him in place, but putting enough of his weight behind the gesture to show him he meant business. "You can argue with me all you want behind closed doors, but the second you take that behavior across my threshold, this is over. You drive me fucking crazy in every goddamn way, but what I want will *never* come before what Jack needs. Never. And what he needs is to live in a place where his neighbors don't gossip about his father. Do you understand?"

Warren's eyes flashed with anger. "So you think it's okay to fucking lie?"

"What the hell are you talking about?" Chris's temple twitched. A headache was setting in. "We were never friends in school. We never hung out. I never even spoke to you unless I had to for class. If you're not causing a scene just to get me to rough you up, then there's a disconnect going on here, and I'm not letting you leave until we've got it figured out. Now…" Chris eased some of the pressure off Warren's chest to test the waters, but stayed alert. If Warren flew off the handle, he'd snap back into action. "Tell me about what I did to make your life so miserable you'd make that Urban Dictionary post to retaliate."

148

Movement caught the corner of his eye. Warren had balled his fists. "You know what you did."

"Wrong answer."

Chris didn't go for Warren's chest this time. He grabbed him by the jaw, holding his head in place. Warren's eyes widened, then narrowed into hateful slits that would've done Chris in had he not been so used to seeing Warren angry.

"Use your words, Reaves," Chris said in the deep, rumbling voice Warren always reacted the best to. "Tell me what I did wrong so I can try to fix it."

The prick of Warren's stubble abraded his skin, but Chris didn't let go. He tightened his grip. If they were ever going to weed out the misconceptions they had of each other, they needed to talk, and they needed to do it now.

But Warren wouldn't speak. He glared at Chris, but there was a glint of uncertainty in it, like he was starting to believe that maybe it was all some big misunderstanding. With a little more pushing, Chris hoped he'd believe it in full... so he kissed Warren. Kissed him hard. Savored the gasp Warren fed to him and endured the pounding of his fists on his chest. No matter what, he would not relent.

Not until the broken past they shared was made right.

At first, Warren buzzed with anger, but soon enough he started to loosen. It made sense. Even rock could be eroded given persistence and time, and Chris was in possession of both.

He indexed the changes as they came.

First, Warren's shoulders relaxed. It wasn't that they slumped—not exactly—but the knots of tension pinching them to his neck undid themselves, and like a corset come undone, Warren's body loosened. Next, a shiver ran through him. Chris would've overlooked it had Warren not made the faintest moan. Eventually, persistence paid off, and Warren began to kiss him back. It was slow at first. Hesitant. Guilty. But soon enough, Warren's lips demanded more. They kissed each other fiercely until they were out of breath, and even then kept going.

By the time Chris pulled away, he'd been made half-crazy by want.

"Try again," he told Warren. "Tell me what I did wrong."

Warren didn't speak right away. He leaned against the wall for support and took a few deep breaths. While he recovered, Chris got a good look at him. The pink in his cheeks had darkened and spread, and his lips were glistening and overplumped from having been kissed too hard, too often. God, was he gorgeous. Infuriating and irresistible. Corporeal temptation. Chris ran his thumb over those plump lips, then let Warren go.

"Tell me," he said again. "I want to know your truth."

Warren let a slow, steady breath out through his nostrils, then shook his head. For a second, Chris thought he wouldn't speak, but then he opened his mouth and detailed the incidents one by one. Smashed macaroni art in kindergarten. A puddle on picture day. Ruthlessness during dodgeball. A pizza lunch sprayed with Axe. There were others, too. Some that were so minor Chris was surprised he remembered them at all, and some that weighed on Warren like they really were the worst memories of his life. An accidental shoulder check in the hallway. Sand art trampled on. An armful of binders knocked to the ground. Chris listened to it all, and although he didn't remember, he did believe.

"What else was there?" Chris asked when Warren trailed off. "Is that all?"

"I can't remember."

"If you do, you tell me." Chris leaned in and kissed him again, softer this time. "You tell me the hurt you feel. You let me listen to it so I know never to do it again. All that shit you just brought up? It didn't even ping my radar back in school. I wasn't doing it on purpose, but that doesn't mean I'm not sorry. No one deserves to be made to feel the way you did, and it being an accident doesn't change that. If I'd known, I would've apologized back then. I would've been more careful."

"You did know," Warren argued, but his usual petulance was gone. He sounded exhausted. "Why else would it be you? Only you. No one else ever fucked me up the way you did."

"No one?"

"Never."

"Do you think there could be another reason for that?"

"What do you mean?"

The pieces had all fallen into place for Chris, but Warren was trapped inside the situation, and until he got some distance from it, he wouldn't be able to see the bigger picture. One day it'd come to him. One day, but not now. It took time to unlearn principles a life-time in the making—Chris would know. The bullshit that'd gone down with Free had taught him as much, but Warren wasn't under the same kind of pressure.

"Use that big college-educated brain of yours, Reaves," Chris said softly before brushing Warren's forehead with his lips. "If you think on it hard enough, I'm sure you'll figure it out. Until then, I'm sorry about what happened when we were in school."

"And I'm sorry for acting out the way I have. And for the doucheweasel thing. I really would fix it if I could."

"I know."

Warren sighed, so Chris drew him into his arms. Up this close, all his favorite parts of Warren were his to enjoy. Chris stole a kiss from the corner of his lips that Warren turned to reciprocate, and they made out in a slow and unhurried way that made Chris more eager than ever to drag Warren back to bed. If only he could. For now, the best he could do was hold him, so he waited until some semblance of tension returned to Warren's limbs before reluctantly letting him go. "You gonna be okay to get home?"

"Yeah."

The look in Warren's eyes. The goddamn look. Like the bliss of orgasm softened by regret. The light coming from the living room had shifted since they'd started to argue, striping his face so the browns of his irises gleamed like bronze. They were the kind of eyes that could undo a man before he knew to brace himself. Weapons in their own right, and a force Chris hadn't been trained to defend himself against.

"Good." Chris's heart was in his throat, his cock standing at attention. The urge to keep Warren there with him was overwhelming—if they spent any more time together, he was sure he'd give in. "I need your ass out. Now." Chris pointed his chin in the direction of the door. "I've got a kid waiting on pickup and an ex-in-law to rescue."

He chose to omit that if Warren kept standing there, someone would need to rescue *him*.

Warren seemed just as begrudging to leave. He lingered a moment longer, looked Chris in the eyes curiously, then headed for the door.

"I'll be waiting in the usual spot next time you're on shift," Chris said after Warren had stepped into the hall. "Don't think this changes anything."

"Of course it doesn't change anything," Warren bit back with none of his usual prickle. "Just because I regret what I did doesn't mean I don't think you're a jerk."

"Likewise."

"So... fuck you." Warren flipped him off and took a few steps back, challenging Chris with his eyes, but Chris had seen the way Warren had looked at him, and he knew better than to fall for it. "Me being here doesn't mean anything."

"You wish it meant something."

"Fuck you."

"Fuck you back."

Warren backed down the hall, birds flipped high, but Chris didn't miss the swagger in his walk, like he was a teen who'd just made it to third base with the most popular girl in school.

"Fuck you sideways," Warren continued, not to be outdone. "With a spiky dildo. And *no* lube."

"A dildo? Yawn. Fuck you with a cactus."

"Fuck you with *two* cactuses!"

"Cacti."

"Fuck you!"

Their bickering drew the attention of an elderly neighbor down the hall, who opened her door and peered at them distrustfully from behind thick-framed glasses. Warren, a weasel in his own right, popped his index fingers up so he was flashing Chris twin peace signs. The little shit. Chris couldn't help but grin.

He closed the door and continued their conversation in private.

Chris: Fuck you harder

Chris: You and only you

Unknown Name: Woe be unto you if I find out you're fucking someone else

Chris: I'm not

Unknown Name: WOE

Unknown Name: And cacti

Chris sent back two cactus emojis, then added Warren's name to his phone.

2 2

WARREN

A flick of Warren's thumb shot rows of cactus pictures across the screen of his phone. By nature, cacti were all fairly phallic, but none of them were phallic enough. He needed more. Not only did his cactus have to look like a dick—preferably with a big old set of balls to drive the point home—but it needed to look *painful.* Cute, fuzzy-looking spines didn't scream intense anal agony. The only cactus that would do was one that looked like it would cut a bitch.

A death cactus.

A *warning.*

"I worry about you sometimes," Libby said out of nowhere, scaring the shit out of him. Warren yelped and clutched his phone to his chest. Mercifully, he'd met his quota of couch falls for the day, so his ass remained planted on the cushion, but his heart still raced like he'd been chucked into the Grand Canyon. "Cactus peens, Wren?" Libby continued. "I know you're mid dry spell, but come on..."

"Jesus, Lib! Are you trying to give me a heart attack?"

"No." Libby folded her arms on top of the couch and grinned at him. "Attack is too harsh a word. I was going for something softer. Like a... hmm... a heart startle. That's a little more fitting."

Warren eyed her. She looked different, but he couldn't put his finger on why. "Did you get a haircut?"

"No."

"Did you just take off one of those bird poop face masks?"

"*No.*"

"… Do you *have* bird poop face masks?" he asked, alarmed.

Libby rolled her eyes. "We're not talking about my *bad* choices right now, Wren. We're talking about my good ones."

"You make good choices?"

She whacked him upside the head. "Them's fightin' words, you cactus pervert. You know, it looks an awful lot like you're in the middle of making a bad decision yourself." Warren was so confused he had nothing to say, which Libby didn't seem to mind, because she plowed forward with the conversation as though Warren wasn't looking at her like she had six heads. "You know, if you'd told me you were Frankensteining a body together for your Quaker Oats lover, I would have been happy to jump in with good dick suggestions. You don't have to go full cactus. There are other phallic objects you can graft onto your dreamoat… uh… dream*boat* if you like it a little freaky. Have you heard of our lord and savior, Bad Dragon?"

Warren's mouth fell open.

"I know, I know, it may seem a little pricey up front, but when you consider how much you'll save from hospital visits to have needles removed from uh… well, you know… it'll be well worth the investment. Plus, I'm pretty sure you'd end up crushing the cactus and having to get another in a never-ending cycle of dildo disappointment. Totally not worth it in my book."

"How about we move on to what's going on with you and never talk about this again?"

"Oh! Sure. But before I do, I need to ask you a question." It was going to be about dildos, wasn't it? "When you said I looked 'different,' did you mean *good* different, or *bad* different? Be honest. It's important."

Thank god, a normal question.

"Good different," Warren clarified. "It's like you did something with your face. You're glowing."

Libby lit up. "I'm so happy to hear you say that. I'm wearing makeup. Isn't that weird?"

"Yeah. What's going on? You going out?"

"I *am*." Libby sighed happily and draped herself over the back of the couch. "You'll never guess what happened."

"You found out they're serving free pancakes at the library?"

"No!" A hopeful sparkle glimmered in her eyes. "Are they, though? Because that would be pretty cool."

"No."

"Darn." She shelved her disappointment and in its absence, her smile came back stronger than ever. "But it doesn't even matter, because Pete and I are going out for dinner."

"Together?"

That earned him another whack.

"Yes, together! And I'm not even creepily following him inside and sitting a few tables away this time. We're going to be sitting together. He even knows to expect me. It doesn't get any more fairy tale than this."

"How the hell did you manage to score a date with Pete?"

Libby waggled an eyebrow. "I did the unthinkable and asked him out first. Now all I've gotta do is woo him with my winning personality, impress him with the fat stacks in my wallet, and wife the *fuck* outta him. This relationship's gonna be my bitch."

Warren shouldn't have snorted, but he did. Libby went to whack him again, but he'd grown wise to her ways, and he intercepted her hand before it could deliver swift justice. "I'm sorry, I'm sorry! I shouldn't have laughed."

"It's the fat stacks, isn't it? I figure I can just cash out a huge wad of singles and put a lonely hundred-dollar bill on top. It's not *technically* a lie if I do it that way—I can't be held accountable for other people's assumptions. And you know what they say about those."

Holding back his laughter was torture. "What *do* they say about assumptions, Libby?"

"Everybody has one."

A beat of silence passed before Warren couldn't take it anymore. He burst out laughing.

"See? Winning personality." Libby grinned and stood straight, brushing the wrinkles out of her top. For the first time in weeks, she wasn't wearing pajamas. Warren was impressed. "As long as Pete's not gay, he's gonna fall head over heels for me."

Warren arched a brow. He actually agreed with her, but he couldn't help but offer up a Chris-ism. "That so?"

"Uh, yeah. Admit it, Wren—if you weren't playing for the other team, you'd *totally* be in love with me. I'm a *delight*."

She wasn't wrong. Warren did love Libby. She was the sister he'd never had and the best friend a guy could ask for. Pete was lucky.

Although Warren was starting to think he wasn't all that unlucky, either.

Stupid cactuses.

… cacti.

"For the record," he said. "Pete's straight. I have suspicions he might be the tiniest bit bi, but if he is, he's never come out and said it."

"Which means butt stuff isn't off the table." Libby's eyes shone. "He's perfect."

"If I had only one chance to turn back time thirty seconds, I'd use it right now so I could unlearn that about you."

"Sorry." She winked. "I'm just so excited about tonight. I feel like I've been pining after him for forever, and now it's finally happening. We're finally going out. All it took was me actually taking initiative. Crazy, right?" She laughed. It didn't last long. A second later her expression crumpled and she threw herself once again across the back of the couch in despair. "Wren, what if he hates me?"

"He won't hate you."

"What if I blow it?"

"I mean, that could work."

The gears turned slowly behind her eyes. When realization finally dawned, she snapped back from the couch and glowered at him. *"Wren!"*

"Kidding. Don't blow it. I know it sounds corny, but just be you. Pete's a good guy. It won't take him long to see that you're the right kind of special—and if he doesn't, you know I'm going to kick his ass, right?"

"You know, I'm not usually the kind of person who endorses capital punishment, but I'm *so* behind you right now."

"You mean corporal punishment?"

Libby shrugged. "Sure. We'll go with that."

Warren laughed again.

"Anyway, I should get going. This whole having-dinner-at-seven thing might be romantic, but I'm starting to think it's also a form of torture. I wanna go back in time and kick old Libby in the ass for suggesting we go out so late." Libby wrinkled her nose. "Hopefully Pete likes girls who gnaw on the table, because by the time the food actually arrives, I'm gonna be starving."

"As long as you don't have a rat dog, you should be good."

"Do raccoons count?"

Warren glared.

"I'm kidding, I'm kidding. No raccoons for this girl. I learned my lesson. Non-human beings with opposable thumbs belong outside, where they can't mess with the thermostat or poop in the pantry. So, uh, I guess I'll see you later. Leave the porch light on, but don't wait up for me."

"Have fun."

Libby had made it to the door, but she turned around to curl her fingers in a wave. "Thanks. You, too. Just, uh, not too much fun. At least not with a cactus. You're a kickass paramedic, but you're not *that* good."

"Thanks."

"Welcome!" She waved one last time, then left. When she was

gone, Warren lifted the phone from his chest and took stock of the cacti on his screen. None of them were good enough. He scrolled on, losing hope with each disappointing new row, until a text from a certain doucheweasel arrived.

Chris: Forgot to tell you earlier it goes both ways
Chris: You're mine, Reaves. All mine. And if I find out you're giving it up for someone else…

A picture of a perfect death cactus loaded in the chat.

Chris: A prickly fate awaits you.
Chris: I don't like to share

23

CHRIS

Time had a way of passing by unnoticed in places like Lethridge, where day in and day out, nothing much changed. At first, with boxes to unpack and jobs to apply to, Chris had resisted falling into tedium, but now that he had stable employment, the days blurred. Every weekday morning at six fifteen, he watched the same red Ford Focus with the rusted grill and the cracked windshield roll out of the Delmar Apartment Complex while he sipped coffee in the few quiet moments he had before Jack woke up and loudly went about getting ready for the day. At noon, lunch bag in hand, Kathleen Sinclair always poked her head into his office to glare at him before tottering off in the direction of Sheriff Sinclair's office. Chris had it on good authority she made lunch for him every day. But for all the monotony that came with being an adult burdened with adult responsibilities, there was one constant Chris looked forward to: every night at half past eight, Warren would send him a text.

Their conversations were predictable. Warren liked to give Chris shit, then act offended when Chris gave it back. Some nights his indignant behavior led to an argument that almost always dissolved into dirty talk, dick pics, and promises to fuck each other up the next time they were in the same place. Some nights it tapered into nothing. The nights Chris was fondest of were the ones where he could tell that he was making Warren squirm. On those nights, whether they ended the conversation coming together or Chris shut things down before Warren could get off, the rest of the world ceased to matter. Even the bullshit with Free fell by the wayside. It was like, for just a little, Chris could be himself.

Warren: Went to Lowe's today. Looked at cacti. Your ass is toast if you're playing me

A picture of a commercial display of cacti followed.

Chris: I'm disappointed. You missed a perfect opportunity for a "your ass is grass" pun. Is the warranty up on your college degree? Might wanna consider a refund
Warren: You succ
Chris: Lame pun is lame
Chris: I stand by what I said about that warranty
Warren: Screw you, Chris. That was funny and you know it
Chris: You wish
Chris: Pretty sure Jack could come up with better wordplay
Warren: I STRONGLY disagree, but whatever. You can think what you want
Warren: But since we're on the topic of Jack, guess who pilfered my cookies again?
Chris: Penance
Warren: Fuck you
Warren: I'll have you know this is the THIRD time I've been robbed.
Chris: Have you asked him to stop?
Warren: Well... no
Chris: Then why are you complaining?

Warren: Because it's basic human courtesy not to demolish someone else's box of cookies
Warren: Are you raising a beast, or a boy?

On the night of this particular exchange, Chris had discovered that all the lunch meat he'd wanted to use for sandwiches had mysteriously disappeared. In unrelated events, his ravenous eight-year-old hadn't been able to finish his dinner. At that point, it wouldn't be a surprise to learn he'd been raising a beast, but until the jungle came to take back its own, he couldn't say for sure.

Chris: What do you expect me to do? Rip through the fabric of time itself to go back and discipline him? If you want to keep your cookies, tell him that you don't appreciate him taking your things without asking. If the problem persists, I'll step in
Warren: You're useless
Chris: You're looking to pick a fight so you'll get laid
Warren: Is it that obvious?
Chris: You're like a goddamn Snickers commercial. Go bust a nut. You're not you when you're horny

Warren started and stopped typing several times. Chris could practically see him squirm. The conversation ended there, but it was all worth it the next day when Warren rushed out of the station after Chris had finished work, sank into the passenger seat, and all but ripped Chris's fly open.

Not all routine had to be soul-sucking.

Chris had learned it could be dick sucking, too.

All good things came to an end. Or at least, that's what Chris had been told. The truth was a shade more ambiguous, especially when it came to public sex. All he knew was that one second Warren was grinding on his lap in the front seat of his SUV after work, and the next he was getting up close and personal with the back floor mats. Chris, heavily aroused and more than a little confused, then spotted Sheriff Sinclair as he crossed the lot, cell phone glued to his ear.

Chris couldn't help but wonder if he was finally calling in a search and rescue for his missing hat.

"Shit, shit, *shiiiit*," Warren whispered from his hidey-hole. "Can you see him? Does it look like he noticed me?"

Chris watched Sinclair kick a cluster of wet fallen leaves, slip, and almost fall on his face. "No, I think you're good."

"Thank fuck."

"You'd be better off thanking the roomy interior of my Acura."

"What are you, a car commercial?"

Chris snorted. "No, but if Sinclair catches us, we could be a teaser clip for *Cops*."

Sinclair, having regained his balance, hurried away from the offending leaf pile. He headed back inside.

"You're clear," Chris said. "Sinclair's gone."

Warren wrested himself up from the floor and climbed into the front seat. Chris narrowly dodged a foot to the face. It stood to reason that Warren would leave immediately and head back to the station if for no other reason than self-preservation, but it seemed that common sense had gone the way of Sinclair's hat and simply disappeared. The dreamy, smitten look in Warren's eyes was almost enough to make Chris forget they'd been seconds away from being caught.

Almost.

Unfortunately for Warren, Chris had long ago learned that thinking with his dick was often more trouble than it was worth. "You need to get going, Reaves."

"But..."

"No buts."

Warren pouted. It was unfairly adorable. "You didn't even come."

"Then you're gonna have to make up for it later, aren't you?"

The shiver that shot through Warren was worth the blue balls. He raked his teeth over his bottom lip and nodded, devouring Chris with lust-sweetened eyes before setting a hand on the door handle. It looked like he had something he wanted to say, but whatever it was never made it past his lips. With a shake of his head, he opened the door and ducked out of the car, leaving Chris to watch as he trekked back to the station.

For a while after he was gone, Chris sat behind the wheel and thought about the way Warren had looked—of the affection in his eyes and the softness that overcame his face whenever he looked Chris's way. He wondered if Warren had started to put the pieces together, but decided it was still too soon. It'd been a little more than a week since Warren's last visit to his apartment, and it would take more time than that for him to realize why Chris had always been at the forefront of his mind.

It was fine. Chris could wait. Until Warren saw the light, Chris would work on being honest with himself.

Having feelings for someone was easy.

Having feelings for an old enemy? Not so much.

But with time and repetition, all things got easier. Love wasn't any exception. With that in mind, Chris turned the key, shifted into reverse, and got going. One of these blurred days he'd wake up and realize that wanting Warren had become so normal, it blended in with the rest of his routine.

That night at half past eight, sprawled on the living room couch while the TV streamed Netflix at a whisper, Chris sent a text to Warren before Warren could text him.

Chris: I've been thinking about what happened today, and I've come to a conclusion
Warren: What?
Chris: You wanted to get caught when we were out in the parking lot
Chris: You're taking too long on purpose
Warren: That's bullshit and you know it

It was, but working Warren into a tizzy was worth the little white lie. Chris hadn't been able to stop thinking about the way Warren had looked after Sinclair had interrupted them—the desire that'd glimmered in his eyes. Jerking off hadn't done shit. What he needed was Warren's mouth. Warren's hands. Warren's ass. *Fuck*, his ass… Chris's cock stirred at the memory.

Chris: Bullshit or not, I'm not willing to put my neck on the line because you can't get to the point and suck me off
Chris: I'm giving you five minutes tomorrow to do the job, then I'm kicking you out of my car. If I don't come, you'll pay for it on your next day off
Warren: Like you'd have the balls to punish me

There it was. Chris had set Warren up, and Warren had returned volley. The ball was back in Chris's court and he had the perfect play in mind.

Chris: You really wanna try me?
Warren: Yeah, because I know you're not gonna see it through
Chris: Fuck you
Warren: Really? That's the best you got? This is what I'm talking about
Warren: you're all bark, no bite
Warren: I don't have anything to be afraid of

166

Chris grinned.

Game, set, match.

Chris: Good. Then you have no reason to turn me down. The timer starts the second you shut the car door. See you tomorrow, Reaves. Don't be late.

24

WARREN

Waiting was not Warren's strong suit. At least, not when it came to promises made via thirst trap texts. To make matters worse, it had been an unusually quiet shift. Without work to distract him, he'd resorted to cleaning the garage—*again*—because if he sat still, he'd lose his mind wondering if Chris would live up to his word.

His one saving grace was Pete, who trailed after Warren wherever he went, hearts in his eyes and a spring in his step. At long last, his curse had been broken. Libby had charmed his socks off... amongst other things.

"Did you know you can be a professional macramér?" Pete asked with a dreamy sigh as he pushed a scrub brush across the floor. He'd been scouring the same section for close to half an hour, but Warren wasn't going to intervene. The longer it took them to finish, the less time he'd spend fighting an erection while lying in his cot, daydreaming about Chris. "I had no idea. What a world we live in. It makes me so ridiculously happy that artists can take their passion for knotting and turn it into a career."

Warren almost choked.

Pete, oblivious, blinked at him. "What?"

"I, uh, I wouldn't go around enthusing about having a passion for knotting online."

"Why?"

That was a conversation best had never. Warren cleared his throat. "So did she show you her Etsy shop?"

"*Yes.*" Pete's confusion lifted and the hearts returned to his eyes. "I'm so amazed at the work she does. I have trouble knotting a tie the right way, and here she is making a living selling sex hammocks."

If Warren choked any more, his stand-up comedy career would sink before it began. "*Excuse me?*"

"What?" Pete asked again, no less confused.

"*Sex hammocks?*"

"Uh, yeah?"

"Christ." If only he could scrub that thought from his mind. Warren could have lived a perfectly happy life not knowing the works in progress in his living room were being shipped to boho sex dungeons across the globe. To distract himself from the news, he plunged his brush into the nearby bucket of soapy water and kept cleaning. "I thought they were for trees."

"I mean, some of them probably are."

"Did Libby tell you they were sex hammocks?"

"Yeah." Pete said it with such a dreamy sigh that Warren couldn't help but wonder if shibari was his thing. "She said that it's a pretty recent venture, but that she's been really drilling down to target a specific audience... and it's paying off. I think it's genius. She's so amazing. Did she tell you that she's branching out into lingerie now, too? Macramé lingerie! How does someone even think of something like that?"

Warren scrubbed harder.

"Ever since we went out, I've been brainstorming things she might want to add to her storefront. You know... to capitalize on all the business she's got flowing in now. Because if people are crazy about sex hammocks, then they'll probably wanna go full steam

170

with other sexy macramé stuff. What do you think about macramé cock cages?"

Warren nearly aspirated his own tongue.

"Hmm. Yeah, I thought so, too. It's probably too soon in the relationship to suggest things like that. I don't want her to think I'm perving on her. I'm not. Not like that, anyway. She's so cute, though. I can't stop thinking about her. Fuck, Wren, why didn't you tell me you had such an amazing roommate? As soon as I'm off shift, I'm swinging by to pick her up and I'm gonna take her to that breakfast place in Cresco. You remember the one? With all the stools lining the counter and the old-fashioned booths?"

"Yeah, I remember."

"I'm gonna bring her some flowers, too. Romance the shit out of her." Pete grinned. "It feels like everything's finally turning around for me. What about you? You've been looking a little happier lately. That Code Three turn out to be a little less DOA than anticipated?"

"No." Warren cleared his throat in the hopes that Pete had run out of choke-worthy material and kept scrubbing. "It's kind of complicated. I don't really want to talk about it."

"Well, if you want help from the Master of Romance, I'm your guy." Pete waggled an eyebrow, then moved on from his exceptionally clean section of floor. "I can't believe I found a girl I want to take on a second date. I'm telling you, Wren, things are changing. Cupid's been let loose in Lethridge and there's no telling where he might strike next, so you'd better watch your ass, or you might find yourself impaled by *love*."

This time Warren didn't choke. He spent the rest of the day wishing that he had.

It was hard to concentrate when Chris was in the station. Dispatchers didn't often get to leave their office, but a closed door didn't bother Warren's imagination, which ran wild speculating about all the things Chris would do to him if he didn't meet his stupid five-minute expectation. After what had happened the last time Warren had gone to his place, nothing was off the table. Chris wouldn't hold back. The sex would be brutal, amazing, and incredible. A struggle-fuck unlike any other. A transcendent experience. Rapture.

Warren was so lost to his daydreams that he didn't notice Pete had taken a seat next to him until he got elbowed in the ribs.

"Earth to Wren?" Pete illustratively lifted the coffee mug in his hand. "Kathleen just finished making coffee. You're gonna wanna get in there before Meatball's finished his reps or you can kiss your caffeine fix goodbye."

"Shit, is it that time already?" Warren glanced at his watch, which confirmed coffee o'clock had arrived. "Did Melody get there yet?"

"Nah. I think she's spotting Meatball. Why?" Pete raised an eyebrow. "You thinking of bringing her coffee? How unexpectedly sweet of you. That Code Three you've been denying all this time... it's not with her, is it? Because that would be *weird*."

Warren shook his head. "Nah. You know I don't swing that way."

"Hmm. Why else would you be asking?" Pete tapped his chin thoughtfully, which was enough to light a fire under Warren's ass and get him going. It wouldn't take much for Pete to jump from Melody to Chris, since she was the one who brought him coffee in the morning, and Warren didn't want to be around when the lightbulb went off and Pete started to ask questions.

But he wasn't quite fast enough.

"Uh, Wren? Are you and the newbie..."

"*Gottacoffeetalklater*," Warren said in a single breath, then darted through the door into the sheriff's department, where Kathleen guarded her coffee station like a dragon would its gold.

As usual, Kathleen was busy with some paperwork when he entered and didn't notice him sidle up to her hoard. While she worked, Warren stole into her space, slipped two mugs out of the secret cubby the rest of the station stashed their coffee paraphernalia in, and hurried to make himself a cup. As long as he could get out before Kathleen clued in to his existence, everything would be fine. If not, she'd chew his ear off and write him up for petty theft, and he really didn't want to add to the stacks upon stacks of coffee violations cluttering Steve's office.

Warren poured the coffee and got the hell outta Dodge before Kathleen spotted him. The high stakes made it easier not to think about why he was going out of his way to bring coffee to Chris. It wasn't like he was doing it to get behind his closed office door where they could have a little privacy. Nope. Not at all. Bringing a coworker coffee was a totally normal and platonic thing to do, especially when they couldn't easily leave their desk.

But not even Pete was buying that excuse. When Warren slunk out of the sheriff's department, he was waiting there with one eyebrow raised. "So... you and the newbie, huh? Didn't see that one coming, but I can't blame you. That is one attractive man. If I were down with the dick, I'd be gay for him, too."

Warren's hands were occupied, so he swung a foot at him—not quite a kick, but more of a polite prodding—and like he'd hoped, Pete hopped back to give him some space.

"It's not like that." Warren advanced toward the dispatch office's door. Pete followed. "All I'm doing is bringing a coworker coffee. What's so weird about that? We do it for each other all the time."

"Yeah, but you and I are partners, which is pretty much like being married without all the sex. Or the passive-aggressive remarks about the right way to do dishes. If you didn't bring me coffee from time to time, we'd have to get work-divorced, and not only would that be messy, but we'd have to trade Meatball on the weekends and it'd break his big squishy heart." Pete gestured at the second mug. "But you and Chris? Not the same at all. You wouldn't even speak to the guy the first couple days he was here, and now you're bringing him coffee? Seems pretty suspicious to me."

"It's just coffee," Warren mumbled. "Melody brings him coffee, too."

"And she's trying to get in his pants. Although I guess that won't be happening any time soon, since they're on someone else's bedroom floor." Pete looked particularly pleased with himself for that one. "You're gonna need my blessing, you know. I'm not gonna let my partner date just anyone. What's his opinion on sex hammocks?"

"Aaand I'm out."

Before Pete could ensnare him in further conversation, Warren made it into the dispatch room.

Like the rest of the Howard County station, the dispatch room was small, meaning Chris's desk—and by extension, Chris—was almost within arm's reach upon entry. It had been a while since Warren had seen the ancient but reliable transmission radio and the other odds and ends that made the room what it was, but as fascinating as they were, his attention was focused elsewhere. Namely, on Chris. He sat behind the desk with a notebook open in front of him and a pen in hand. Warren had no idea what he was doing, but it didn't matter. Whatever it was, Chris looked more handsome than usual doing it. Being behind a desk, he concluded, was the inverse equivalent to the scene in every romcom where the leading lady plucked the glasses from her face and shook out her ponytail. Chris was hot, but when he was on the job, he was hot as hell.

"I, uh…" Warren realized he'd been slack-jawed, so he swallowed and took a second to calm down before he continued. "I brought you coffee."

Chris eyed the mug for a second, then went back to devouring Warren with his eyes. "Melody know you're here?"

"No. She's, um, spotting Meatball, I think. I'll let her know you're already caffeinated when she's done." Warren set the mug on Chris's desk, heart hammering like he was a third grader working up the courage to speak to his crush. "I figured you'd appreciate having your coffee a little earlier today. You know. So you'll be properly energized all day long. It'd be a shame if you dragged ass this morning and weren't at the top of your game for... whatever it is you'll be doing after work."

Chris folded his arms on the desk and leaned forward, eyes ever on Warren. "How thoughtful of you."

"And, I, uh..." What was it he'd wanted to say again? Stupid sexy desk. "I... have some for myself, too. Because it'd be equally bad if I wasn't ready to tackle whatever came my way this afternoon."

"You really think something will be coming this afternoon?" The low, sardonic tone of Chris's voice was ice water on a hot day, so wholly satisfying that Warren got the chills. It was one thing to argue over text, where he could spend time composing his thoughts. It was another entirely to look in Chris's eyes while knowing full well what was going to happen.

Five minutes wasn't going to cut it.

Chris knew it as well as Warren.

Warren would try, of course, but he'd fail. Not even his best would cut it when Chris knew to expect him. Once that happened, Chris would punish him, and oh, the thought of it made Warren want to squirm. After a lifetime of lackluster relationships and forgettable hookups with men who didn't quite get him, he'd found someone fluent in his love language.

Not that it was love, but...

Warren brushed the thought aside. It was just supposed to be a coffee break, damn it. Love had no business butting in.

To show it who was boss, Warren squared his shoulders and launched back into the conversation determined not to let Chris gain the upper hand. "Yeah, actually, I do. Unlike some people, I'm on shift until early tomorrow morning, and that means I'm giving the next twenty-four hours everything I've got."

Chris arched a brow and raised his mug to take a sip, but Warren still caught the corners of his lips as they curled into a smirk. "Is that so? Well. All right then. Call me a skeptic, but I'll believe it when I see it."

25

CHRIS

Five minutes into the most intense blowjob of his life, Chris's cell phone alarm went off. Chris scrambled to snag it off the dash and silenced it, then threw it back down and grabbed fistfuls of Warren's hair. Fuck the timer—Warren couldn't stop now. That mouth of his was too damned good, his tongue too eager, his lips too taut. And the way Warren had teased him this morning? Fucking perfection. It'd been torture waiting for his shift to end knowing what was about to happen.

Not willing to let Warren go, Chris bucked his hips and fucked into Warren's throat. It constricted around him, hot and wet and so goddamn good. "You fucked up, Reaves," Chris rasped as he owned Warren's mouth. "Oh, did you fuck up..."

Warren emitted a sound of outrage but made no attempt to pull away.

"Couldn't get me off in five minutes." Chris squeezed his eyes shut and bucked several times in rapid succession, each thrust marked by a new spike of frenzied pleasure. Warren grabbed him by the thigh and dug his fingernails through Chris's denim, but he didn't signal asking Chris to stop. He could take it—*wanted* to take it

177

—and Chris loved to let him have it. "Gonna have to show you what happens when you misbehave."

He pushed Warren's head down with all his strength and at the same time lifted his hips to bury himself all the way in Warren's throat. Warren coughed and sputtered, but he didn't fight. He wanted to choke. Chris would've come right then and there had he not promised himself he wouldn't. Instead, he ripped Warren off his dick and tucked himself back into his pants. "You off tomorrow?"

Warren sank bonelessly into his seat, hazy-eyed. "Yeah."

"Stop by my apartment at five and make sure you're ready for me. I'm not fucking around."

"Fuck you," Warren said, but it was just as boneless as he was.

"Fuck you, too," Chris said back.

Warren spared him a lingering look, something significant in his eyes, then left the car. As always, Chris watched him walk all the way back to the station through his rearview mirror.

Of all the routines he'd established since coming back to Lethridge, that one would never get old.

The text pinged Chris's phone only a few minutes after Jack had gone to bed. It was a damned good thing it arrived when it did, because if Jack had caught sight of the face he'd made upon reading it, he would have had to explain himself, and that was one conversation Chris wasn't ready to have.

Warren: My limits are knife play and scat
Chris: What the hell?
Chris: You didn't accidentally message me while trying to hook up with someone else, did you? Because that shit's not gonna fly
Warren: I mean, I just said shit was my limit, so…

178

Chris snorted. Asshole or not, Warren could be funny.

Warren: But no, it's not an accident. You said you were gonna "punish" me tomorrow. Now you know how far I'm willing to go

Oh, fuck. Chris's dick twitched. He shifted his hips to adjust himself and get more comfortable, then grabbed the remote and increased the volume on the TV a bar or two. Like that would help. Fuck, he wasn't thinking straight.

Although with Warren around, he never was.

Chris: You're seriously hard thinking about tomorrow, aren't you?
Chris: Fuckin dirty boy
Warren: If you think me texting you with my limits is dirty, I have low hopes for tomorrow's performance
Chris: Fuck you. I'm gonna blow your fucking mind, Reaves
Warren: Prove it
Warren: My safe word is pineapple
Warren: If I'm not screaming it by the time you're done, you're not going hard enough

26

WARREN

Come prepared. *Come prepared.* Warren sat on the floor and rooted through the plastic tote he kept under his bed, at a loss for what to do. Chris wanted him prepped and ready to fuck, but wearing the same plug twice in a row felt too boring for the enormity of what was set to happen this evening. It would be like showing up to the Met Gala in the same dress two years in a row. Warren's asshole deserved better than that.

But which of his plugs would it be?

Nothing too small. Warren typically liked the pain of being stretched open on a fat cock after prepping with a plug too narrow, but Chris wasn't going to be impressed if he wore anything tinier than before. Going too big wasn't all that great an idea, either—Warren wanted to *feel* when Chris punished him.

Not that it was a sure thing that Chris was going to punish him with his dick, but, well… that was certainly going to be part of it.

Whatever he chose had to be big—but not *too* big—and impressive enough to be eye-catching. A boring silicone base wasn't going to cut it. What he needed was a little pizazz.

The answer came to him all at once.

Warren selected the plug from amongst the others and weighed it on his palm. It was satisfyingly heavy, and better yet, captivating. When Chris saw it—*if* he saw it before pulling it out and throwing it aside—he'd be wowed.

With one less thing to worry about, he closed the box and slid it back under the bed. All that was left to do was see if he could squeeze in a couple hours of sleep before five o'clock hit. After his little chat with Chris, he had a feeling he'd need it.

A few minutes before five, Warren headed up the musty stairwell of the old Delmar apartment, through the door to the third floor, and down the hall. The exterior of apartment 304 was no different than last time, its numbers bronzed and its three crooked, but the way Warren felt while standing in front of it had changed. There was no more pinch of apprehension in the back of his mind, no more fear that he was making a mistake. He raised his hand to knock, but there was no need—the door opened, and there was Chris.

He stole Warren's breath away.

It wasn't that he looked any different than usual. His fitted t-shirt and relaxed jeans were staples of his wardrobe. Chris's body was equally familiar—broad shoulders, a strong chest, sleekly muscular arms. What stopped Warren was the look in his eyes. Steely, cold, and hungry, it set the mood in a visceral way that words couldn't and told Warren that tonight, he'd get everything he wanted.

Every. Last. Depraved. Thing.

For a while, all that moved was time. Chris held Warren pinned with his gaze, those hungry eyes devouring him, possessing him in ways he'd never known. The tension between them thickened. It weighed in the air and solidified in the empty parts inside him—his lungs, his heart, his stomach—until there was nothing but it and the man in front of him. The embodiment of Warren's darkest dreams wrapped in an illicit package.

"You're late, Reaves." Chris's voice was different when he was aroused. Lower. Rockier. It rumbled in Warren's chest like thunder that had struck too close or the thud of bass at a concert. Goosebumps inducing. Warren resisted a shiver, feigning strength, but it was futile—with a single look, Chris had already disarmed him.

Another tense moment passed. Chris slid his hands into his pockets and glanced down Warren's body. It looked a hell of a lot like he was sizing up Warren's cock. Heart aflutter, Warren followed his line of sight and saw what Chris did—that he was tenting his jeans.

"Well, would you look at that." Chris stepped forward, and as he did, Warren's gaze snapped up to watch him. It wasn't that he was afraid of what Chris would do, but that he didn't want to miss a second of it. But Chris didn't get any farther than the doorway. He simply stood there and ate Warren up with his eyes, a hint of a smirk perking his lips. "We'd better get you inside."

It was a good idea in theory, but not one that worked in practice. Warren's feet were glued in place. It wasn't that he was scared—far from it—but the look in Chris's eyes... the *look*. It made Warren's heart race like he was staring out the open door of a skydiving plane cruising at altitude, knowing in seconds he'd be in free fall.

"Reaves?" Chris came closer and took him by the wrist, his thick, calloused fingers anchoring them together. All it took was the slightest tug to send Warren stumbling into his arms, and from there it was like he'd fallen into a dream. Chris's lips met his. Warren closed his eyes and grabbed the front of Chris's shirt with his free hand, desperate to stay close. They moved. Warren couldn't tell how far, but he heard the door rattle in its jamb as it shut. After that, there was nothing, because the kiss became all lips and teeth and hands, distracting him from everything else.

"Shirt off," Chris growled into Warren's mouth.

Warren shivered and lifted his arms obediently, and off came his shirt. No sooner did it hit the floor than Chris was back on him, kissing him hard enough to bruise. A hand snaked through his hair and tugged. Another lifted his captive wrist and pinned it over his head. The frenzied beat of Warren's heart rushed in his ears and dampened the sounds around them, but he didn't miss the hiss of satisfaction that Chris made when he boldly tugged Chris's bottom lip between his teeth.

"Tell me what you did to get ready for me," Chris said when Warren was so breathless, darkness speckled his vision. "I wanna hear how you think I'm gonna punish you tonight."

Warren's cock twitched. Breathing hard, he chased Chris's lips, brain too scrambled to think of a reply. He managed to reclaim them briefly, but Chris didn't let him have his way for long. One scorching kiss later, Chris pulled away. "No. Not yet. I wanna hear what you have to say. What have you done to get ready for me, Reaves? Use your words. Don't tell me you can't."

Irritation prickled somewhere within the hazy depths of Warren's mind, enough that his upper lip pulled back in a would-be snarl. "Fuck you."

"You wanna try?" Chris huffed a laugh and tilted his head to rake his teeth down Warren's neck. "Good luck."

Warren shivered and arched his back, pushing into Chris in need of more. So much more. But even horny as hell, he was stubborn. The more they fought, the harder they'd fuck, and the better his punishment would be. "I could fucking top you if I wanted!"

"Yeah?" Chris nipped his neck, chasing a gasp out of him, then drew back to look at Warren with those damned blue eyes of his, the sharp smugness in them piercing him like needles. "You wanna own my ass, then? Throw me down and fuck me senseless? Come inside me? Because I don't think you have the balls to do it." Chris carded his fingers through Warren's hair and gripped it tight. "I don't think you can bear the thought of having sex with someone whose cock isn't inside of you."

It was the truth, but Warren would never admit it. He bared his teeth and struggled, and Chris indulged him by tightening his grip. When Chris tugged his head back using his grip on his hair, Warren stopped struggling and glared at him. "You think you know me, but you don't have the faintest idea what you're talking about."

"Yes, I do."

"You fucking arrogant bastard."

"Yeah?" Slowly, Chris closed the distance between their lips until they were touching, but not quite kissing. Warren whimpered, caught between needing to kiss him senseless and wanting to resist in order to prove his point. "Funny. You've never said or done anything to make me believe otherwise. You wanna top me, Reaves? Go a-fucking-head. But know that I'm not an easy lay. If you want my ass, you're gonna have to fight me for it."

Chris stopped speaking to kiss him, and Warren whimpered again.

"But that's not what you want, is it?" Chris whispered in the seconds after the kiss had ended, letting Warren feel his words. "I see right through you. You like to talk a big game, but when push comes to shove, you're always face down and ass up, begging to be fucked. You can't tell me it's not true. So what's it gonna be?" He smirked. "Are you gonna tell me how you prepared for your punishment tonight, or are you gonna hold your tongue and force me to figure it out for myself?"

"Fucking fight me and find out," Warren seethed, then kissed Chris fiercely, no longer able to hold back.

27

CHRIS

Warren's mouth was on his, and Chris couldn't get enough. He growled and abandoned his hold on Warren's hair and wrist to grab him by the hips, then dragged him off the wall as their teeth clacked and their lips met again and again. They fumbled down the hall, one violent kiss after the next, until Chris couldn't take it anymore. Driven wild with lust, he threw Warren up against the wall and grabbed the buckle of his belt, yanking it off while Warren kissed him senseless.

Warren was his now—all his—and Chris was going to prove it.

He thumbed open the button of Warren's fly and yanked down the zipper beneath it. Warren's jeans pooled at his feet. Like before, he was nude underneath. All he had left were his shoes, which kept his jeans shackled around his ankles.

"Shoes off," Chris growled into his mouth. "Socks too."

"Don't fucking tell me what to do."

"Yeah?" Chris grabbed him by the chin. "You think that's how this works? You really are looking to be punished, aren't you? Take your shoes off, Reaves. I'm not gonna ask again."

Warren opened his mouth, but unless he'd become a wizard overnight, shoe removal didn't involve semantic components, so

187

Chris shut him down before he could begin by hooking his thumb into Warren's mouth. Warren's eyes widened and he tried to jerk his head away, but Chris held firm. Lo and behold, Warren stepped on the back of one shoe, then the other, and kicked them away.

"And your socks," Chris insisted, sliding his thumb along Warren's tongue until he'd secured a grip on the front of his jaw. Warren made a sound of consternation but did as he was told, and off went his socks the same as his shoes. "Much better."

Chris didn't relinquish his grip, though. Not yet. Not until Warren decided to knock off the tough guy act and fold for him. It wouldn't take much. Warren was already at his mercy. With a little time, he'd figure out he'd been bested and give it all up, but until then, Chris wouldn't relent.

But Warren had other plans.

With a hummed note of irritation, he grabbed fistfuls of Chris's shirt, twisting until the neckline cut against the back of his neck. The pressure burned, and Chris had no choice but to release him with a snarl. He ducked out of the shirt while Warren was still holding it, leaving him to throw it wherever he saw fit... which ended up being at Chris's face.

"Fuck!" Chris tried to swat it out of the air, but he hadn't been braced for an attack, and it struck him dead on. Did Warren actually want a fight? Because it was on.

He snatched the shirt from his face and tossed it to the floor, but by the time he had, Warren was already on the move. He bolted in the direction of the bedroom hallway, bare feet slapping the wood floor. There was a glint of something in the valley of his ass, but Chris didn't focus on it—couldn't—because instinct took over.

He sprinted after Warren like a hound in pursuit of a fox.

Chase.

Hunt.

Grab.

Chris was faster and heavier than his target, and it took little more than a second for him to gain the upper hand. He grappled

Warren from the side and tugged him through the nearest door into the bathroom. They crashed onto the counter together, knocking the hand soap dispenser into the sink and sending the toothbrush holder flying. Warren gasped, and before he could turn it into a shout, Chris kissed the sound out of him. They slid down the side of the counter and landed on the cold tile, Warren on his ass and Chris on his knees in front of him, where the kiss turned feral. Chris wasn't sure who was responsible—if it was he who'd grabbed Warren and crushed their lips together, or if Warren had wrenched him forward and demanded worship from Chris's mouth—but it didn't matter. He was too enamored to care.

"Fuck you," Warren whispered. It was praise passed off as an insult—affection from a man who spoke a love language few understood. Chris let it nourish him, accepting it for what it was, and kissed him until the tile was too uncomfortable on his knees and he had to stand. He dragged Warren to his feet as he did, taking the opportunity to look him head to toe.

Their game of cat and mouse had mussed Warren's hair and flushed his cheeks. A dreamy, blissed-out look had replaced the ire once in his eyes. But for as soft as his expression was, his body was a study in strength. He was no soldier, but his arms were leanly muscular and his core was impressively tight. There was a sleekness to him that Chris lacked, but it only served to amplify his build. The man was fit. He liked to play the part of a little brat, but there was nothing little about him.

Chris's gaze dipped south.

Nothing.

When they were both on their feet, Chris dragged Warren in front of the sink, over which hung the bathroom's only mirror. Chris had some height on Warren and he used it to his advantage, keeping Warren drawn to his chest while he snaked his arms around him. One of his hands followed the trail of hair leading to his groin and wrapped around his cock while the other went north, where it pinched and rolled his nipple. A desperate, breathy whine broke in

Warren's throat, and *fuck*, did it make Chris throb. He nipped Warren's neck and pinched a little harder. Like he'd hoped, Warren gave him more.

"Tell me what's inside you right now." Chris let the words caress the tender skin of Warren's neck over the reddened spots of irritation he'd made with his teeth. "I saw it glittering when you tried to run from me. Did you think I wouldn't notice?"

Warren shivered, and Chris watched in the mirror as a ripple of pleasure spread across his face. Bit by bit, Warren was coming undone for him. It wouldn't be long before his tough guy act crumbled and he became the dreamy-eyed innocent that Chris fantasized about late at night while he pumped himself to completion.

But no sooner had pleasure softened his face than irritation hardened it. Warren scowled. "You wanna find out? Then look for yourself."

"Wrong answer." Chris let go of Warren's shaft and took him by the balls instead, tightening his grip steadily until Warren tensed. "What's in your ass, Reaves? I want to hear you say it."

"A plug."

Chris tightened his grip.

"A plug!" Warren gasped. "It's a goddamn plug! I swear to god. What else do you think would be in my ass, genius? A chandelier?"

"That's a lot of snark coming from someone who's got their balls in a vise." Chris squeezed, prompting Warren to let loose with a warbling cry edged with desperate arousal. "Tell me more about it," Chris said when it was quiet. He grazed Warren's neck with his teeth. "I wanna hear every last detail."

"Fuck you."

"Really?" Chris nipped his neck in warning, then drew back to check Warren's expression in the mirror. While he was pale and trembling, lips loosened with the promise of untold pleasure yet to come, there was still a glint of resistance in his eyes. Chris hadn't pushed him far enough yet. "Well, don't say I didn't give you a chance. I asked and you shot me down. Now you're gonna find out what happens to boys who don't play nice."

Warren opened his mouth to speak, but Chris was through with talking. He let go of the more sensitive parts of Warren's anatomy to wrench him away from the counter. Warren gasped and flailed, latching on to the only thing within reach—the shower curtain. The tension rod holding it up buckled beneath his bodyweight and came down with a clatter, taking Warren with it. He landed on his arms on the lip of the tub, trapping swaths of plastic curtain beneath him. Before he could get his footing, Chris grabbed him by the thighs and yanked him into position.

If Warren wanted to play the game, they were going to fucking play.

"*Shit,*" Warren croaked as he recovered. He laid his head on his folded arms like he'd finally given in, but Chris didn't believe that for a second. Not after the stunt he'd pulled in the hall. He waited to see if that would change, and when it didn't, he moved forward with his plan.

"Clumsy boy," Chris scolded. He kept Warren in place with one hand and used the other to trace over the treasure he found between his cheeks—the jeweled base of a plug. "You just can't seem to stop getting in trouble, can you? It's a good thing you have me here to teach you a lesson."

Warren moaned and seemed to perk his ass, so Chris didn't hold back—he smoothed a hand over Warren's cheek in warning, then spanked him hard. Warren muffled a cry into his arms and went right back to presenting himself.

The bastard liked it.

And damn if Chris didn't like it, too.

"You need to do better," Chris growled, tracing the redness on Warren's otherwise pale skin with his fingertips. "You need to start behaving, or this is gonna happen again." He spanked Warren for emphasis hard enough that Warren lurched forward, but a second later his ass was tilted and asking for more. "So I'm gonna teach you a lesson today, and if you don't learn from it, then I'll have to punish you again."

Another spank.

Warren let loose with a truncated cry, like his jaw had been clenched through the scream. Again and again he lifted his ass for Chris until Chris had decorated both cheeks with bright red hand-prints. By the time Warren sagged rather than bounced back, Chris was throbbing for him. He needed inside Warren, and he needed inside now.

The plug had to go.

Chris wanted to take its place.

He grasped the ridiculous rainbow-hued jewel base and pulled, watching as the bulb stretched Warren open.

"Fuck," Warren whimpered. The fallen shower curtains crinkled, and Chris looked up in time to see Warren try to lift himself onto his shaking arms. Before he could get far, Chris pushed the plug back in, filling Warren back up. Warren cried out and sank onto the tub. His thighs trembled. All the signs pointed in the same direction —if Chris kept pushing, he'd come.

So he pulled instead.

Warren's body stretched and stretched around the stainless-steel bulb until Chris was sure it had no more give. It maxed out at an obscene three inches at its widest, then tapered down to nothing. The thought of it buried in Warren, stretching him from the inside where no one could see, was the hottest damned thing Chris had ever imagined.

And yet Warren had taken it like it was nothing.

"That's not your biggest plug, is it?" Chris asked as he let go of Warren.

"No."

"How much more can you take?"

Warren made a noise, but didn't otherwise respond.

Fuck this. Chris couldn't wait. He'd been patient so far, but he'd reached his limit. *"How much more can you take?"*

192

"Screw you," Warren bit back, but Chris heard through the deception and saw it for what it was—a plea to go harder, to be stricter, and to take whatever he wanted.

Warren wasn't going to back down.

Luckily for him, neither was Chris.

28

WARREN

There was no warning but the rip of a zipper before Chris pushed inside, stretching Warren on his cock. If it hadn't been for the prep he'd done to fit the plug it would've been painful, but Warren had come ready. Rough sex wasn't enough to throw him. If Chris wanted him to tap out, he was going to have to go hard.

Which wasn't to say it didn't feel good, because *fuck,* was it amazing.

Warren squeezed his eyes shut and perked his sore ass, helping Chris target his prostate. The uncomfortable fullness and aching stretch of being well and thoroughly fucked was worth it if he could just get Chris into position. He was close—so close—but he could do better. With just a little more effort, he could—*"Fuck!"*

Chris had changed his angle, and now with every thrust rubbed into Warren's prostate. Pleasure burst inside of him and all other thoughts fell by the wayside. All that remained was a craving for more.

Delirious, Warren fucked back onto Chris. In his haste, his arms slipped on the shower curtain and sent him sliding forward, but Chris was quick to grab him. He kept pumping, one savage thrust after another, until all Warren could do was hang over the edge of the tub and take what he was given. If they kept going like this, he was going to come. "Oh, *fuck!* Fuckfuckfuck, *Chris...*"

"You like it?" Chris lurched forward and surprised Warren by grabbing his hair and tugging Warren's head. The pain that bloomed across his scalp melted into pleasure with each new thrust, and Warren cried out, unable to hold back. "You like it when I fuck you?"

Yes.

Yes, yes, yes.

Warren choked out a laugh that sounded like a sob and ground against Chris as his fat cock tried to split him open. Words were impossible when Chris was fucking him. Using him. *Destroying* him. Soon enough Warren would lose strength in his legs and crumple, and Chris would fuck him into the tile the same way he'd fucked him into the living room floor.

No one had ever dared do something like that to him before, but Chris? Chris was perfection dressed in wolf's clothing. The lover Warren had never known he needed.

As if to agree, his knees went out and he buckled onto the floor. For a second he was painfully empty, but then Chris was on top of him again, his cock sliding right back where it belonged. Warren gasped in relief and pushed back into him as best he could, then let Chris screw him against the side of the tub.

"This is what happens when you misbehave." Chris strained the words through a grunt, shoving Warren chest-first into the porcelain. "This is what fucking happens when you try to run from me, Reaves. When you don't fucking answer me when I'm speaking to you. This—all of this—is all on you."

Drunk on the fantasy Chris had created, Warren gasped and squirmed like he was trying to get away. Chris knew his safe word—knew that he'd use it if it got to be too much—but they weren't there yet. Warren needed more.

"Fuck." Chris nipped his shoulder hard enough to bruise, then, once he had his teeth in Warren, picked up the pace. It was brutal, selfish, amazing, and Warren, overcome by it, grasped the shower curtain in a feeble attempt to hold out for as long as he could. It didn't help. Pleasure tightened in his gut. He knew he was going to come. "Fuck, Reaves, just... *fuck.*"

Chris wrenched him away from the tub and slipped an arm around his body. He grasped Warren's cock and started to pump. With tight heat wrapped around his dick, Warren was a lost cause. His balls churned, and as Chris slammed into him from behind, he came, striping the side of the tub.

Out of his mind in the midst of his orgasm, Warren relentlessly rode Chris. The sounds of sex filled the bathroom—slapping skin, panted breaths, and the gasps and groans of men getting exactly what they wanted. Warren shot again, and again, until he was so empty he ached, but it still wasn't enough. He needed Chris to finish. Needed to know he'd loved it, too.

It wasn't long before he got his wish.

"Goddamn, Reaves... oh, fuck. Here it comes. You wanted it so bad, and here it fucking comes..."

Chris had warned him, but Warren still moaned when he felt it.

The sudden thickening.

The twitch.

The flood of warmth.

Chris drove it into him in short, urgent thrusts that brought Warren to the brink all over again. A second wave of orgasm hit, this one dry. When it was over, he slumped onto Chris.

"Was it good?" Chris asked. He'd started to soften, but hadn't pulled out. Warren wished he never would. "You made a damned mess of my bathroom."

Screw the bathroom.

Screw everything.

Warren hadn't used his safe word, but it'd still been the most mind-blowing sex of his life. Cleanup could wait. He was too high from the fun they'd just had to want to do anything but enjoy the quiet that came after release.

Words continued to fail him, so he wiggled his hips and sank down on Chris's cock in the hopes Chris would catch his meaning. It seemed to work, because Chris chuckled and wrapped his arms over Warren's chest, holding him in place while he thrust. It was lackluster work at best—Chris had gone flaccid and Warren was a slippery mess—but Warren appreciated the gesture.

"I'm glad to see you're not done yet," Chris said against the back of his ear in a dark whisper that snapped Warren right out of his state of post-orgasmic bliss. "I'd hate to think that I spent all this time getting you ready for you to be finished so soon."

Warren stilled and turned his head to judge Chris's expression, but it was too late. Chris slipped out of him and pushed him against the side of the tub. Warren heard him stand, felt his hand tighten over his arm, and knew that he was being dragged to his feet, but had trouble following along with what was happening.

What Chris had said... he couldn't mean...

"What? You look surprised. Did you really think that's the best I've got?" Chris tugged him toward the bathroom door. "We're not done yet, Reaves. We're not even close."

It was a short distance from the bathroom to Chris's bedroom, and an even shorter journey from the door to the bed. Chris's room was small and utilitarian—a bed, a dresser, an end table. Blackout curtains covered the window, creating pervasive darkness Chris chased away by flipping on the overhead light. With it on, the room's details—or lack thereof—came into view. The walls were white and bare. The curtains were a forgettable gray. The bedsheets were plain, and the blanket topping them was similarly monochromatic. Warren noticed a laundry basket tucked between the legs of the dresser and a small garbage pail hidden next to the bed, blocked in by the end table.

Nothing within sight told him anything about the kind of man Chris was behind closed doors.

Nothing but the framed crayon drawing by his bedside.

Before Warren could get a better look at it, Chris placed a hand on his shoulder and pushed him onto the bed. The mattress dipped beneath his weight, then dipped again as Chris climbed on after him, kissing him firmly before pushing him into the sheets. Warren braced for the inevitable rough treatment to follow, but it never came. Instead, Chris sweetened the kiss.

"You think this is punishment?" Warren asked in a whisper as heat rose into his cheeks. They'd been kissing for a while now. The entire time, Chris had treated Warren like he might break. There was no hair pulling, no nipple torture, no teeth. It was like he'd run out of steam. Like every other hookup, Chris had talked a big game, but had failed to live up to his own hype. It was disappointing, but not deal breaking. Maybe it was the orgasm talking, but Warren kind of liked the way it felt to be in Chris's arms.

"Hmm?" Chris asked lazily. He rolled them over so he was on top and Warren was beneath him, then kissed him again and again until Warren was breathless and dizzy.

What had they been talking about?

Everything was fuzzy.

It wasn't like him to want affection, but the way Chris was kissing him, the way their bodies felt together... Warren didn't want it to end. He lifted himself and captured Chris's lips again, not stopping until a new sensation distracted him—Chris was starting to get hard.

"Already?" Warren asked, grinning. "What are you, a teenager?"

"Have you seen your ass?"

Warren snorted and Chris hastened to steal the sound from his lips, kissing him soundly while their hands slotted together. It was nice. Unexpected, but nice all the same. Chris could be sweet when he wanted to be, and while this wasn't what Warren had signed up for, he'd take it all the same.

Kissing led to touching. Chris palmed Warren's cock and stroked it to partial stiffness, prompting Warren to spread his thighs and lift his ass. Chris might not have taken school seriously, but he was smart enough to get Warren's meaning—soon enough, Warren's legs were pinned back, and Chris was busy coaxing his semi back to full mast while he worked it inside Warren's body. After that, Warren didn't spend much time worrying about anything. How could he when Chris felt so good? What mattered was the way Chris stretched him, the pinpricks of excitement that tingled up his arms and down his spine when they touched, and the pleasure they shared.

But what started soft and sweet didn't stay that way forever.

Contented noises of pleasure turned into groans. The bedsprings started to creak. Chris's cock reached full stiffness inside him, and Warren welcomed the ache it brought. He tightened around Chris, squeezing and releasing to coax him into coming, and Chris rewarded him for his willingness by grabbing him by the undersides of his thighs and shoving them back, lifting Warren's ass in the process. Once Warren was folded over, their pace grew frantic. Chris sank deeper. Warren moaned.

"You like that?" Chris rasped. "Like the way I feel inside you?"

"Yeah. Don't fucking stop."

"Never?"

"Never."

"Not even when I do this?"

There was the click of a plastic lid being snapped open. Chris stilled his hips. Was he drizzling more lube on his cock? The mess in Warren's ass wasn't starting to dry out, so there was no reason why he'd need more unless he wanted to get sloppy.

Mm, sloppy.

Warren could get behind sloppy.

Fuck, if it meant Chris would get rough, he could get behind just about anything.

Curious, he lifted his head to see what was going on in time to spot Chris tossing the lube aside. He met Warren's eyes, the same dark look in them Warren had seen in the bathroom, then barred his thighs with one arm to hold him in place while the other...

Warren's eyes widened.

The other traced a line from his balls to the stretched ring of his ass, leaving a trail of lube in its wake.

"I told you we weren't done yet," Chris scolded while mapping the point where Warren's ass gave way to his cock. "You didn't think I'd let you off that easy, did you?"

Warren opened his mouth, but had nothing to say.

He knew where this was going.

"If all you'd done was fail to get me off that time in the parking lot, maybe I wouldn't have to do this. But that's not all you've done, is it? You've been bad—so bad—since you got here. Let me list the ways." Chris's finger ran back and forth, back and forth, pushing just enough to make Warren whimper, but never enough to breach his hole. "Mouthing off, for one." More pressure. Warren squeezed his eyes shut and choked back a groan. "Making me chase you down the hall." The pressure increased again, and Warren did groan this time. "Pulling down my shower curtain." Warren gasped and squirmed, but it was no use—when Chris next increased the pressure, his finger slipped inside. "And worst of all, not answering a simple, direct question when asked." Unable to do anything but take everything Chris was giving him, Warren covered his face with his hands and opened his mouth in a silent scream. The stretch. God, the *stretch*. No plug could have prepared him for what he knew was coming.

Because now that Chris had put one finger inside, others were sure to follow.

Chris's finger curled, stretching him further. There was no going back now. Chris had stuffed him full of cock, and now he was going to fill him until he broke.

"So how big of a plug can you take, Reaves?" Another finger slid in, and this time Warren wasn't so silent. He muffled his howl of pain and pleasure in his palms as Chris pushed onward. "It's about time I found out."

29

WARREN

The bedsheets crumpled in Warren's fists, peaks of creased Egyptian cotton protruding lewdly from each side. The noises that had started to spill from his mouth would have been embarrassing if he'd been in the right frame of mind, but decency had been thrown out the window the moment Chris had flipped the script. It shouldn't have surprised Warren that a reformed weasel could come up with such a devious plan, but the haze of post-orgasmic bliss had made him careless, and he hadn't stopped to think that maybe—just maybe—Chris's nice guy act was a ruse.

He was paying for that oversight now.

Chris's finger curled, and Warren let loose with a noise that Chris clamped a hand over his mouth to contain. To reach him, he'd had to lunge forward, and his cock bumped a spot in Warren that transformed his discomfort to ecstasy.

"Quiet," Chris ordered as his hips established a slow but steady pace. "You're not done yet. You're not even close to done. You're going to take me one finger at a time until you can't anymore, and if that means that I have to fist you while I'm fucking you, then so be it."

As if to drive the point home, a third finger traced over his rim.

The pressure it put on him grew and grew until Warren knew it would slip inside, too. He blinked away tears. Taking any more would be insanity, but no one had ever broken him before.

No one had ever tried.

But Chris?

Warren didn't think he'd hold back. If anyone could push him to his limit, it would be him.

The possibility was ripe and plump and tantalizing, but still just out of Warren's reach. If he could have more, just a little more...

"Three," Chris said by way of warning, then shoved the finger in.

Three fingers.

Three twisting, curling fingers lodged in him alongside Chris's cock.

Warren screamed, but it came out as a silent puff of air. Chris would go all the way if he didn't say anything—would fist him and fuck him at the same time.

It was too much.

Too fucking much.

Warren knew that he would break.

The stretch. The burn. The pleasure.

It threatened to swallow him whole.

If he could distract himself from it, maybe he'd be able to hold on. He clenched his trembling jaw and squeezed his fists tight, but no matter how sturdy his grip, he couldn't escape the pulsing agony of being overly full.

As if he knew, Chris traced his fourth finger along Warren's hole like he was trying to find its weakest point.

Then, pressure.

"Four," Chris breathed, and it was all Warren could take.

He opened his mouth in a silent scream and twisted his hips to the side, coming messily over himself as he croaked, "Pineapple, pineapple, *pineapple!*"

30

CHRIS

Warren was a trembling, teary mess when Chris pulled free, but god, was he beautiful. Chris laid him down as gently as he could, and once he was comfortable sat back to look him over and make sure nothing was visibly wrong. He was glad that he had. In the time since Chris had brought him to bed, Warren's skin had gone from blush-tinged to pallid. His shoulders, once staunchly resistant, were clenched and angled inward. His taut stomach had hollowed. Worse, he kept shivering.

Maybe Chris had pushed too far.

He laid a hand apprehensively on Warren's calf, not sure what to do. As a paramedic, he hoped Warren would speak up if he needed medical assistance, but the man wouldn't even look at him, and there was a glassy sheen in his eyes that made him seem vacant.

"Hey, you okay?" Chris asked. He waited for a reply, but received none. A silent tear slid down Warren's cheek.

Fuck.

"Hey," Chris tried again. "Warren?"

Nothing.

It was as if Warren had checked out and had no plans of coming back.

For an agonizing moment, it reminded Chris of the first time he'd discovered Free after learning the truth. The emptiness was the same, but the circumstances were different. So different. Chris pushed the thought aside and lowered himself to the bed so they were face to face. "I've got you," he murmured. "I'm here now. It's over. You're safe."

Warren shifted a little closer but wouldn't stop shivering, so Chris snagged the blanket and tucked them both in. Like he did with Jack, he made sure that all his exposed skin, from his feet to his shoulders, was covered, then tugged Warren firmly to his chest. "This okay?"

Warren didn't reply, but he stopped shivering. Chris took it to be a good sign.

"You're such a stubborn fuck, you know that?" Chris pressed a kiss to his forehead. "Safe word out earlier next time, numbnuts."

Nothing.

Well, that was concerning—it wasn't like Warren to pass up a round of name calling. Chris frowned and took hold of Warren's wrist, which he guided to his bare hip. "If I went so hard on your ass that I accidentally broke your vocal cords in the process, pinch me to let me know you're not okay."

Warren didn't pinch, but he did snuggle closer, hooking his arm over the dip of Chris's waist and hiding his face against his chest. It was sweet and unexpected, and it left Chris at a loss for what to do. After a tense moment of indecision, he concluded the best course of action was to let it happen. It wasn't exactly a hardship to hold Warren. As incendiary as he could be, he was sweet like this.

Wrapped safe in Chris's arms, Warren began to stir. As he did, he tucked his head beneath Chris's chin like Chris could protect him from whatever was wrong. The idea that Chris could be his hero was tempting, which was absurd, but then again, wanting Warren at all was insanity. Of all the people in the world, Chris had never imagined that he'd start to have feelings for someone like him.

Chris closed his eyes and tried not to think about it, but with every breath he took, Warren's scent was there, mingled inextricably with his own. Shampoo and sex and bodywash—masculine notes he didn't associate with his own. Smitten with them, he held Warren closer and kissed the crown of his head, but the longer Warren stayed in his arms, the more Chris got to feel him. *Really* feel him. Not with brief, unforgiving contact, but with tenderness.

He discovered the planes of Warren's back and how caressing the dip of his spine made him shiver. Marveled at the gentle swell of his body where his lean and muscular build ended and the curve of his ass began. By the time Warren regained enough autonomy to pull back and look him in the eyes, Chris was enamored. Judging by the look of adoration on Warren's face, the feeling was mutual.

"What happened just now?" Chris asked softly. "One second you were fine and the next you weren't. Are you hurt?"

"No."

"But you went catatonic."

Warren grinned in a goofy, dreamy kind of way, like mind-shattering emotional trauma was his idea of a good time. "Yeah."

"Okay... I don't get it. You're gonna have to explain it to me in virgin. What the hell is going on?"

"You're not a virgin."

"Right, because *that* was my point." Chris sighed. "*Pretend* I'm a virgin. I don't get why you falling to pieces like that is a good thing."

Warren untangled himself from Chris and flopped onto the bed. He was silent for such a long time that Chris wasn't sure he'd ever answer, then, just as Chris had come to terms with never knowing the truth, he spoke. "You ever watch horror movies?"

"Yeah."

"Then you already kind of understand where I'm coming from." Warren tucked his arms beneath his head, disturbing the blanket in the process. "You don't turn on a horror movie expecting to have fun. Not in the traditional sense of the word. You do it because you want to be pants-shittingly terrified—because you want to experience that lightheaded, heart-pounding high that comes along with being afraid. The thing is, if the movie never gives you a chance to breathe, the high takes a hell of a lot out of you, and you get worn out. Your body can't handle so much at once, and it burns through all your resources and leaves you kind of empty." The goofy grin made a reappearance. "What you did just now drained me of everything I had. You took me on one hell of a ride and my body is paying the price, but I wouldn't trade it for anything."

Chris wasn't sure what to think of that, but Warren didn't give him much time to reflect. He rolled onto his side and took Chris's hand, guiding it so that his fingers wove through Warren's limp, sex-mussed hair.

"So, to tie it back to the horror movie explanation, when you do something like this…" He tugged on Chris's hand, making him pull his hair. "Or when you pin me or force me onto my knees… it's my version of getting enjoyment from being spooked by a movie. And it gets me the hell off. It just so happens that I like to be spooked so hard, I reach a tipping point, so if I'm crying by the time we're done, it means you've done a good job."

Chris's cock throbbed. "Yeah?"

"Yeah." Warren came closer, letting their lips brush. "All you have to remember is that since you're the one who broke me, you're the one who has to put me back together. You did so great today, tucking me in and holding me close. It was perfect. *You* were perfect."

The words had an unexpected impact—Chris's heart fluttered. Heat rose to his cheeks. Seeking a distraction, he touched the tip of his nose to Warren's, lips parted in want of a kiss he wasn't brave enough to take. "Fuck off… You're just saying that."

Like he'd hoped, a smile sweetened Warren's voice. "Fuck you."

"Fuck you more."

"I fucking hate you." Warren kissed him, smiling more broadly than ever. "Hate, hate, hate…"

It was everything Chris needed to hear.

"Hate you, too," he said, heart brimming, then rolled them over and pressed Warren into the bed.

From there, temptation took hold. Lips found lips. Fingers interlocked. Conversation gave way to hushed moans. Warren parted his thighs, Chris pushed inside, and they made hate that verged dangerously close to love.

Half an hour and an orgasm later, while Chris kissed Warren senseless, there came the angry buzz of a phone ignored.

"Shit," Chris groaned, pulling reluctantly away from Warren. "Jack."

"You told Libby you'd be late, didn't you?"

"Yeah, but—"

"Then shut up and keep kissing me."

Well, when Warren put it like that...

They fell back into old habits, kissing each other while Warren ground against Chris's thigh and Chris fondled his ass, but whoever was calling wouldn't stop. The phone buzzed, and buzzed, and buzzed until not even Warren's lips could distract him. Liberty wasn't the type to spam call over nothing—something had to be wrong.

"I gotta go." Chris detached from Warren and left the bed, snagging a pair of boxers from his dresser on the way out. He stepped into them in the hall, and by the time he answered his phone—which was doing its best to jackhammer through the bathroom tile—he was decent enough not to feel weird speaking to his ex-sister-in-law. "Hey."

"Hey," said a voice that wasn't Liberty's. The sound of it turned Chris's fear into dread.

31

CHRIS

"What do you want, Free?" Chris asked as he picked up the clothing left in the bathroom before returning to the hall. "There'd better be a damned good reason you're calling."

"Oh my god, Chris, chill out for a second, okay?" Free sighed in frustration. "You're always so uptight about everything. I wouldn't call you unless it was important. Look... they kinda let me out early, and I'm scrambling to find a place to stay. Do you think you could loan me like, fifty bucks to make up what I'm missing on my security deposit? You know I'm good to pay you back."

Chris headed toward the door to collect the rest of his and Warren's clothing. "Oh, really? That's news to me."

"What are you even talking about? When haven't I paid you back for something?"

The fucking audacity. Chris clenched his jaw, but didn't fall for her trap. He'd learned a thing or two since Warren had wormed his way into his life, and he already knew the argument wouldn't be worth having. Free wanted to get him emotional so she'd have the upper hand, and Chris couldn't let that happen. He had to stay calm and collected, if not for himself, then for Jack. "We're not having a conversation about that right now. Since when did they let you out?"

"Oh." Free trumpeted her lips. "It's, uh, it's pretty recent. It's actually kind of crazy. Turns out I was doing so well with my program that they fast-tracked me through it. Great, right? But it means all that time I would've had to prepare for life in the real world was kinda stolen from me, so I'm in a tight spot. I managed to find this great little studio apartment that's super affordable, but because of my credit score they want last month, first month, and a security deposit up front, and I just don't have enough. I was able to get some help from my parents, but you know they're super strapped for cash, so I'm trying to find the rest, and I figured you'd be willing to help me... y'know, so I'm not homeless or anything."

God, she'd gotten to be such an effortless liar. Chris took a grounding breath and collected the last of his and Warren's clothing, then headed to the bedroom. Warren was draped like an old-world Hollywood starlet across the sheets when he entered, hips angled to show off the curve of his hip, all legs and skin and sex.

"Chris?" Free insisted, dragging him out of his fantasies. "I can't hear you if you're talking. Is the connection bad? I can call back if it is."

Chris considered saying nothing at all, blocking her number when she hung up, and crawling back into bed with Warren, but nothing good ever came out of ignoring Free. If he blocked her number, she'd call from another phone. If he turned his phone off, she'd resort to something underhanded—like finally returning Jack's calls. The kid had been up early every day trying to reach her, and Liberty had confided to him that he was also calling after school. Free knew what she was doing, even though she pretended that she didn't. She'd use him in a heartbeat if it meant she could get what she wanted, and Chris couldn't allow that to happen. If it meant he had to endure her to keep Jack safe, so be it.

"I'm here." He gave Warren a lingering look, then tossed the clothes on the bed and grabbed his t-shirt from the pile. "I can hear you."

"Oh, I'm so glad the call didn't cut! Connection's been kinda funky around here. So, you'll give me the money?"

"No."

"What the hell?!"

Chris took the phone from his ear long enough to shrug into his shirt, then left the room. Behind him came a shuffle of bare skin on bedsheets and the creak of the old metal bedframe—Warren was likely getting up to follow him. He had to be confused. Chris had never told him about the divorce. Hadn't told anyone, really. The less he thought about what had happened—what he'd *let* happen—the better.

He continued the conversation with Free on his way down the hall. "Don't act like you're surprised. You knew this was gonna happen. There's no security deposit, Free. I know it. You know it. Pretending there is won't change anything." Chris crossed the living room, entered the kitchen, and jostled the balcony door open. "Rehab doesn't let you out early. That's not the way it works."

"Says who?"

"Says everyone. It's a verifiable fact. You can look it up."

"Uh, no, you can't. You're such a liar, Chris. You're so fucking greedy. Why can't you just be happy for me?"

The door slammed into its off-kilter jamb. Chris nudged it with his foot to make sure it was shut, then crossed the shitty, rusted flooring to lean on the balcony. It was too damned cold to be outside in boxers and a t-shirt, but if he went back inside, he'd explode. The chill kept his temper from reaching a rolling boil. "Stop it, Free. I'm serious. I'm not giving you the money."

"Are you being serious right now?" Free sounded close to boiling over herself. "You're such a fucking dick. I'm trying my hardest. I'm working hard and staying clean, and what are you doing? Trying to undermine me with your bullshit. And it *is* bullshit, Chris. I'm for real this time. But you don't care, do you? You don't care because this is what you always wanted. You *love* to see me fail. You'd shoot me up yourself just for the satisfaction of watching me struggle. Because that's what gets you off, isn't it? Coming out on top. Looking like a *hero.*" She sneered that last word, weaponizing it like she always did when she got angry. "Stop being so goddamn high and mighty and give me the fifty bucks. Or do you want to be the one who has to explain to Jack why his mommy is homeless?"

Chris clenched his teeth. "If you fucking dare—"

"If I dare what? Tell the truth? You want me to lie, Chris? You want me to tell him everything's all flowers and rainbows when I'm out on the streets because *you* can't pull your head out of your ass long enough to support me while I'm getting clean?"

"I'm so fucking tired of this." Chris gripped the railing, squeezing as hard as he could. Corroding metal bit into the undersides of his knuckles and scraped across his palms. He welcomed the sting. "Do you think after two years of the same old shit I can't see what you're doing? Look, if this whole security deposit thing is real, then I'll be first in line to help you, but the burden of proof is on you. Send me a picture of your lease or the address and phone number of the property manager's office—the one you can find on the website, not some unlisted bullshit. If you're serious, you should have both those things on hand. I just need one of them. Just one, Free. You do it, I'll send you the money."

"Fuck you."

It was all the answer he needed. Chris released the railing to rest both elbows on it, back hunched and head down.

Two years.

Two years and it still hurt.

The love he'd had for her was gone, but his heart ached for Jack, who was too young to understand what was going on or why she would never come home. The idea of divorce didn't mean much to a kid who'd spent his life missing a dad deployed half a world away. All he wanted was his mom, but she was gone now. She was gone, and nothing Chris did could make her come back.

"You mentioned talking to Jack like you do it all the time, but did you know he's been calling you every day?" It was a struggle to keep his voice from breaking, but he pushed through because she needed to know. "He's been getting up early in the hopes you won't be so 'busy.' I hear he's been calling you after school, too. It would mean the world to him if you answered one of these days. All he wants is to say hello. To tell you how much he loves and misses you. To hear you say it back."

"Fuck you," Free snarled, more vehemently than before.

The call disconnected.

Chris did, too.

It was a long while before the balcony door creaked open and bare footsteps padded across the worn grating. Warren slotted into place at his side, but didn't touch him. Didn't try to.

"It's cold out here," he remarked after a long moment of silence.

"Yeah."

"You wanna come in and talk about what happened?"

Chris didn't want to—dreaded so much as thinking about it—but when he opened his mouth, the catch in his voice said yes even when his lips said no.

3 2

WARREN

On the way from the balcony to the bedroom, Chris told Warren about Free. Some of it Warren already knew, like how he and Free had been high school sweethearts who'd married after graduation and left their little town so Chris could join the military. Some of it Warren didn't. Basic training hadn't been good on their marriage, Chris told him as they settled on the bed. Free had never loved being a small-town girl, but she hated following Chris from base to base even more. Their relationship had fizzled, and he'd realized too late that what they were missing wasn't a baby, but a spark. By then, his frequent deployments had put serious strain on what was already a fragile relationship and pushed it past the point of no return.

"But that wasn't where it ended," Chris admitted in hushed tones as Warren pulled him into his arms. "I should've called it there, but I didn't. I thought I could make it work. I didn't want Jack to fall through the cracks, and so I tried to hold everything together, but I did more harm than good. Free, she just... she checked out. I kept trying to make things work, but she wasn't willing to meet me half-way. I, uh... I was deployed when it happened." The small, hollow sound of Chris's voice made Warren's heart ache. "I didn't realize anything was wrong until I came back home, but by then, it was too late. The money was gone, the woman I'd married wasn't the same person anymore, and Jack... *fuck*." Chris's voice quivered. It was as close to crying as Warren had ever heard him come, and the sound of it took the ache in his heart and multiplied it a thousandfold.

"When I got home, he was different, too. Hungry. He, uh..." Chris had to stop and take a breath. "He was eating everything I put in front of him, and that's saying something, because I'm not the best cook. I just figured he was going through a growth spurt. I told myself it wasn't all that unusual. But then things started going missing from the pantry. Weird things. The gross whole-grain crackers Free likes that taste like cardboard, half a box of granola bars, a jar of peanut butter. I thought Free was behind it, because she'd been acting so fucking strange, but then I found the jar of peanut butter in Jack's room while I was cleaning, globs scooped out of it like he was eating it straight off his fingers..." He shook his head, expression gaunt. "But I still didn't get it. Not really. It didn't click until my card declined one day when I was out with Jack. I called the bank, found out Free had made a cash withdrawal that'd drained the last of our savings. I went home after that and started digging. There was a paper trail of ATM transactions dating back almost a year—money I couldn't account for. All of it taken by Free. I tried calling, but she wouldn't answer her phone, and Jack told me"—he laughed, but it was thin and strained—"he told me that it was probably because she was sleeping. She'd been doing that a lot since I was last deployed, apparently. Because she 'missed' me. Because it made her sad. He told me that when she was sleeping like that, nothing could wake her up. Not the phone, not her alarm, not anything, and he knew because he'd already tried."

The story was eerily familiar. Warren looked Chris over, searching his face for clues, but came up empty. He had a feeling he knew what "sleeping" meant, but he didn't want to put words in Chris's mouth.

"It was like dominoes after that," Chris continued. "One revelation sent me crashing straight into another, and all that was left in the end was a mess I had to clean up. I learned that one of Jack's classmates had been sharing his lunch with him because Free was too busy 'sleeping' to prepare meals, and that Jack had been hoarding food from the pantry when he could find it, squirreling it away in his bedroom so he had something to eat when his mom couldn't be there for him. I dropped Jack off at a friend's place so I could confront her in private, and when she came home, she ripped into me. Said it was all my fault. Told me that if I'd been a better husband, none of this would've happened—that she wouldn't have needed to find comfort in other things."

"Other things?"

Chris sighed in resignation and lowered his gaze. "She got addicted to drugs while I was away—was shooting up and nodding out when she should have been looking after Jack."

Warren had been right on the money, but he wished he hadn't been. He'd seen the way addiction destroyed families while on call to treat suspected overdoses, and there was never anything glamorous about it. To know Jack was caught up in it was even more heartbreaking. "Jesus Christ, Chris... I'm sorry."

Chris shook his head. "It's not your fault. I'm trying to remind myself that it isn't my fault, either, but I haven't quite gotten there yet. Like all things, it'll take time. I need to catch my breath before I can firmly put it in my past, and I haven't been able to do that yet. Everything's been moving so fast. The divorce, the custody hearings, getting Jack into therapy... I couldn't balance life as a single dad with my military career, so I had to make a choice. We left Fort Hood as soon as the custody ruling came down in my favor and moved here. Back home. I knew that it'd be a dead end for me, but it was the only place I could think to go where I knew Jack would have people who'd care for him if I fell short."

So that was why he'd come back. Warren's heart hurt to know it. When he'd stormed up to Chris's apartment that first day, he'd attacked him for making those hard choices, not understanding the

219

reason behind them. He regretted it now. "I didn't know. Libby never told me. I'm sorry that I said what I did. You should've kicked my fucking ass."

"Mm, well, I fucked it instead. Oh well." Chris grinned, breaking the somber mood. "But, seriously, it's fine. No one outside the family knows what happened. Jack only half understands what went on, and I don't want him to know more until he's old enough to get it. He knows that Free and I are divorced, but he doesn't understand why she had to go away. How do you explain something like drug addiction to a kid? I haven't been able to figure it out. And even if I did know, then what? The false hope he'd get every time her parents check her into rehab would break him. She never sticks with it long. She's not ready to get clean yet. Nothing will change until she's the one who takes responsibility for her actions, and I don't know how long that will take. Months? Years? I'm not in love with her anymore, but when I get calls from numbers I don't recognize, the bottom drops out of my stomach thinking it'll be news she OD'd. How can I live with myself knowing I've passed that same fear on to my son? I can't. I don't know what to do."

All was quiet for a moment. Warren listened to the hum of the central heating and reflected on what he'd heard. The Chris he'd known in high school was the kind of guy who shirked responsibility, but maybe he'd been a little too quick to judge. Not only about that, but about other things.

Use that big college-educated brain of yours, Reaves, Chris had told him. And now, as he reframed his perception of Chris from weasel to devoted father, Warren was starting to catch on to what he'd meant.

The silence ended when Chris sighed, and after a moment, he continued from where he'd left off. "Jack's rationalized it in his own way. He assumes she's been deployed, just like I used to be. He gets anxious sometimes thinking she won't know where we are when she 'comes home.' He doesn't see the wrong in what she did to him. He loves her too much. I know, deep down, she loves him, too, but there's so much shit she has to wade through before she'll be in a place where she can prove it. One day, maybe, when he knows the truth and she's ready, we can work on repairing the damage she's done, but for now it's still too fresh. There's still too much shit to unpack. It's not something that gets better overnight."

When had Chris gotten to be so admirable? Warren bit the inside of his lip to keep from saying any of the million stupid things floating around in his head. Not only was Chris not the man he'd thought he was, but he was genuinely a kind and loving person. Yeah, he could throw down with the best of them, and he knew how to make Warren's blood boil, but he wasn't evil. Warren was starting to believe he'd meant what he said about never having targeted him.

But if that was the case, then it meant that Warren had been the one in the wrong, and that meant...

That meant what he'd been feeling all this time hadn't actually been hate.

Back then, it'd certainly felt like it. How else was he supposed to articulate a feeling like that? It'd burned hot and bright inside of him all through their childhood, prickling under his skin like fire eating through wood. Hatred had been the easiest answer. It was supposed to feel fiery and eat him up from the inside.

At that age, he hadn't known that love could do the same.

"So I guess that's it," Chris concluded. "I don't know what else there is to say. You know the rest already. Here I am back in town, living in this shitty apartment while I start my life over from scratch. Divorced at thirty, a single dad, pulling myself up by the fucking bootstraps as life tries to kick me back down. But the most miserable part about all this? About starting over fresh?" Chris let out a laugh that could easily have been misconstrued as a sob. "All the people I used to be friends with are gone and here you are, the one guy high school me would have been happy to never see again, only now I can't get you out of my fucking head. It's like I've lived my whole life backward—I loved the girl I should've hated and hated the boy I should've loved."

The fire was back, and it burned. Warren was helpless against it. Unable to speak, he caressed Chris's cheek and acknowledged him through touch.

Was a fire burning in Chris, too?

Warren's eyelids sank. He closed the scant space between them and kissed Chris to check for himself. The heat between them—the way the air itself seemed to crackle when they touched—made him think he wasn't alone.

When their shared inferno had devoured all the air in the room and Warren was too breathless to continue, he pulled away from Chris and let the flames flicker low. "I, um... I'm free... all day tomorrow. But especially at five. And, uh... after five, too. So we could... you know. Meet up again."

"Yeah?" Chris said it with a cocky, enamored little smirk that made Warren's heart ignite.

Warren tilted his head to the side as he brought their lips closer. "Yeah."

The kiss that followed was slow and sweet. When it was over, Chris cupped Warren's cheek and ran his thumb across its swell. "You know I can't say no to you."

Warren's lips parted in a silent, "Oh," prompting Chris to kiss him again.

"If it weren't for Jack," Chris whispered when the kiss ended, "I'd give you a preview of what I'm going to do to you next time you're here, but I guess it'll have to wait. Put your clothes on, Warren. It's time to go. I'll see you again tomorrow."

33

CHRIS

Half an hour after getting home from Liberty's place, Chris's phone pinged with an incoming text. At first he didn't pay it any attention —he was wrist deep in soapy water, getting a head start on dishes while dinner defrosted—but when another two texts arrived in rapid succession, he ditched the sudsy mess in the sink to check what was going on.

Warren: Houston, we have a problem

Before Chris read any further, he checked to see what Jack was up to. Warren had yet to send him explicit messages during the day, but with a curious kid around, Chris could never be too careful. Fortunately, Jack was too wrapped up in Minecraft to notice much of anything. Better yet, Billie was with him, which practically guaranteed Jack wouldn't be lured away from the screen. Safe in the knowledge that his son was safe from whatever depraved messages were waiting, Chris leaned against the sink and read Warren's other texts.

Warren: I left my butt plug in your bathtub

Warren: I will never be able to look your son in the face if he finds it

In the second it took to read both texts, the bottom dropped out of Chris's stomach. He launched himself out of the kitchen and bolted across the living room.

"Dad?" Jack popped up over the back of the couch as Chris passed, his eyes narrowed curiously. "What's wrong?"

"*Nothing.*"

"Then why are you running?"

"*I'll tell you later.*"

Chris hadn't quite finished speaking when he flung himself into the bathroom, but he didn't let that stop him from slamming the door shut. As he locked it, he heard Jack shimmy off the couch and make his way down the hall.

"Dad?" he asked from the other side of the door. "Are you okay? You're not sick, are you?"

"I'll be fine, champ. Just need a second. Why don't you go back to your game?"

There was a pause. "Was it something you ate? Jacob from my class got real sick when his mom forgot to put an ice pack in with his sandwich and he had to stay in the bathroom all afternoon until his dad could come pick him up."

The universe was smiling down on him. Chris almost let out a sigh of relief. Jack would sooner believe his own narrative than whatever excuse Chris could come up with.

Chris would have to send Jacob's family a thank-you card.

And some Pepto-Bismol.

"It, uh, it might've been. I'm gonna need to be in here for a little while, so why don't you go back to your game? I'm sure I'll be feeling better in no time."

"Okay. I hope you feel better soon, Dad."

"Thanks. Me too."

By the sounds of it, Jack patted the bathroom door a few times in

224

the same way someone might reassuringly pat a friend on the back, then left. Chris waited until he heard the telltale rustling of a young body climbing onto the couch before he dared move, inching toward the tub in the same way a plucky paleontologist might approach a pack of velociraptors.

"You've got this, Chris," he muttered to himself as he curled a hand around the edge of the shower curtain. "If it's there, no harm done. If it's not..." He couldn't think of a way to cap that sentence that wasn't horrible, so he ripped off the Band-Aid and yanked the shower curtain back.

Nothing.

Absolutely nothing.

The plug was gone.

Chris released the curtain. Where the hell could the plug have gone if it wasn't here? So help him god, if Jack had found it and taken it to his room...

But then a telltale twinkle caught his eye.

The plug, ridiculous bejeweled base and all, glittered at him near the drain, where it had blended in with the stainless-steel stopper.

Chris snapped a picture and sent it to Warren.

Chris: Got it

Chris: Would you care to explain why you own a diamond plug?

Warren: Uh, are you trying to start a fight, loverboy?

Warren: In what world is that a diamond?

Chris: Christ

Warren: It's marketed as a "Rainbow Princess" plug. Diamonds are white. Mostly. The jewel on my plug is multi-colored and changes depending on how the light hits it

Chris: Are you trying to pick a fight with me over the plastic gem in a butt plug?

Warren: Yes.

Chris: FFS

Warren: Is it working?

Whether it was the relief of knowing that Jack wasn't the proud owner of a used "Rainbow Princess" butt plug or the sudden rush of dopamine now that the stress was over, Chris didn't know, but his mood lifted. He snorted.

Chris: You don't have to go making trouble. You're already in it. How the hell am I supposed to get it out of the bathroom without Jack seeing?
Warren: Hide the plug under your shirt
Chris: Are you kidding me? With this kid? He already knows something's up. There's no way I'm sneaking past him with a bulge under my shirt
Warren: I mean, there's another place you could hide it where he wouldn't ever see...
Warren: ;)
Chris: FUCK. NO.
Chris: IT WAS INSIDE OF YOU
Warren: Hey, I didn't say it was a GOOD idea
Warren: Maybe rinse it off and stash it on top of the medicine cabinet where he can't see? I'll pick it up tomorrow

It was their best bet. Chris plucked the plug from the tub by its base and carried it to the sink, sitting it in the basin while the water ran.

How did people clean things like this, anyway? Soap? He eyed the dispenser. It made no comment, but the way the overhead light glinted off its metal pump looked a little devious, like it was more into the idea than it ought to be.

Chris decided that soap was a bad idea.

He pushed the plug under the heating water and let the flow cleanse the shiny metal. While it did, he resumed the conversation to grump playfully at Warren.

Chris: I cannot believe I'm washing your butt plug

Warren: You're a dad. Don't tell me you haven't done worse

Chris: There's a difference

Warren: Would it help if I called you Daddy?

Chris: Don't you dare

Warren: Not my kink anyway, so that's fine

Chris: You mean there's a kink you don't have?

Warren: Hey, no kink shaming

Warren: And yes. Several. Daddy kink is nice and all, but Daddies care too much. I want the guy I'm with not to be afraid to take what he wants. I don't want to be coddled. I want to be treated rough

It wasn't any big surprise after their earlier conversation, but Chris's dick twitched anyway.

Chris: Yeah? That so?

Warren: Big shock, huh?

Warren: I understand if it's too much for your delicate sensibilities and you have to let me go. I mean, what kind of monster likes being wrestled to the floor, forcibly stripped of their clothes, and brutally fucked?

Chris: The same one I want to carry to bed afterward, wrap up in my arms, and put back together piece by piece

Warren didn't reply to that, but after Chris was done screwing him into the floor the next day, he did let Chris carry him to bed and snuggle the fuck out of him. Eventually, gentle kisses turned into sex, and Chris made love to him soft and sweet. He plundered the moans from Warren's lips and filled him with cum in exchange.

Warren forgot his plug again, so on top of the medicine cabinet it stayed. Chris didn't really mind. It gave Warren an excuse to come back. Which he did. Again, and again, and again.

34

WARREN

Dreary October days gave way to unusually cold November nights. Frost cracked patterns across windows and froze the morning dew, and after a bout of rain that threatened to turn into snow, ice joined it, covering the town in slick, sparkling sheets. Warren didn't enjoy winter. He wasn't fond of the way the cold crept into his bones when he was out on calls or how treacherous the roads became when the temperatures plummeted. Any season the sun hated enough to fuck right off until it was over was a disaster in his books, but this year, winter was a little different.

This year, Warren had Chris.

"Had" was, perhaps, a strong word. They hadn't discussed what they were. By the same token, they hadn't discussed what they weren't, so Warren's imagination was free to wreak as much emotional havoc as it wanted, and wreak it did. On nights when his bed felt too empty, he imagined the familiar weight of Chris's body next to him. At work, he hit their ramshackle gym often enough that Pete started to call him Mini-Meatball. Warren joked it away, claiming he was preemptively working off Thanksgiving dinner, but Thanksgiving came and went and his routine didn't change. He'd never tell Pete the real reason he was pumping more iron than ever was that he'd gotten it in his head that one of these days Chris would leave the dispatch office and find him mid-workout, sweat glistening on his brow and muscles taut from exertion. Thinking about the wild look in Chris's eyes were that to happen was enough to get Warren out of bed and into work on those dark, chilly mornings.

Chris hadn't stumbled across him working out just yet, but Warren didn't mind. He was in it for the long haul. Besides, the unexpected benefits were too good to pass up—the first time Chris had noticed that he was putting on muscle mass, his cock could've cut diamonds. Luckily, Warren's ass was Rainbow Princess grade, so he made it out with his life.

"You try'na look good for me, Reaves?" Chris had asked breathlessly after they'd both come, nipping at Warren's earlobe. "So fuckin' dirty. You shouldn't be encouraging me. You're not supposed to like the things I do to you."

It was a lie, but Warren loved the games they played, so he'd told a tale about how he was training so he could overthrow Chris and fuck him for a change. That little fib had earned him another round of aggressive sex, after which Chris apologized for his bruised knees and skinned palms by carrying him to bed and kissing him until Warren didn't feel the sting anymore.

Warren's imagination didn't need to wreak anything when Chris touched him like that.

Libby and Pete were at least partially to blame for how bad it'd gotten. Their happiness was infectious, and Warren was not immune. Which made it hard to pretend he wasn't lovesick when, one December day, Chris remarked, "It's snowing."

"So?" Warren didn't bother to check. He'd claimed his favorite spot in Chris's bed—the side Chris liked to sleep on, where his scent clung strongest to the sheets and pillows—and he wasn't about to be tricked into being ousted.

"It's the first snow of the season." Chris stood by the window, his very fine ass hugged by a pair of Calvin Kleins Warren had "accidentally" ordered for him during the Great Tequila Wobble of 2020. Just like in 2018, it had never actually happened, but pretending it had made it easier for Chris to accept all the junior boy's clothing Warren "accidentally" bought for Jack. "It's coming down pretty powdery and gusting everywhere," Chris elaborated. "The roads look bad."

"Mmhm."

"So I think you should stay here tonight."

That got Warren's attention. He bolted upright and, ever eloquent, cawed, "*What?*"

"Stay the night." Chris put his back to the window and leaned on the ledge. "Here. With me. In my bed."

Warren opened his mouth, but couldn't speak—his heart was too busy racing a mile a minute to let any other part of his body steal the show. It pumped blood into all kinds of places it shouldn't have been prioritizing—Warren's ears, for one. They burned like he'd just come in after a long time out in the cold. Not to be outdone, Warren's cheeks heated up, too. If his face was any hue duller than tomato, it would be a miracle.

Unfortunately, part of the heart-pumping package included express delivery to his dick, which immediately decided staying the night was a very good idea. Warren fisted a handful of blanket, yanked it over the star player on #TeamSeriouslyMisguided, and gaped at Chris.

Chris shrugged. "Why drive when you know how bad the roads get? Stay here and wait for things to clear out. Tomorrow's Saturday, which means Jack doesn't have school and I'm off work. You're off, too, so none of us have anywhere we need to be. You might as well."

Warren had no idea where his heart was going, but wherever it was, it had to be important, because it left his tongue in its dust. He looked at Chris, who looked at him, and managed a meager, "Jack?"

"Jack has wanted us to be friends since the first time he met you. He'd be thrilled to know we're having a sleepover."

Warren's silver tongue continued to dazzle. *"Free?"* he squawked.

Chris worked his jaw to the side and eased off the window ledge. He came to sit by Warren on the bed. "She's not in the picture anymore. You know that. If you're worried she'll find out and use you against me, don't be. My parents have known about my sexuality since uh, well, let's just say they know, and everyone at work is supportive of you, so I'm sure they'd be supportive of me."

There was a fair amount to unpack from Chris's sudden invitation, and Warren wasn't sure he had the fortitude to grasp it all. It seemed to him that Chris was opening the door to make their unspoken thing spoken, and that...

That excited and terrified him all at once.

Since that one vulnerable day in October, they hadn't brought up the L word. It wasn't a dirty secret so much as something Warren was still struggling to come to terms with. Chris had been nothing but patient with him, but it seemed that patience was starting to run out. He wanted Warren in his bed not just for an hour when Jack was out of the house on Warren's odd days off, but all night long.

Little fires lit in Warren at the thought.

"Not that I think she's in a place where she'd be able to find out about us," Chris added. "I haven't heard from her since October, and the last I heard from her parents, she'd been arrested for possession and was facing third degree felony charges. We're not on her radar and I don't think we'll ever be. She has way bigger fish to fry. Her story has nothing to do with ours. And if, years from now, she does find out and decides to cause trouble, nothing she can do can hurt us. If she threatens to tell Jack, so what? He and I have already had a talk about what it means to be gay, and he's not gonna think any differently of me for—"

Chris stopped himself abruptly and cleared his throat, but Warren's mind was catching up with his heart, and it beat Chris to the end of his sentence. He'd been about to say "loving who I love." Warren had seen the way his tongue had lifted to tap the roof of his mouth—how his lips had rounded ever so slightly in anticipation of the word. But that couldn't be right, because they were just fucking. Hate fucking. The kind that involved lots of angry sex on all kinds of unlikely surfaces.

Sure, there was some kissing, and cuddling, and sometimes sex of the non-hate variety... but it was more like something guilty they both liked to indulge in. Hate with a healthy dose of love on the side. If given a choice between Chris and a swarm of angry bees, Warren knew which prick he'd prefer.

Chris, hands down.

Wait, that wasn't right.

The bees. It was supposed to be the *bees.*

While Warren struggled with the newfound knowledge that he and Nicholas Cage had more in common than he'd previously believed, Chris laid a reassuring hand on his thigh. "For having you around," he concluded, but it was too late. He'd waited too long. Warren didn't want the bees anymore, and it was terrible.

He really was in love, wasn't he?

In love with Chris fucking Donnelly.

The Quaker Oats man was officially back on the market. Maybe he could make it work with Warren's neglected bees.

"So why don't we cut the bullshit?" Chris squeezed Warren's knee. "No more sneaking around. Stay tonight. Once you do, you can come here whenever you want—stay whenever you want—and then we won't have to rush our afternoons. I can have you all night long instead."

Warren had to look one more declaration away from swearing off honey forever, because Chris finally shook his head and got up from the bed. He put on a good act, but Warren read pain in the pinched corners of his lips.

Great.

Not only had he managed to freak himself out, but he'd hurt Chris while doing it. "Chris, I—"

"No, it's cool. I've gotta go hop in a quick shower before I go get Jack, so think about it and let me know when I'm back. You don't need to explain your choice." He didn't smile—not exactly—but the pain on his face vanished. Where it went, Warren didn't know, but he didn't think it was gone. "If you wanna go home but think the roads are too bad to drive, I'll give you a lift back to your place and you can come get your car tomorrow. It's all good. I'll be back in five."

Chris left to shower. When he was gone, Warren collapsed dramatically onto the bed and sighed, but what he really wanted to do was scream.

Love.

No wonder why little Warren had decided to boycott Chris—this shit sucked. Love was supposed to be for people like Libby and Pete, who sent each other flowers, wrote each other poems, and pelted each other's bedroom windows with pebbles before busting out their best raccoon-inspired love song. It wasn't for people like Warren, whose idea of a romantic gesture was being thrown over a kitchen counter and made to come until it hurt.

If Chris wanted sweeping declarations, he was going to be hurt.

Did he know it?

Did he care?

Warren traced his fingers over the wrinkles in the blanket, smoothing them out one by one.

The only way he'd find out was to ask.

At long last, his racing heart arrived at its destination.

He knew what he needed to do.

35

WARREN

Seven minutes later—not five, the liar—Chris returned from the bathroom dripping wet and deliciously naked. He was carrying a towel. Warren had been nervous that after his little soul-searching episode seeing him would be hard, but it turned out those whisperings had been courtesy of his #misguided dick. To hide his shame, Warren bunched a few extra fistfuls of blanket over his crotch and sat up straighter, looking Chris in the eyes. "I'll stay on one condition."

"Which is?"

"Tonight, after Jack's gone to bed, I want to discuss a few things. Is that okay?"

"Sure." Chris busied himself with rubbing the towel through his hair, but Warren saw right through him. He was trying—and failing —to hide a smile. "You need me to pick up anything from your place while I'm over there?"

Warren eyed the door. "Does your lock work?"

"Yeah."

"Then unless you're worried Jack will climb in through the window to get to our slumber party, I'm good."

Chris tossed the towel into the laundry basket, then moved to the dresser and pulled out a pair of briefs. "You planning on sleeping naked?"

"You planning on letting me stay clothed?"

That earned him a chuckle. A second later, a pair of cotton pajama bottoms landed on the bed just short of Warren's knee.

They were camouflage print. How trite. Warren arched a brow. "Seriously?"

"What?" Chris stepped into his briefs and returned to the bed, where he braced his hands on Warren's thighs and leaned in close. Warren's heart couldn't take any more. He closed his eyes and parted his lips for a kiss that never came. Chris plied him with words instead. "You telling me you're too good for my clothes, Reaves? No one's gonna make you wear them, but if you won't, then tell me... how else should I show the world you're mine?"

On second thought, camouflage was good. Camouflage was *so* good. Warren kissed Chris to prove it, and Chris returned his affection because that was what people in love did. The weirdos.

The thought made Warren laugh, and once he started, he couldn't stop. Chris kissed him anyway, clumsily pressing their lips together until he started laughing, too.

Warren couldn't remember a time his heart had felt so light.

Maybe—in small doses—this whole love thing wouldn't be so bad.

One did not simply stay the night in the home of an eight-year-old boy. The second Jack noticed Warren sitting in the living room, all bets were off. In a maelstrom of hastily flung jackets and flying winter boots, he charged from the door to the couch, leapt at it from a distance, and landed in a heap to Warren's left. From his mess of tangled limbs, Jack looked up at Warren and grinned. "Hi, Wren."

"Hey."

"What are you doing in my house?"

"Your dad invited me over. We're gonna give this whole friend-ship thing a try."

Jack made a noise that guaranteed puberty was still a long way off, then narrowed his eyes suspiciously. "Did he let you shower, too?"

"Uh…" On Chris's advice, Warren had washed to rid himself of the smell of sex. He hadn't counted on Jack noticing his wet hair. "Yeah, he sure did."

"Was it because of the snow?" Jack gestured at his own hair, which glistened with waterdrops. "It got in my hair, too, and now I'm all wet. I hate wet hair. It smells gross."

Thank god. An excuse. Warren flicked a droplet out of Jack's mane and arched a brow. "You don't say. Me too. It's why your dad let me use the shower. He's a pretty nice guy once you get to know him… kinda like you."

The compliment had the desired effect—it made Jack forget all about Warren's wet hair. "You think I'm nice?"

"Yup."

"Do you *really?*"

"Well, I mean, when you don't eat my cookies…"

Jack unfolded himself from his awkward position and sat cross-legged facing Warren. "I won't anymore."

"You've got that right," Chris said as he walked by on his way to the kitchen. "Because if Warren tells me you're eating his cookies again, there's gonna be trouble."

"I won't!"

Ah, an old weasel classic. Warren had to smile. "I'll believe it when I see it, but until then, yeah, I think you're nice."

Jack screwed up his face in thought, then straightened his back and threw back his shoulders like he wanted to make a good impression. "I want you to think I'm nice all the time, so I'll prove that I won't eat your cookies anymore. The only thing is, to do that you need to stay for dinner. *Are* you staying for dinner? Dad, can

Wren stay for dinner, please? I know I said that I wouldn't invite strangers over anymore, but Wren said that you're friends now, so this is different. Plus, I really need him to stay so I can prove that I'm not gonna eat any of the cookies he has for dessert." There was a pause. "So, can we also have cookies for dessert if he stays? I would really, really appreciate it."

Chris, who'd fished out a pot from an under-counter cabinet while Jack had been monologuing, set it in the sink and turned on the tap. Water pelted the metal bottom, the tinny *plink!* fading away as it filled. "Yes, we can have cookies for dessert tonight, and yes, Warren is staying for dinner. In fact, I've already invited him to stay the night. We're gonna have a sleepover."

Jack leapt off the couch and punched the air. It was flattering in a weird kind of way that an eight-year-old was so invested in Warren's friendship with his father, but Warren had been a weird kid once, too, and he appreciated Jack's enthusiasm.

"It's going to be about twenty minutes before dinner's ready," Chris said as he shut off the water. "Jack, you wanna show our guest around?"

"*Yes!*"

Jack grabbed Warren's hand and tugged him to his feet, and thus began an evening of adventure. The Donnelly apartment was small, but Jack made it feel big. They bypassed the wonders of the kitchen and the man cooking spaghetti in it to marvel at the stunning vista offered by the balcony. When it got too cold to stand on the metal grating in their socks, Jack showed Warren the living room—in case he'd missed it the first time—then moved on to the bathroom, where Warren's plug had secretly claimed squatter's rights to the medicine cabinet. From there it was off to the bedrooms. Jack hand-waved away Chris's room and dragged Warren into his room, where he regaled him with tales of his favorite Minecraft plushies and showed off an old laptop Chris had given him to use as his personal computer.

It was, surprisingly, a good time.

When dinner came, Jack escorted Warren to the kitchen table, where they ate undercooked spaghetti served with sauce from a jar. If this whole sleepover thing was going to become a regular occurrence, Warren was going to have to take over kitchen duties. Slightly crunchy pasta was *not* his bag.

Jack didn't seem to mind it, though. He shoveled noodles into his face at blinding speeds and went back for seconds before Warren was halfway done with his first plate. Despite breaking pasta speed-eating records, he still managed to chatter about anything and everything, but particularly about how excited he was for Warren's visit, and how he hoped there would be enough snow tomorrow for a snowball fight.

While Jack monopolized the conversation, Warren occupied himself in other ways. Chiefly, stealing glances across the table at Chris. The man couldn't cook worth a damn, but he sure made up for it in other ways. And not just by being attractive. The pride in his eyes when he looked at Jack did things to Warren he couldn't fully explain.

Maybe Daddy kink *was* his thing.

Just… you know. In a roundabout kind of way.

"Can we watch a movie?" Jack asked abruptly, startling Warren out of a Chris-based stupor. "Please, Dad? *Please?* I don't have school tomorrow, so I don't need to go to bed as early. We have time."

"What do you think, Warren?" Chris looked from his son to Warren, and the pride in his expression sweetened in ways that made Warren's stomach flip. "Do you want to watch a movie?"

"Please, Wren?" Jack begged. "*Please?* We can all watch it together. I'll even let you pick."

College had prepared Warren for all kinds of uncomfortable things, but selecting age-appropriate movies for young boys wasn't one of them. He gave Chris a pointed look, hoping he'd take over the parenting lead, but the bastard just raised an eyebrow like he couldn't wait to see how this would play out.

Warren kicked his shin.

Chris kicked back.

"Wren?" Jack asked when Warren didn't reply. "You okay?"

"Yeah! Sure am." Warren kicked Chris again. It was a fool's errand to pick a fight with a soldier, but the loss was worth it when Chris grinned at him like that. "And I'd love to watch a movie, but I'm terrible at picking them, so why don't you go ahead and find something you'd like to watch? I'm sure whatever you choose will be amazing."

"Sure!" Jack cleared his dishes from the table and put them in the sink, then hurried into the living room and fired up the Xbox. While he browsed Netflix, Warren and Chris finished the last of their meal. When they were done, Chris quietly rose from the table and collected his plate, then came around to Warren's side and leaned in close under the pretext of collecting his as well.

"You're gonna pay for that, Reaves," he whispered against the back of Warren's ear, nudging his calf to make sure Warren didn't mistake what he meant. "Kicking me? Really? I thought you were beyond basic playground bullshit. Don't think you're going to get away with this just because Jack's here."

Warren's lips parted. His eyes closed. He was glad he was sitting with his back to the living room, because the things those words did to him bumped his rating from G to R real fast.

He went to lean into Chris, but no sooner did his shoulder brush Chris's arm than Chris was gone. Warren watched him carry their plates to the sink and run the water.

Busboys had never been sexier.

"Wren!" Jack chirped from the living room, startling Warren out of his blatant ogling. "Have you seen *Spider-Man*?"

"Which one?"

"Any, but especially the Spider-Verse one."

"Not yet."

"Then I know what we're watching!" Jack sprinted from the living room to the kitchen table and grabbed Warren by the arm.

"C'mon! Dad can see the TV from the sink, so we can start the movie while he's washing dishes. He can come sit with us later."

Well, it was time to hope that his dick was behaving. Warren said a small prayer and stood. He was lucky—there were no unwelcome visitors pitching tents in his pants—but even if there had been, Jack was so excited to watch a movie that Warren doubted he would have noticed.

He dragged Warren into the living room and soon enough, it was show time. Warren leaned against the arm of the couch he'd been fucked on and tried diligently not to think about how Chris had slammed into him so hard, he'd knocked him onto the floor.

It didn't go so well.

By the time Chris had finished in the kitchen, Warren had no idea what was going on in the movie, but thanks to his efforts to stay distracted, he *could* list all fifty states and their capitals.

Except for New Jersey.

Thank *god* for New Jersey.

Scanning his memory for its obscure state capital had kept him from looking like a total perv. How did Chris do it? This whole family-friendly thing was way harder than it looked.

"I brought cookies," Chris said as he sat on the opposite end of the couch, sandwiching Jack between them. "Chocolate chip. Three each."

He put the communal plate on Jack's lap.

Bold move.

Warren watched from the corner of his eye and kept count as Jack shoveled cookies into his mouth. It was a little mindless, but way more fun than thinking about Newark. Or was it Jersey City? Whatever. It didn't matter. There were cookies to be counted. Jack was halfway through his second and had already picked up his third.

After the second cookie bit the dust, Warren stretched and made a show of adjusting his position so he could keep better watch over the plate.

The third cookie was gone in two bites. Jack's hand twitched. He reached for another, then sighed and stopped himself before making contact.

Tough kid.

Warren was impressed.

It seemed Chris was, too, because he wrapped an arm around Jack's shoulders and tugged him into a side hug that Jack promptly melted into. Warren removed the plate from his lap and set it aside, and when he looked back, he saw that Chris was looking at him. Their eyes met, and Chris smiled.

Just smiled.

No subtext. No flirty looks or sultry undertones... only happiness.

The movie went on, but Warren didn't care enough to follow it. There was a story unfolding beside him, and it mattered more than all the Spider-Verses combined.

Jack was asleep by the time the credits rolled, head on Chris's lap. Chris petted his hair until he stirred.

"Dad?"

"Hey, champ. You fell asleep. Let's go get you ready for bed, okay?"

"Okay." Jack slid off the couch, tipping himself over the edge of the seat until gravity took over. Warren was afraid he'd fall, but kids were like bony, death-defying cats, and Jack had no problem landing on his feet.

"Night, Wren," he said once he was upright.

Warren smiled. "Night."

Jack toddled off. When he was gone, Chris got up, stretched, and followed him. He kissed the top of Warren's head as he passed by. "Thank you for being so patient. I'm gonna go tuck him in. After that, my night is yours. While I'm gone, why don't you go get comfy in the bedroom? I'll be there as soon as I can, and then we can have that talk."

Talk?

Oh, right. The talk. It seemed almost pointless to have it now that Warren was a little more on board with life's simpler pleasures, but he needed to stick to his guns. As happy as he was right now, he didn't want to risk losing interest and checking out of the relationship like Free had. If they were going to be happy, he needed to know that Chris could commit to satisfying the part of him that liked things a little less than romantic.

"Yeah," Warren said. "Thanks for remembering. I'll be there. See you soon."

Hoping for the best, he waited until Chris was gone, then headed for the bedroom.

36

CHRIS

After halfheartedly brushing his teeth, Jack trudged into his bedroom and toppled into bed. He punted the blankets down with a few kicks of feet and slipped his ankles beneath them, yawned hugely, and buried his face in his pillows. It was important, Jack had once said, to make sure that your ankles were covered before falling asleep. That way monsters couldn't get you. Chris wasn't so sure about that, but he kept his opinions to himself. If Jack wanted to risk dangling a hand into monster territory, that was his prerogative. It had to be an Owens thing—no Donnelly would ever be so foolhardy.

"Dad?" Jack asked in a small, sleepy voice as Chris came to tuck him in. "Can we have pancakes for breakfast tomorrow since Wren is here?"

"Sure."

"Mm." Jack dragged a pillow into his arms. "Yay."

"Love you."

"Love you, too."

Chris pulled the blanket over Jack's shoulders and tucked him in the way he liked. He made sure to squeeze each of Jack's ankles when he finished to prove they were hidden from all things that went bump in the night, then kissed the swirl of his hair and went to turn out the light. While he did, Jack mumbled something incomprehensible and promptly fell asleep.

Done with dad duties for the day, Chris killed the lights and closed the door. He double-checked the front door was locked, then went to be with Warren. Since they'd parted ways, Warren had changed out of his daywear and into his pajama pants. He'd always been physically fit, but he'd been putting on muscle lately, and it was never more obvious than when he was shirtless. Taut abs. Toned arms. The most delicious taper from his chest to his hips. Conversation be damned, Chris needed him. He made sure the bedroom door was locked, then stalked to the bed and climbed onto it, straddling Warren's thighs and pushing him down amongst the sheets.

"It was a mistake to give you those pajama pants," Chris uttered as he brushed his nose along Warren's. "You're so fucking hot when you wear my clothes. Can't keep my hands off you."

Warren wrapped his arms around Chris's neck and arched his back, pushing up into him. In turn, Chris ground down against him. His stiffened cock rubbed on Warren's, the thin fabric of his pajama pants giving Chris a good feel of what was waiting beneath.

"Can't keep your cock off, either," Warren retorted playfully. He ran his thigh along Chris's side. "You gonna put it inside me, or is that erection of yours just for show?"

Chris pawed the waistband of Warren's pajamas and shoved them down. "You sure you don't wanna have that talk first?"

"Who's saying we can't do both?"

"At the same time?"

"Unless I make you too horny to think straight, which... well, come to think of it, I probably do, don't I?"

Cocky bastard. Chris kissed him to shut him up, then pulled his pajama pants off completely. Once he'd cast them onto the floor, he tugged off his own shirt and undid his fly. Warren, spread on the bed before him, watched with one eyebrow cocked as he undressed and grabbed the lube from the bedside table drawer. Chris clicked the cap open and coated himself, then tossed the tube away.

"You wanna say that again?" he asked as he pushed Warren's legs back and slid in. *Fuck,* was he tight. And the way he clenched and released like he was trying to milk Chris dry? Heaven on earth. He pushed in deep and made it his. "Tell me about how I can't listen. I dare you."

"Oh, *fuck.*" Warren clamped a hand over his own mouth, cutting off what would have been a moan.

"You good?"

Warren mewled behind his hand, then dropped it from his face and looked up at Chris with sex-starved eyes. "M'good if you are."

"I'll manage."

"I just… mm, fuck. I wanna make sure we're on the same page about where this thing between us is going."

"Yeah?"

"Yeah." He cut himself short as his face crumpled with pleasure. "Oh, fuck, you feel good. Can we always have serious conversations like this? Please?"

"We'll see." He pushed Warren's legs forward and leaned over him to steal a hot little kiss, hoping it would get them back on track. "Depends on if you keep stalling. Fess up. What did you wanna talk about?"

"Mm…" Warren's face flushed. "It sounds stupid to bring it up now after what you did at dinner, but"—he hissed in pleasure, in no small part because Chris had made it a point to thrust into him —"I… I was afraid we might lose what we have if we stopped sneaking around. Being treated rough like that is something I need to be happy, and if that doesn't gel with your long-term plans, then maybe… maybe we should cut this off before it gets any more serious."

"No." It was out of his mouth before he had time to think, a foreboding, dangerous sound meant to shut shit down before it could get started. "Fuck that."

Warren closed his eyes and parted his lips as if in bliss and rolled his head back, emphasizing the arch of his neck. He looked at Chris down the bridge of his nose, eyes gone dark with desire. It was an invitation, Chris realized as he wrapped a hand around Warren's neck. A plea. Words could only prove so much—what Warren needed was action. So Chris tightened his hand and let him feel everything he couldn't say.

"I'm not giving you up," he growled as Warren's pulse thrummed against his fingers. "I'm not letting you get away."

Warren made a breathy noise and closed his eyes. Chris wasn't squeezing hard enough to choke, but he still felt the lift as Warren inhaled and the glide of his Adam's apple as he swallowed. If he wanted to, he could have told Chris to stop, but he didn't. He took what he was given. Enjoyed it. So Chris enjoyed him, holding him by the neck as his hips picked up a steady pace.

"Our lives may change in small ways from here on out," Chris told him, leaning in so his lips brushed Warren's jaw. "But what's between us never will."

Warren shivered, then tangled his fingers loosely in Chris's hair and tugged him up to kiss him hard. From there, it was all grunts and groans and gasps, thrusting hips and steady hands, as pleasure took over.

The next morning, Warren wore Chris's pajamas to breakfast. It was no ring, but damn if it didn't make Chris feel like the luckiest guy in the world.

37

WARREN

When Warren came home from what was hands-down the hottest night of his life, he discovered there was something different about the living room. Something... odd. The couch, which typically occupied the space in front of the television, had been dragged right up to the front door. An end table was squished between its arm and the wall, with what appeared to be a steaming cup of tea resting on it. On the very middle of the couch sat a pajama-clad Libby, her hair twisted in a messy bun. Warren stared at her. Libby stared back. The pajamas, he noticed, were patterned with magnifying glasses and question marks which, which... where did someone ever get pajamas like those?

Unfortunately for him, Libby hadn't come to spill the secrets of her pajama collection. When he stepped through the door, she looked him over and lifted an eyebrow, then picked up her steaming mug from the end table. "Well, well, well. Home at last. Looks like someone had fun last night." She took a dramatic, if slightly noisy, sip of tea. "Care to explain yourself, mister?"

Warren stared a little harder, expression flattening. "What are you, my mom?"

"No. I'm a detective." The cold air from the open door chased her feet off the floor. She tucked her legs beneath herself and raised her arched eyebrow even higher. "Where were you the night of... yesterday?"

"Oh my god." Warren stomped the snow off the bottom of his shoes before kicking them off. When he moved them to the shoe mat, he noticed it was wet. The culprit was Libby's boots—the ones with the ridiculously fluffy faux-fur trim. Their soles were shiny from melted snow. "Hmm. Weird. Looks like I'm not the only one who just got in after a night out. Where were *you* last night, Libby?"

"Don't try to redirect the conversation! I'm the one doing the questioning around here." Libby gestured at the couch. "See? I had to hustle to drag the couch over and everything. Do you even know how hard it was to time making tea so it'd still be steaming when you got home? I'll tell you. *Very.* So, dish. I didn't go through all this effort for you to notice that I, too, was out all night having fun."

"I cannot with you." Warren tried to keep a straight face, but the corners of his lips twitched, betraying him. "You never called me out on any of my other hookups. What's so different about this one?"

"Aha! Another attempted redirection!" Libby took another sip of tea and wiggled an eyebrow. "You're definitely hiding something, Mr. Reaves, and I'm going to get to the bottom of it."

The mention of his last name sent heat straight to Warren's groin, and it was even more awful than the loss of his bees. "Libby, I love you, but I would die a happy man if you never called me that again."

"A *clue!*" Libby leaned forward, squinting at him. Her tea threatened to slosh over the rim of the mug. "Hmm. Curiouser and curiouser. What could your last name have to do with where you went last night?"

While she tried to figure it out, Warren attempted to sneak by the couch and into the kitchen. He didn't get far. No sooner did he start inching forward than out shot one of Libby's legs, blocking his way.

"I'm not done with you yet," Libby said. "I've been informed by an anonymous source that you've been up to some funny business with a certain persona non grata at the station, and I'm not stopping until I get to the bottom of it."

There was only one anonymous source Warren could think of who'd tip Libby off. He groaned. *"Pete."*

"Hey! Don't go naming anonymous sources! That's probably against some kind of code of conduct."

Warren opened his mouth, then closed it again. Nope. Not touching that one.

"But anyway, you wanna go have a pantry talk? We haven't had one of those in a while." Libby lowered her tea and offered him a reassuring smile. "It'll be just you, me, and those potatoes that've probably gone bad because we keep forgetting to eat them."

For all Libby's faults, if he said no, he knew she'd leave him be. But what was the point of hiding anymore? What was going on with Chris had evolved into more than just a fling. If she didn't hear the news from him, she'd connect the dots when Jack told her about all the fun they'd had watching movies when Warren had spent the night. It was better that he be the one to share the news. "Sure. But on one condition."

"Shoot."

"What gets said in the pantry stays in the pantry."

Libby trumpeted her lips and waved a hand dismissively. "Is that all? Wren, the pantry is hallowed ground. Do you really think I'd desecrate such a sacred place by using the sweet, sweet knowledge gained within to gossip?" She hopped off the couch. Her tea made another break for the rim of her mug, but sloshed back into place as if by magic. "I'm not gonna spill your secrets. I promise. Now c'mon. Let's go. There are some lonely potatoes waiting for us, and it's high time we paid them a visit."

It was too late. The potatoes were dead. A clear, brown-tinged slime had accumulated in the bottom of their bag and their corpses had sprouted so many eyes that had they not met an untimely fate, they would have known all Warren's secrets. Warren helped Libby dispose of their bodies, and once they'd scrubbed away all evidence of the crime scene, Libby closed the pantry door.

"So." She leaned against the shelf with their canned goods, her thigh butting up against the pack of toilet paper that jutted out from the bottommost level. "You and CD? Are you serious?"

Warren didn't know what to say, so he said nothing.

"It's totally not a big deal to me, if that's why you're being so quiet." Libby set her cup of tea beside their stockpile of tomato purée. "I know that things didn't go so well between Chris and my sister, but... I'm kinda on Chris's side, to be honest. Free really screwed up. I mean, *really* screwed up. Like, she's-in-prison-now kind of screwed up. And while I will always love and support my sister, I'm not gonna be able to forgive her for a really long time. Chris didn't do anything wrong. The only reason I didn't like him was because you didn't like him, so if you guys have literally kissed and made up, it's all good by me."

Warren dodged what needed to be said by dragging the step stool out from the corner and unfolding it. He used the top step as a seat. "It's more complicated than that. We didn't really make up. It's..." Vague and somewhat frantic hand gestures followed. "*Different.*"

"Different how?"

Warren stared at his knees. "Making up implies that both of us were in the wrong, but that's not true. There was only one asshole this whole time, and it was me." He hesitated, then in a smaller and more uncertain voice asked, "Why didn't you tell me?"

"Wren..." Libby sidestepped around a year's worth of vegetable oil and patted the top of his head. "Don't be so hard on yourself. People hate on other people all the time for no reason. Like celebrities. I mean, Chris isn't a *celebrity*, but he was popular, so it's pretty much the same thing."

"Not helping."

"Then I'll say it straight—you're not an asshole."

"I accused him of bullying me when he wasn't."

Libby sighed. "That doesn't mean you're an asshole. It just means you were misguided. People make mistakes, Wren. It's what you do when you realize you were wrong that determines what kind of a person you are."

Warren looked up from his knees and managed a thin smile. "I needed to hear that. I love you, Libby. Thank you for being you."

"I have my moments." She clasped her hands and rubbed them together eagerly. "Now, since you're not so down on yourself anymore, it's time to get into the juicy details. Spill. We're not leaving until you tell me exactly what happened that would make you change your mind about Chris. Also… did you *literally* literally kiss, or what? Because I had no idea that he was gay. I mean, he married Free and made a kid, so he must be at least a little straight, but I'm assuming since you spent the night that it wasn't all pizza and pillow fights."

Warren gestured at the pack of toilet paper. "You might wanna grab a seat. This is gonna take a while."

Libby nodded and wrangled the pack, and soon enough, Warren was spilling the beans. Her mug, forgotten, cooled on the shelf behind her. It wasn't such a big deal. The tea Warren was spilling was so hot and delicious, her Earl Grey would have paled in comparison.

38

WARREN

By the time Warren had finished filling Libby in on what had happened, Libby's eyes had narrowed into slits.

"So you're telling me that all this time, Chris was bi?" she asked when he'd run out of things to say.

He nodded.

"I never would have guessed."

"Do you routinely sit around guessing people's sexuality?"

Libby scrunched her nose and waved him off. "No. But I mean, he was over at my parents' place almost every day acting like a caveman while he was dating Free. I guess I assumed guys who act like that only swing one way. My bad. But you know, I'm glad I was wrong, because if anyone deserves a Neanderthal in their life, it's you. You deserve it."

It was flattering in a Libby kind of way. "Thanks."

"So, when's the wedding?" She beamed at him. "Can I be your best man?"

"We're not getting married."

"You mean you're not getting married *yet*. But that's okay. I can be patient. I'll wait. Does Jack know about you two yet?"

"Not yet."

"Are you going to tell him?"

"It's, um, a little complicated." Warren raked his teeth over his bottom lip to buy himself a second to think. He'd used broad strokes to paint the picture that was his relationship with Chris, but now that he'd laid his colors out, it was time to go back in and add some of the more uncomfortable details. "These are hallowed grounds, right?"

"Yeah."

"Okay. Well. I may not have told you *everything* going on between Chris and me. We've been hinting at having feelings for each other, but we haven't really, um, gone ahead and..." Warren rolled his hand illustratively. "Made anything official. So we're kind of just... fucking. With extra steps."

Libby gaped at him.

"So we'll tell Jack eventually," Warren concluded. "But before we do, we need to have a talk and lay everything out in a straightforward way, because right now it's all very abstract. We're, uh, we're not so good at words."

Libby's whole face pinched inward like she'd bitten into a lemon. She batted her hands at her face and shook her head, then gasped for breath and glared at him. Irritation crept into her voice. "Wren, do you mean to tell me that you're sleeping at his house—"

"Yeah."

"Hanging out with his son—"

Warren held up a finger. "That one doesn't count. Jack's over here all the time, and we've hung out on more than one occasion."

"Not the point." Libby retaliated with a finger of her own and swatted his like they were wielding tiny swords. "It's different when a guy brings you into his house when his kid's home. It's like the single dad version of meeting his parents. Jack has officially been introduced to the concept of you being in the apartment and sleeping in Chris's bed, and that's *huge*. I find it hard to believe neither of you have discussed making things official if that's happening."

256

Warren scratched the back of his neck and ducked his head. "Sorry?"

"You are a hopeless case, Wren." Libby swept up from her toilet paper perch and nudged it beneath the bottom shelf. "He's been giving you all the right signs. Tell him how you feel! If he's serious enough about you to introduce you to Jack, you're not gonna get rejected. And before you get caught up spinning those wheels of yours questioning how you really feel, consider this: you chose to stay at his place last night knowing that it wasn't going to be some wild kinky sex party. You were happy enough then to hang around with him and his kid, no dicks involved. If you enjoyed yourself, then it's not a stretch to say you'll keep enjoying yourself. Don't let your head get in the way of your heart." Libby looked him in the eyes, and for once, she was serious. "I know I haven't been around as much lately, but don't think I haven't noticed how you've changed. You come home from your super-gross sex romps glowing. You, *glowing!* Who would've thought?"

Warren went back to staring at his knees, this time for an entirely different reason—the heat in his cheeks was embarrassing.

"So go for what makes you happy," Libby said with some finality. "Be bold. It doesn't have to be scary. Take a breath and let the universe guide you. Or, you know, your cosmic leader of choice. If it ends up not working out, dump his ass and that'll be that."

Apparently, Libby had evoked the universe with her decree, because the thought of dumping Chris tied Warren's stomach up in knots. "I'll talk to him the next time we're together. I promise."

"Good." Libby clapped her hands in what Warren could only describe as a self high-five. "Well, I think that about concludes my investigation. This has been an amazing pantry talk. We should come talk here more often—maybe then we won't end up losing so many potatoes."

Warren lifted his head. Libby was smiling, lit up from behind by the dangling overhead light. The messy bun atop her head was starting to droop and her pajamas were a little baggy, but he

257

couldn't help but think that she looked happier, too. It was like love had brushed out all the cobwebs from behind her eyes, thrown open the curtains, and shown the world everything she'd been hiding inside. Was that how he looked, too? Warren scratched his jaw. Stubble prickled his fingers—he needed to shave. A little coarseness wouldn't have bothered him a year ago, but like Libby, who'd dolled herself up to impress Pete, Warren had found a good reason to look his best, too.

And on the subject of Pete, that traitor. "One last thing before we go."

"Yeah?"

"I need you to slap Pete's ass for me the next time you see him. Not in a sexy way, but in an, 'I can't believe you'd rat me out to Libby' way. Put some muscle in it. He can take it."

Libby wiggled an eyebrow. "Consider it done. Although, for the record, I would've eventually figured it out without him. You're not as sneaky as you think. If you wanna outfox me, you're gonna have to tone down the Quaker Oats staring sessions a bit. And maybe quit looking so forlornly at cactus dicks."

"Okay. Pantry talk officially over." With a clap of his hands to his thighs, Warren stood. "Do you need help moving the couch back across the room? I was gonna grab a glass of water and head upstairs to nap, so if you need the extra muscle, now's the time to ask."

"Nope. This girl can take care of heavy furniture all on her own, thanks." The statement was punctuated by the creak of the pantry door. Libby stepped out into the kitchen and stretched, lifting the bottom hem of her shirt. There, tucked in the waistband of her pajama pants, was an honest-to-god magnifying glass. Warren gawked at it for a second, then shook his head and grabbed the forgotten mug of tea before following her out. When Libby wanted something, she really went for it. It was time he did the same.

39

CHRIS

Nights were lonelier without Warren there. Chris lay awake in bed, lounged in the glow of his phone screen, and distracted himself from the empty space at his side with pointless internet searches. Forgotten nineties cartoon characters. Best shows on Netflix for eight-year-olds. How to cook bacon in a microwave. Somewhere between an investigation into local urban legends and looking up the world's strangest-looking vegetables, an advertisement for Calvin Klein popped up, and suddenly Romanesco broccoli wasn't all that appealing anymore.

From then on, all Chris could think about was Warren.

Unable to shake the feeling, Chris sent him a text.

Chris: Next time I get you alone, I'm gonna make you come so hard your knees will give out and you won't be able to leave the bed
Chris: You're mine

Fabio he was not, but Warren was no bodice-ripper heroine. Their romance was read between the admittedly filthy lines. If Warren was worried they were in danger of losing their spark,

Chris would do what it took to prove he had no intention of snuffing it—sexts and all.

Chris waited a minute or two, hoping to see the icon at the bottom of their conversation switch from sent to read, but when nothing changed he laid his phone on his chest and stared at the ceiling through the dark. Warren was probably asleep. It was late, and they'd stayed up longer than they should have fooling around.

Before he could get too wrapped up in his thoughts, his phone vibrated. He snatched it from his chest to check it, hoping to see correspondence from Warren.

He was in luck.

Warren: Yeah? I find the whole knee thing pretty hard to believe considering you haven't managed it yet
Warren: I'll be waiting

The nerve of him. Chris grinned.

Chris: Keep pushing your luck. See how that turns out for you.
Chris: Oh, wait. You already did. What was that word again? Something fruity, I think? 'Pineapple'?
Warren: Fuck you
Chris: Fuck you, too
Warren: I'm going to sleep now so I won't have to put up with your bullshitty machismo
Chris: Machismo, huh? Looks like that college education wasn't entirely worthless
Warren: I swear to god, next time I see you I'm gonna let you have it
Chris: Bring it. Best me at wrestling and you get a free pass at my ass
Warren: Fine. I will. And don't think you can weasel out of it, because I'm screenshotting this conversation as proof

Chris: Fine by me
Chris: Now go get some sleep, Reaves. I'll see you at work on Monday
Warren: Goodnight, asshole
Chris: Night

Chris set his phone to silent and left it on the bedside table to charge. His bed was no less empty than it had been before, but his heart was a little fuller, and for now, that was enough.

Over the weekend the temperature yo-yoed. The ice from Friday melted, but by Sunday new storms had rolled in and brought precipitation that turned into freezing rain. By Monday morning Lethridge looked like a skating rink, and it took Chris an extra ten minutes to drop Jack off at school and make it in to work. Caroline, who manned the night shift, was slumped over the desk when he arrived, a cup of Kathleen's finest within arm's reach. It was still steaming.

"Tough night?" Chris asked as she dragged herself off the desk.

Caroline fixed him with a look of a woman who was well and truly tired of a man's bullshit. "You don't know the half of it."

She was right, but by the end of the day, Chris had a pretty good feeling he'd at least partially figured it out. Their sleepy little station was hammered with calls, more than one of them proper emergencies. Most of them got off lucky. Some didn't. It was the first time Chris had to call in to Mercy Medical Center in Des Moines to let them know a patient would be arriving by medivac.

It was also the first time he'd seen Warren in action.

Chris had just come back from pilfering a cup of coffee from Kathleen when the ambulance pulled into the garage, and he took a second to watch from the doorway while Pete and Warren worked in tandem to unload the patient from the vehicle and wheel them to the elevator leading to the helipad. Until that moment, he hadn't made the connection between Warren—bratty, mouthy Warren—and the medical professional. The contrast was striking. Warren's face had become solemn and his frame somehow fuller. All his softer features were gone. His voice was deep and cutting, and he spoke in short, brisk sentences, like words were in scarce supply and had to be rationed.

In him, Chris saw some of himself.

Hot nights spent in the desert, his body an extension of the weapon he wielded.

The switch between soldier and civilian was every bit as jarring, but it was needed. Sometimes, there was no other way to keep sane than to turn your brain off and trust in your instincts. He figured it was the same with Warren, too.

Chris watched until the elevator doors closed. When Warren was gone, he went back to his desk and sent him a text.

Chris: Stay safe out there. I'm thinking of you

The reply came an hour later.

Warren: Safe in Des Moines. Patient is stable. Thinking about you, too.

A fresh sheet of hell arrived on Wednesday morning. Or was it ice? It was starting to get difficult to tell which was which. In any case, Chris watched it glint beneath the orange glow of the streetlights while he sipped his coffee. The red Ford Focus with the rusted grill crept across the parking lot at a snail's pace, but ended up skidding around the corner onto the street despite the driver's best intentions. Chris took it as a sign of another busy day at work. He was starting to understand why the job paid so much—the stress would have him going gray before the winter was through.

But a mane of silver hair wasn't the only downside of this morning's horrible road conditions. Warren was about to finish his shift, which meant he'd be free when Chris got off work. He'd wanted to have him stay the night, but asking him to drive beyond what was absolutely necessary was too irresponsible. Still, Chris didn't want Warren to think that he'd lost interest, so as he finished his coffee, he sent Warren a text.

Chris: I wanted to have you over tonight, but I don't want you driving any more than you have to
Warren: And I don't want you coming to pick me up for the same reason. It's hell out there
Chris: Then we're in agreement that today's a wash, but if the roads are better tomorrow, I want you to spend the night
Warren: Sounds good. There's something I wanna talk to you about anyway, so I'll make sure it happens ASAP
Chris: You wanna talk about it now?
Warren: Nah, it's an in-person kind of talk… hopefully the kind we have with your dick up my ass
Chris: I'll see what I can do

The conversation ended there. Either Warren had been distracted by something going on in the station, or he had nothing else to say. Chris didn't let the uncertainty get to him. He pocketed his phone and went to wake his son, who'd be disappointed to know school hadn't been canceled. Again. A little ice had never been enough to keep kids home during Chris's school days, and it seemed not all that much had changed.

Jack wasn't thrilled to be woken, and was even less thrilled to know he wouldn't get to spend the day at home playing Minecraft. He grouched and grumbled his way to the bathroom while Chris fixed him a quick breakfast, then scowled at his cereal one spoonful at a time while he ate.

"Do I have to go to school today, Dad?" he asked, a dripping heap of Froot Loops stationed in front of his mouth. "I'm so tired and it's dark outside. Can I stay home just once?"

"No can do, champ." Chris kissed his head in passing. Now that Jack was done with the bathroom, it was his turn to get ready. "I've gotta work today, and you can't be home alone. Christmas break will be here before you know it. You're gonna have to hang in there until then."

Jack huffed and kept eating, so Chris took his leave of the kitchen and finished up his morning routine. Soon enough they were both dressed and ready to go. After one final check to make sure they both had everything they needed—school bag, lunch, car keys, wallet—Chris herded Jack down to the ground floor and across the slippery parking lot. Jack buckled himself into the back seat, Chris turned on the car to let it warm up, and soon enough he was chipping ice off the windshield and knocking sheets of it off the roof.

"What are you excited to do today in class?" he asked Jack once he was behind the wheel. He took the parking lot at a crawl. The ice was no joke.

Jack made a noncommittal noise. "I dunno. Recess, maybe?"

"Bud."

"It's too early to think about school, Dad. It's still dark outside. It should be against the law to have school before the sun comes up."

A young Chris would have adamantly agreed with him. As an adult, Chris still agreed with him, but he knew better than to admit it. While they made their way to the bridge connecting the east and west banks of Lethridge, he tried to find a compromise. "Do you think that getting up early for school even when you don't want to will help you in the future?"

"No."

"There's gonna be a lot of stuff later in life you're not gonna want to do, champ. What if school is preparing you for that?"

"If it is, then it's a stupid way to do it." Chris watched through the rearview mirror as Jack yawned and cuddled into his seat. "Besides, they don't test us on any of that kind of stuff. If that was why they were making us come in so early, they'd give us tests on it for sure."

The kid had a point. Chris mulled it over until they turned onto the bridge, then focused only on driving. The stone was slippery when not bone dry, and the ice only made it worse. Chris hadn't lived in town in years, but he'd grown up here, and he knew how to take it slow and steady to keep from skidding. Frozen bridges didn't faze him. But the sudden screech of brakes from an oncoming minivan barreling around the corner did.

Chris was blinded by its headlights. Heard Jack's shrill scream. Felt the crumple as the front of his car imploded. Tasted the blood on his tongue when he clamped his jaw shut and yanked the wheel to the side to keep Jack far, far away from the crash.

But after that, there was nothing, and the world ceased to be.

4 0

WARREN

Warren was barely through the door when his phone went off.

"You've got Reaves," he said when the call connected.

Alicia, one of the paramedics from the team who worked the shift after his, responded. Her voice was unusually stiff. "Wren, there's been an accident that requires emergency transport to Mercy Medical. Are you in?"

The drive home had been dark and gloomy and starless—an indication that cloud coverage was thick. That alone would make flight conditions poor, if not impossible. There was a chance Pete would decline the flight based on that alone. Exhausted, he sagged against the doorframe and closed his eyes. "Have you heard from Pete about whether he's willing to fly?"

"Not yet. I'm calling him next."

Warren stifled a yawn. "Okay. If he's in, I'm in. I'm on my way back to the station. If he turns the flight down, I'll sleep there until conditions improve."

"Roger that."

The call ended. Warren peeled himself off the doorframe and headed back outside. In order to fly, both he and Pete needed to agree that it was safe. With the current conditions, it didn't seem likely, but Warren would rather be at the station and ready to fly than sleeping at home when the cloud coverage broke—especially since no details about the patient or the incident could be released until they both agreed that it was safe to make the trip. There was no way to tell what difference a few seconds could make in a medical emergency, and Warren wouldn't put himself in a position where his slow ass ended up costing someone their life. The sooner they could get airborne, the better.

On the way in to work, he found himself doubly glad he'd made that decision. There'd been an accident on the bridge. It looked like one of the vehicles involved had crashed through the guardrail and plummeted into the creek. A crew was positioned on the shore of the bank, heavy machinery still on site, but the vehicle itself nowhere to be seen. Sinclair was there, mustache twitching as he filled in an incident report. The other emergency responders were already gone.

All the commotion had brought traffic to a standstill. Warren glanced at the scene of the incident one final time, sighed, and sank into his seat. It was going to be a busy day.

The station was strangely silent when Warren arrived. No one was in the gym and the television was switched off. Not even Kathleen was where she should have been—her treasured coffee had been left unguarded. If Warren hadn't been banking on catching a few hours of sleep, he would have slipped in and fixed himself a cup just for the novelty of not having to worry about being caught.

"Anyone here?" he called into the empty common room. When he was met with no response, he shrugged and headed for his bunk. There'd probably been another call. He'd catch up with everyone when they got back. Until then, he'd chill out and wait for Pete.

Warren's buzzing phone woke him from a dead sleep. He snatched it from its place on the mattress and checked the screen from behind mostly lidded eyes.

Libby: WHERE THE HELL ARE YOU?
Warren: Got called into work, sorry

Libby kept typing. While she did, another text arrived.

Pete: We're flying in five. Get your ass in the copter.

Warren sat up and rubbed the sleep from his eyes. Not much time had passed since he'd arrived at the station, and he doubted conditions had changed. It wasn't like Pete to want to fly when cloud coverage was so thick, but if he was up for it, Warren was game. He tucked his phone into his pocket, hopped out of bed, and jogged from the bunk room to the garage. Pete was waiting there by the elevator to the helipad, his cheeks pink from the cold and his hair windswept. Snow clung to the bottoms of his boots and had started to melt in little puddles under his feet. There was an unusually tense look on his face. Warren had seen him get serious while responding to a call, but never like this.

"We're flying?" Warren asked as he joined him. "Did the clouds clear up?"

"No."

"You sound... off. What's going on?"

Pete shook his head and ran a hand over his mouth, but didn't reply. There was a look in his eyes—fear—that made the hairs on the back of Warren's neck stand on end.

"Pete?" he tried again. "What's going on? Is it someone you know? Your mom?"

"No, Wren. That's not it. It's—"

The doors linking the common room with the garage burst open. Alicia and Gary swooped in, wheeling a stretcher between them. The patient on it was blanketed, only the crown of his head visible from where Warren stood. What Warren could see were the chest tubes emerging from his pleural cavity, one of which fed into a sealed drainage container positioned on the stretcher. He recognized the setup—they'd performed an emergency pericardial tap. The red stains on Alicia's scrubs gave it away. She must have attempted a needle decompression and discovered a cardiac tamponade. Never pleasant. It was no wonder Pete had wanted to get in the air as quickly as possible—prognosis for an injury like that wasn't good. A collapsed lung was serious enough on its own, but when paired with damage to the heart… well, Warren would be surprised if the patient made it through transit.

As Alicia and Gary approached with the stretcher, Pete pressed the button to open the elevator doors. Warren stepped out of the way to give them room to pass, and as he did, Pete fell into place beside him and blocked his view of the stretcher.

"Look," Pete said tersely. "We don't have much time. I'm gonna fly as goddamn fast as I can, but we're a team, and flying alone isn't going to keep him alive. I need you on top of your game."

It was an odd thing to say. Warren grimaced. "Why wouldn't I be on top of my game?"

"You didn't see?"

"See what?"

The stretcher jostled as it crossed over the threshold of the elevator. Warren went to step around Pete and join Alicia and Gary in the cabin, but Pete grabbed him by the arm and pulled him back. He wasn't gentle about it.

"What the fuck!" Warren grabbed his shoulder to keep from falling. "*Pete!*"

"Wren." Pete's voice was stern, but there was a shimmer in his eyes that looked an awful lot like tears. "It's Chris."

The bottom dropped out of Warren's stomach. He stared at Pete, unable to speak. There had to be some mistake.

"Get in the elevator!" Alicia shouted. "We need to go!"

"It was a car crash. The one on the bridge you probably saw on your way back to the station. Jack is okay. He made it out with a couple scrapes and bruises," Pete elaborated, not yet letting Warren go. "He's home with Libby, shaken, but otherwise okay. I need you to be okay, too."

"Pete, Wren, *we need to go!*"

Voices.

Pete's. Alicia's.

They surrounded him. Thundered in his ears. Had meaning, but made no sense. Warren stood still while they reverberated inside of him. It felt like if he moved, they'd rip him apart.

Yes, they needed to go, but Chris couldn't be the one on that stretcher. It didn't make sense. They'd just been talking this morning, making plans, going about their lives as normal. Chris couldn't have been hurt.

But why would Pete lie?

When Warren next blinked, tears slid down his cheeks. An uncomfortable tightness clenched in his chest and locked itself around an uncomfortable pearl of truth: Pete had no reason to lie to him.

Chris really was on the stretcher.

Really was at risk of not making it through.

"You've got this," Pete said in a hushed voice. "*We've* got this. We're a team. He's gonna make it out of this okay."

Warren nodded. He had nothing to say. Couldn't speak if he tried.

"*Boys!*" Alicia warned.

Pete jerked his chin toward the elevator. "Let's go."

Warren knew he needed to, but he couldn't.

Couldn't move.

Couldn't breathe.

Couldn't bear the thought of stepping into the elevator and seeing Chris's face sallow, chest fitted with tubes, body almost broken.

Not the Chris you know.

Warren's stomach turned. He braced an arm on the wall and took a few steadying breaths, but it didn't help. His throat constricted like he was going to be sick.

"Wren," Pete said nervously. "Hey. Hang in there. You can do this. We're gonna make it through this together. I need you to be brave."

Brave? Chris was the brave one. The strong one. The one who kept Warren in check and made sure he was okay. It was like the rug had been pulled out from beneath him, only instead of flooring to break his fall, there was a bottomless pit.

"What the hell is going on?" Alicia demanded as she leaned out of the elevator. "We need to get moving!"

"C'mon, Wren." Pete put a hand on Warren's back. "It's just me and you, and I can't do this alone. I need your help. *He* needs your help."

Warren nodded. Bottomless pit or not, he had a duty to uphold. There was no one around who could take his place. Yes, there was a chance Chris would die, but if Warren didn't fly chance would have nothing to do with it. He'd succumb to his injuries. There would be no bringing him back. Warren was the only one who could save him. No matter how bad it hurt, he had to try.

"I'm ready," he rasped as he pushed off the wall and wiped away his tears. "I'm okay. We've got a patient in need of urgent transport. Let's get our asses in gear."

Pete punched his shoulder. "That's the Wren I know. You've got this. I'm aiming for a forty-five-minute flight time. Think you can manage?"

"Yeah."

Pete clapped him on the shoulder, Warren nodded, and they hurried into the elevator. It was going to take every damned thing he had, but Warren was prepared to give it all if it meant the man he loved would live.

WARREN

The whir of the helicopter's turbine engine and the lop of its blades as they gained speed were welcome familiarities. Warren let them drown out his racing thoughts while he ran his final checks. When he was sure that all his equipment was strapped down and the stretcher was locked into place, he flicked on the microphone on the headset connecting him with Pete, who was in the cockpit. "Testing," he said as he strapped himself into the four-point harness nearest the stretcher. "Testing. Pete, do you copy?"

"I copy ya loud and clear. We set for takeoff?"

"Roger that."

"Then off we go."

A gentle feeling of weightlessness swelled in Warren's gut. Pete had begun his ascent. While they climbed, Warren zeroed in on the on-board patient monitor displaying Chris's vitals. They were stable at the moment, but with the shift in altitude, there was a very real chance his condition would worsen. There were too many things that could go wrong—too many variables and unknowns. If he was going to get Chris through this, he needed to stay on his toes.

Pete's voice crackled in his ear as he got in touch with air traffic control. "This is MediWing, an EC130 medical helicopter out of

Howard County, Iowa. We are currently in transit to Mercy Hospital Medical Center in Des Moines. I repeat, this is MediWing, an EC130 medical helicopter out of Howard County, Iowa. We are currently in transit to Mercy Hospital Medical Center in Des Moines. Please stand by for further communication."

While Pete established contact, Warren rested his head against the padded backing of his jump seat and counted the seconds as they climbed.

One.

Two.

Three.

With a patient on board, they wouldn't rise far. Higher altitudes put more stress on the body than they could risk.

Four.

Five.

A blip on the patient monitor sent Warren's heart racing, but it was a trick of the eye. Nothing unusual was going on. The pericardial tap was doing its job. As long as they could make good time, everything would be okay.

Six.

Seven.

Eight.

Tears clouded Warren's eyes. He frantically blinked them away. Now was not the time to lose his shit. Chris wasn't safe. Not yet.

Nine.

Ten.

Somewhere after eleven but before twenty, the weightless sensation in Warren's gut settled—Pete had reached a cruising altitude. Chris remained stable. With no imminent threat to manage, Warren's attention wandered from the cardiac monitor to the man it was hooked into. It was a mistake. Chris's skin was waxy, so pale it didn't look real. Alicia and Gary had done a great job setting his chest tubes, but the sight of them snaking out from beneath the blankets turned Warren's stomach.

He looked away.

"How are we holding up?" he asked Pete a good half hour later when staring holes through the cardiac monitor made him feel like one more blip would drive him batty.

Pete snorted. "It's like flying through a lint trap that's never been cleaned. Not sure when we'll hit the screen, but I'll keep you updated. How are you holding up back there?"

"Stable."

"You know that's not what I meant."

Warren brushed new tears away with the side of his wrist. So much for being brave. "I'm hanging in there."

"For the record, you and I are getting drunk as hell after this. I don't care if it's nine in the morning."

"Nah. I should, uh, I should go home after this and..." Warren trailed off while he thought about how to conclude the sentence. What he wanted to say was, "Vomit into the toilet and cry until I pass out on the bathroom floor, no alcohol needed," but he didn't want to make Pete any more worried than he already was, so he settled on, "Be alone for a while."

"The only reason I'll agree to let you be is because Libby will be there to keep an eye on you. You shouldn't be alone right now. If I were in your shoes... if that were Libby..."

"It's fine. This is what we signed up for, right? When you work in a small town, you shouldn't be surprised when your patients are people you know." More tears threatened to fall. Warren was quick to wipe them away. If he gave in and broke down now, he wouldn't be able to pull himself back together. "I'm really not up to talking about this right now. Can we talk about something else? What's our ETA?"

"Twenty minutes. We're pretty much breaking sky speed records. Fuck you, clouds. Poor visibility can suck my dick."

Warren's lips wobbled, which was as close to a smile as he could manage. "Poor visibility's pretty much the only way anyone's ever gonna suck your dick."

"I walked right into that one, didn't I?"

"You did."

"Well—" Pete prattled on about something, but Warren didn't hear what it was. The heart rate displayed by the patient monitor spiked and Chris, who'd been unresponsive, jolted awake. He ripped back the blankets, grasped at the tap protruding from his chest, and yanked.

42

CHRIS

Jack.

Where the fuck was Jack?!

Chris's vision was blurred. Shapes, lights, and colors blended into one. A deafening roar surrounded him—rushing wind, like speeding down at top speed from the highest drop of a rollercoaster.

Where was this?

Where was he?

Copper.

The taste of it stained his tongue. Dirty pennies kids sucked on when parents weren't looking, flattened on railroad tracks by freight trains shipping grain beneath the scorching summer sun.

He *burned.*

Burned with it.

Burned from the inside.

Why did it hurt the way it did? Bone deep. It wouldn't go away. He snatched at it. Found tubing. Discovered it buried in his chest.

Inside.

Inside.

It was *inside of him.*

He needed to get it out.

Get it the *fuck out.*

He grabbed it. Ripped it out. Tried to, at least. It was lodged tight, so deep he couldn't make it budge. Before he could readjust his grip to get a better handle on it, something grabbed his wrist. Made him stop.

Skin. A palm. Clamping fingers. Someone's hand.

"*Jack?*" Chris croaked, but it couldn't be. The hand was too big. Calloused. Strong. Jack's hands were still small and soft. The kind he could wrap in his fist when they were crossing the street. Not like this. Never so rough.

There was no response. The roaring noise in the background drowned out everything else. Combat noises. Like a UH-60 Black Hawk. Whirring and clipping and the rush of rapidly moving air. A helicopter. Was he dreaming? He'd left that life behind.

But the pain in his chest…

The *pain.*

It made him think the life he knew—the shit with Free, his perfect life with Warren—had been a dream.

Something pinched his wrist. A tingling spread down his arm and into his legs. Chris blinked slowly a few times. His vision cleared enough that he recognized the shape hovering over him.

Warren.

His messy blond hair tumbled out around a headset, its large earpieces positioned like bolts on the sides of his head. His heart-shaped lips, usually pink, were almost red, like he'd been biting them. His cheeks were flushed. His eyes misted over.

Chris blinked again, his eyelids heavier this time. The pain in his chest had almost gone. His tongue felt clumsy. It was Warren's hand on his wrist, and when Warren took it away from the tube and laid it by his side, Chris couldn't lift it again.

What was happening to him?

Where was Jack?

Jack.

Despite how numb he was becoming, Chris felt his heart speed up.

His boy. Where was his boy?

Warren's eyes got wide and panicked. Chris's eyelids drooped. Sleep tempted him, but a voice in his head told him that if he closed his eyes, he'd never see Warren again. After a groggy minute spent struggling against his failing body, Chris found the strength to open his eyes all the way and look at the man he loved. Warren had started to cry.

"It's okay," Chris told him, but it didn't look like Warren had heard. "It's okay. You're okay. Don't cry. I love you."

Warren didn't stop crying. He opened his mouth like he was speaking, too, mouthing the same words over and over. The pressure in Chris's chest became rhythmic—almost unbearable. His eyelids felt too heavy to keep open.

What was Warren trying to say?

Chris moved his lips in tandem, trying to figure it out. He kept it up as his eyelids shut. Kept it up as prickling darkness crept into his head.

I love you. I love you. I love you.

That was it, wasn't it? What Warren was saying.

Words he'd never said before.

I love you.

Chris smiled. "Love you, too. So much."

There was nothing left to worry about. Warren was there. He loved Chris. He would make sure Jack was safe.

Chris's body was heavy, and his head was starting to get heavy, too. He was losing the war. Sleep wrapped him up safe and warm, and he gave in to it.

I love you. I love you. I love you.

Warren loved him, and that meant everything would be okay.

43

WARREN

"We need boots on the ground *right fucking now*," Warren spat as the sedative dragged Chris under.

"We're closing in on Mercy Medical," Pete replied. "I'm going as fast as I can, Wren. We have to work with air traffic control over Des Moines. They're telling us to circle."

"Tell them to go fuck themselves! He's crashing. We need to land *right now*."

"Let me see what I can do."

The patient monitor was going crazy. Tachycardia. Hypotension. Chris's oxygen levels were plummeting, but any noninvasive or standard mechanical ventilation would form positive pressure that would fuck him over and do more harm than good. It was all fucked. So fucked. What else was he supposed to do? The pericardial tap was supposed to have held until they arrived at Mercy Medical, but it'd been knocked out of place when Chris had grabbed it. It was a miracle he hadn't punctured his own heart.

"We're losing him, Pete. He tried to pull out his own tap. We need to get him into the OR. Tell air traffic control to let us through."

"They're rerouting traffic for us. Waiting on confirmation we can approach and touch down. Hold tight. Five minutes max and we'll be on the ground."

It was five minutes too many. Chris was crashing. But what could he do? The tube draining the fluid from around his heart wasn't kinked or clogged. There was no reason to believe it wasn't doing its job. Something else had to be wrong—something that'd happened when Chris had jolted awake.

Think. *Think.*

Tachycardia, hypotension, and plummeting oxygen levels were signs of respiratory failure. They'd only manifested after Chris had tugged on his tap. It stood to reason that what Chris had done had caused his symptoms, and that meant...

Warren's eyes widened, and he scrambled away from the stretcher and toward his supplies.

He knew what he had to do.

Back at the station, he'd suspected Alicia had performed a needle decompression to relieve the pressure from Chris's collapsed lung only to discover a cardiac tamponade. The work she'd done had no doubt relieved the increased pressure in Chris's chest cavity, but now that he'd yanked his chest tubes out of place, those measures had been undone. Air was flooding into his chest and getting trapped there all over again, crushing his damaged lungs in the process. It was unconventional in the extreme, but if Warren wanted to save him, he'd need to perform another needle decompression and get that air out before it killed him.

Needle decompressions weren't heavily technical. All Warren needed were three things: a long, large-bore cannula; antiseptic solution to clean the skin around where he'd be working; and a pair of sterile gloves. He snapped the gloves on first, then swabbed the area on Chris's chest he needed to work with and braced himself for what was to come.

"Second intercostal space, midclavicular line," he mumbled under his breath as he prepared the cannula. It was like he was on his first rotation again, still green and uncertain, scared he'd make a wrong move. "Use a ninety-degree angle and a single motion. It may require forceful entry. You'll know you've done it when you feel a pop."

The noise from the helicopter would drown out the hiss of escaping air, but Warren would be able to feel it with his thumb if everything went according to plan.

And it would go according to plan. There was no alternative.

More afraid than he'd ever been, Warren lifted his hand, took a deep breath, and forced the cannula into Chris's chest.

There was a pop. Air hissed against the pad of Warren's thumb as it escaped through the hollow of the needle. Chris's vital signs improved. Bleeding was minimal. Warren, stomach twisted into knots, openly wept as he held the needle in place.

The helicopter began to descend.

"Bringing her in. Brace for landing," Pete warned.

It was unhygienic, and Warren would be reprimanded for it if anyone were there to see, but he couldn't hold himself up anymore. He grabbed Chris's hand and slid down the side of the stretcher so he was seated with his back to it, one arm raised over his head so he could keep his fingers locked with his lover's. The tears came on harder now—the dam had been broken and there was no holding them back. He'd done everything he could. Every damned thing. All he could do now was pray that Chris would pull through.

An eternity passed before the bump as the helicopter's landing skids made contact with the helipad. The engine wound down. The blades stopped spinning. Warren knew he had seconds before Pete and the Mercy Medical team unlocked the door and swept in to retrieve the patient—*Chris*—but he couldn't bring himself to stand. The tears hadn't stopped. The thighs of his jumpsuit were speckled with their ghosts, little wet reminders of his pain. Warren's sinuses flushed, and he ran his arm under his nose as he sobbed.

It could be the last time he held Chris's hand.

The last time he saw him alive.

"I love you," he managed to say through racking sobs. "I fucking love you. Don't leave me."

There was a dull clunk as the metal lock on the door disengaged, and in rushed the medical team. Seeing them made it real. Warren broke down, not caring if they saw. Not caring what they thought of him. He held Chris's hand until it was taken from him. Until he was wheeled away. Alone, Warren tucked his knees to his chest and curled into himself. He cried harder than ever.

It was done now. He didn't have to keep being brave. Chris's care was out of his hands, and from there... from there, who knew what would happen. He'd done the best he could, but he had no idea if it had been enough.

One of the Mercy Medical emergency staff had stayed behind. He placed a hand on Warren's shoulder. "You gonna be okay?" he asked. "We can issue you some alprazolam if you need help calming down."

Warren shook his head. He buried his face against his knees. Drugs would only take the edge off—the pain he felt couldn't be prescribed away.

"Then let us know if you need anything," he said kindly, then, like the rest of the Mercy Medical crew, he was gone.

In the end, it was Pete who sat down next to him and butted their shoulders together. "Hey, Wren. You ready to go home?"

No, he wasn't.

If he had his way, he'd wait here for Chris to come out of the OR and sit by his bedside while he recovered. He'd spend his nights sleeping in the awful plastic chairs of the waiting room and survive on reheated cafeteria pizza and soggy, prepackaged salads.

But he couldn't.

Wasn't family.

Wouldn't be recognized as Chris's partner.

There was nothing left to do here. He had to leave Chris on his own.

Drained and helpless to improve his situation, he latched on to

Pete and sobbed into his shirt. Pete wrapped a brotherly arm around him and rested his head on top of Warren's.

"It'll be okay," Pete promised in a whisper. "We did everything we could. Chris is tough. He'll pull through. If he can stomach dating you, I'm pretty sure he can survive just about anything."

The burn was so unexpected that Warren actually laughed, but it was short-lived—his voice cracked with a sob, and soon enough he was crying again.

Pete ruffled his hair. "I heard that laugh. I knew you were still in there somewhere. Now, come on. Get up. I'm bringing you with me to the cockpit. It's time for us to go home."

Warren didn't resist being herded out of the medical bay and into Pete's domain, but he did take off his headset. He didn't have it in him to have a conversation. Not now. Not when he didn't know if Chris would ever hear him say that he loved him, too, and that he was a fool for not having said it earlier.

44

WARREN

The house was quiet when Warren came home. He stood by the door for a moment, listening for signs of life, but heard none. Libby must have taken Jack to Des Moines to be with Chris. It was just as well. Right now he needed to be alone.

One by one, Warren unlaced his boots and kicked them off. He needed out of his work clothes. Out of clothing in general.

Fuck clothing.

In fact, fuck his whole outfit.

Warren tore off his outer layer and cast it aside, then yanked his shirt over his head, balled it up, and chucked it in the direction of the stairs. It was the shirt he'd worn the day Chris had pulled him onto his lap and kissed him for the first time, and thinking about how stupid and happy he'd been back then made him want to slam his fist through the wall. He settled for wrenching his phone from his pocket and hurling it at the couch. It wasn't quite as satisfying as shattering it into a million pieces, but it was the best he could do given he was still on call.

Warren's pants, now phoneless, were his next victim. He tossed them in the same direction as his shirt, although they didn't get all that far. Which was fine. Fuck pants. They could lie there alone and wrinkled, legs splayed at odd angles, and think about what they'd done. Warren sent a balled sock after them. Then another. If he hadn't been worried that Libby and Jack might come home to an eyeful of accidental peen, he'd have pitched his boxers at them, too.

Why had it happened like this?

Why did it have to be Chris?

Anger hit Warren so suddenly that he didn't have time to brace for it. Why the hell had he been so stubborn? All he'd needed to do was tell Chris that he loved him. That was it. Words. Fucking simple words he could have said at any time, but hadn't, because his head had been so far up his ass that it was a wonder Chris had been able to fuck him. And now it was too late. Chris didn't know and might never know. There was no fixing a fuck-up like that.

On the verge of another breakdown, Warren left his spot by the door and sank onto the couch, where he mashed his face into the seat cushions.

"Turn off your brain," he muttered, like saying it out loud would convince his subconscious to stop fixating. "You're not being fair to yourself."

But that was what worried mothers told their heartbroken teenagers after a bad breakup, and this... this wasn't anything close. Warren kept his face buried, sniffing as needed to clear his nose, and tried to reason with himself. He couldn't change the past, but he could learn from it. No matter what happened, he'd walk away a better, more honest person. If Chris recovered, he wouldn't wait to tell him how he felt. If he didn't...

A new wave of crippling sorrow washed through him, and he hid his head beneath one of Libby's fiddly throw pillows to ride it out.

If Chris didn't recover, he'd have to figure it out one day at a time, because he couldn't imagine what his life would be like without him.

Sleep came, but not easily. After hours spent building himself up just to tear himself back down, Warren brought out the big guns— an irresponsible dose of Nyquil. After that it was lights out. He passed out mid-episode of *Parks and Recreation* and woke up to find himself bathed in sunlight, which sounded romantic, but was actually terrible. Not so much because of the sunlight, but because it felt like someone—maybe the sun, but he wasn't about to point fingers —had come round with a baseball bat and beat the shit out of his neck and spine. Sleeping on the couch had been a mistake. Past Warren was a sad, sorry asshole, and current Warren didn't like him very much at all.

The situation was not helped by the fact that his arm—which was dangling over the side of the couch—was touching something that was neither furniture nor floor. Warren couldn't tell exactly what it was, but he got the impression that it was alive.

Please don't be a raccoon, he thought to himself as his fingers brushed something soft and fur-like. *I can't handle rabies shots on top of everything else I'm going through.*

Luck prevailed. The something was not a raccoon—it was a mini-weasel.

Jack popped up and looked at Warren. The kid wasn't his usual smiley self and had dark bags under his eyes like he hadn't slept at all since yesterday, but he was fully dressed, which meant he was taking it better than Warren was. He'd come out of the accident with a couple scrapes, the worst of which was on his cheek. It'd been bandaged by someone who had no concept of how much medical tape was *too* much medical tape. Libby, probably. At least the dressing looked clean.

"Hi, Wren," Jack said in a small, somber voice.

"Hey."

"Aunt Libby said that I shouldn't disturb you because..." His voice hitched, breaking Warren's heart. "Because you worked really hard to save my dad, and you deserved some sleep."

What little good a drugged night's sleep had done for Warren was instantly rendered useless. His throat constricted with the onset of tears. Hoping to buy himself time to get his emotions under control, he scrambled up into a seated position and was surprised to discover that he was dressed. Libby must have been responsible, because he was wearing one of his old, stretched-out t-shirts that'd somehow found its way into her laundry and never made it back. "You're not disturbing me," he said in a quiet voice as soon as he was able. "Not at all. If I was in the way, you could've woken me up. The living room is for everyone, not just me."

"You're not in the way." Jack rubbed his eyes, brushing away tears that wouldn't stop falling. His voice wobbled. "You're not in the way at all. I didn't wanna sit on the couch or anything. I just... I wanted to be here when you woke up so I could say thank you. You saved my dad. He's really hurt, but he's gonna be okay because of what you did. I'm so glad that you're my friend."

Warren clamped a hand over his mouth and squeezed his eyes shut, but nothing he did could keep his tears at bay. They fell in fat streams down his cheeks, over his fingers, and fell from his jaw.

Chris was going to be okay.

The cushion beside him shifted, and a Jack-sized shape glommed onto his side. Tears soaked through his shirt—not his own. Jack was crying, too.

"It's okay," Warren said through his tears as he wrapped Jack in his arms and shielded him from the world. "It's all gonna be okay. I'm here for you and your dad. I'll keep you both safe, I promise. You're not alone."

Jack started to sob. He grabbed fistfuls of Warren's shirt and clung to him as his shoulders heaved and his body shook. Warren held him tight through it all and cried silently with him. Eventually, Jack's sobbing started to even out and his body began to relax. When he was silent and his breathing had slowed and softened, Warren kissed the top of his head and gathered him in his arms. He carried Jack from the living room to the guest bedroom and tucked him in.

"It will get better," he whispered to a sleeping Jack. "It's hard now, I know, but it'll be a little easier every day. We'll get through this together."

The promise stuck with him on the way from the guest room to the couch. Once there, he fished his phone out from where it'd become lodged in the cushions and fired a text off to Pete.

Warren: I have an idea, but I'm gonna need your help
Pete: You have no idea how good it is to hear from you
Pete: Anyway, I'm in. What kind of trouble are you about to get us into?

Warren wiped the last tears from his eyes and got to typing. It was going to take a while to explain and a fair amount of work to wrangle everyone he needed to wrangle, but he was up to the challenge. Just like Jack had people in his life who'd help him through the worst, so did Chris, and Warren would be the one to bring them all together.

45

CHRIS

Chris woke to an unfamiliar ceiling. Neatly arranged holes on off-white tile—the kind you might count while a dentist poked at your mouth. But Chris wasn't at the dentist. He was in a bed, body tingling and near numb, brain foggy. Wherever it was, it was safe and warm. Busy. A machine beeped somewhere nearby. In the distance came the muffled sounds of scuffed shoes and human voices. Conversations. A trill of laughter. A distant knock.

Hospital, he realized. Then, far more urgently, *Jack.*

Chris tried to sit up, but his body wouldn't cooperate. He managed to turn his head to the side and saw he was surrounded by curtains. Pale blue.

"Jack?" he croaked. *"Jack?"*

A door opened, groaning on its hinges, and a few seconds later a nurse stepped into his curtained enclosure. Her scrubs were pink, and she wore a smile that suggested she'd been the one laughing out in the hall. "Good afternoon, Mr. Donnelly. We weren't expecting you up so soon. I'm Renée, and I'm your day shift nurse. Now, why don't we get you settled? You've been through quite a lot over the last few days. You need some more time to recover."

"My son," Chris rasped. His mouth was dry and it hurt to talk. "Where is my son? Is he safe?"

"Safe as can be." Renée fiddled with the IV bag by the bed. "He's with your wife, I think. Pretty brunette girl? They've been here to see you every day."

Chris's heart stopped. The Owens had told him Free was in prison. There was no way she could be here. Not now.

"Was she wearing pajamas?" he asked. "The woman with my son?"

"Oh. You know, I think she was." Renée clicked her tongue. "Cute ones, too, I think. We have all kinds of folks who pass through here wearing all kinds of things, and half the time I'm looking a hot mess myself, so I don't judge. But I think you're right."

"Liberty," Chris said, sighing in relief.

"Maybe. Never got her name. Quirky little thing, though. It's always a little more interesting when she's around. Now, I've given you something to help take the edge off a little, but you need to be careful with that heart of yours, Mr. Donnelly. The doctors patched you up, but it's up to you to take care of the stitches, so to speak."

"Stitches?" Chris mumbled. The world was starting to make less sense. One thought blended into the next in disjointed, dreamlike ways.

When Chris next blinked, his eyes stayed closed. Renée kept chatting, but he couldn't tell what about. Squeaking sneakers made their way down the hall. Laughter and conversation continued. The hospital was all around him, but Chris's mind was somewhere better—in bed, back in his apartment. Warren was with him, stripped down to his underwear. He sat with his back to the headboard, legs stretched out in front of him and crossed at the ankle. When Chris looked his way, he angled his head and smirked, and there was a glint in his eyes like he was up to something. God, was he gorgeous. A sight for sore eyes. Chris slid a hand over his thigh, eager to feel him again.

"You know," Warren said as he leaned in and teased Chris with something that wasn't quite a kiss, "it's not wrong to fall apart sometimes. Everyone does. It's okay. I put you back together once, and I'll do it again if I have to."

How delicate were stitches that held together a heart? It was a mystery best saved for another day. Right now what mattered was Warren, so Chris stayed silent and basked in his presence until the dream shifted and the sounds of the hospital faded away.

The next time Chris woke up, a pajama-clad Liberty—not Free—was sleeping in the chair beside him. One section of her messy, lopsided bun had come out of its clip. It hung over her open mouth, where it flapped wildly every time she snored.

"Liberty?" Chris's voice was sore from disuse. He cleared his throat and tried again. "Hey, Liberty?"

Liberty snored at him.

"*Lib.*"

"Dad?"

The question hadn't come from Liberty, who was one snore away from asphyxiating on her hair, but from a voice at the foot of his bed. Chris lifted his head and spotted Jack, who'd been sleeping on his bed near his feet. When Jack saw he was awake and responsive, he flung himself over the guardrail and onto the floor, then rushed to Chris's side. "*Dad!*"

Chris smiled. "Hey, champ. It's really good to see you. Have you been good for Aunt Libby?"

"Yeah." Jack grinned. "I missed you so much, Dad. I was really afraid when you didn't wake up for so long, but Wren told me it was because you needed time to get better."

"Did he now?" Chris reached out and ruffled Jack's hair. "Have you two been hanging out?"

"Mmhm. We watched *all* the Spider-Man movies while Aunt Libby worked on her macramee."

295

"Macramé," moaned a sleeping Liberty.

"Macramé," Jack agreed. "We also worked on homework together, and I keep getting better and better at math. Wren is a really good teacher. He could be doing other things that are way more fun, but he takes the time to help me when I don't understand. I'm really glad that you're his friend now. Did you know that he saved—"

"*CHRIS!*" Liberty sprang up from where she'd been sitting, lost her footing, and almost fell over. Jack gasped and rushed to help her, but it was too late. There was no way to save her from herself. Arms flailing, she hopped a few paces, folded her legs, and dropped into a seated position on the floor. All things considered, it was surprisingly graceful. What happened next wasn't. With a little hiss of pain, Libby grabbed her leg and started to rock, almost rolling onto her side. "Oh my god, pins and needles," she moaned. "Sleeping in that chair was a bad life decision. I regret everything. *Everything.*"

It was a little over the top, even for her. Chris narrowed his eyes suspiciously. It was quite the coincidence she'd sprung up right when Jack had been about to bring up Warren.

"Are you okay, Aunt Libby?" Jack asked, who was much less suspicious.

"I will be. I need a sec." She hissed and tried to stretch her leg out, then quickly changed her mind. "Maybe a little more than a sec. You know what? Jack, buddy, I think I need your help."

That clinched it—something was definitely going on. Chris eyed Liberty, but she was doing a great job at not looking his way.

"What do you need me to do?" Jack asked.

Liberty let go of her leg and whisked a credit card out of her back pocket. She presented it to Jack. "You know the vending machine down the hall we've been using? I need you to go get me a big bottle of water. It'll help me feel better. Then, while you're there, I'd love if you'd get me a snack. I'm not picky about what as long as it's good. While you're there, you can get a little something for yourself, too."

The lure of the credit card proved irresistible. Jack accepted it like it was a delicate treasure to be protected, then looked over his shoulder at Chris apologetically. "I'll be right back, Dad. I promise. Can you please not go back to sleep until after I get back?"

"You got it."

Jack nodded, very serious, and off he went on the adventure of a lifetime. Liberty waited until he was out of the room before she stood and approached the bedside. All signs of her pins and needles were gone. "Sorry for the theatrics. I, um, well, there are some things you shouldn't hear from an eight-year-old. You up for a talk?"

Chris nodded. "Yeah."

"What's the last thing you remember?"

"There was a..." Chris's mouth wanted to continue, but it didn't know the words to use. He'd thought he'd known what had happened, but now that he was trying to talk about it, he couldn't remember at all. What was the last thing he'd been doing before he woke up here? Orange streetlights. Ice sloughed off his windshield. Jack and something about recess. He winced. It wouldn't come back to him. "I... I don't know. Getting Jack bundled into the car to head for school, I guess. It's foggy."

"Okay." Liberty hummed anxiously. "Well, there was an accident. Probably not all that surprising. You don't usually wake up in the hospital when everything's hunky-dory."

A scream—Jack's shrill voice.

Chris closed his eyes, but it didn't come back to him. It was probably for the best. "How bad?"

"We, um, we almost lost you," Liberty admitted. "You were struck by an oncoming vehicle that lost control while making the turn onto the bridge. It hit you with so much force that it sent your car through the guardrail. It wasn't all that far a drop, but your car's toast. You broke a couple ribs and suffered from some serious impact-related trauma, but Jack got out with just a few scrapes and bruises."

297

Chris laid a hand experimentally on his chest, but they had to be giving him the good shit, because there was no pain. "What kind of impact-related trauma are we talking about?"

"One of your lungs collapsed and apparently your heart started leaking. I don't know how a heart can leak and not, you know, kill you, but I guess it's a thing that happens. I'm no doctor. You'll have to ask Wren about it, because it's *way* over my head."

Warren. The thought of him made Chris's leaky heart ache. "He wasn't the one to respond to the accident, was he?"

Before Liberty could respond, the door opened. Both of them froze, listening, and sure enough, the sound of Jack's footsteps approached. He nudged the curtains open with his shoulder, a huge bottle of water tucked under his arm and a box of raisins clenched in his hand. He presented both to Liberty. "Here you go, Aunt Libby. I needta go back a second time because I ran out of hands."

"If only you'd been born an octopus." Liberty ruffled his hair. "Now scoot and go get yourself something good. Take advantage— it's not every day your favorite aunt surrenders her credit card."

Jack left a second time. When he was gone, Liberty picked up the conversation from where they'd left off.

"No, it wasn't Wren who responded to the call. Another EMS team did. But you needed to be air lifted, so he was called in to fly you out here, to Des Moines."

A sour taste rose in Chris's throat. What kind of panic had Warren felt when he realized what was going on? How hard had it been to administer care knowing there was a chance Chris could die? The thought turned his stomach. He needed to ask, but couldn't. No one knew they were together and he couldn't out Warren to Liberty.

It seemed that Liberty read some of the discomfort on his face, because she reached over to squeeze his hand. "I know about you two, by the way," Liberty said softly. "Pete and I kind of figured it out together a while back. You don't have to pretend to hate him for my sake."

"How is he?" Chris blurted. "Is he okay?"

"He's okay. I mean, he's not great. It's been hard for him. But he's been hanging in there, and he's really stepped up to take care of Jack while you've been gone." She slid her phone out of her pocket and tapped away at the screen. "He's not able to come visit because they don't allow people who aren't family into the rooms, but he asked me to give you this video he made." She handed him the phone, which was opened to her media player. Warren was in the thumbnail, framed from the chest up. Exhaustion weighed on his face and darkened the skin beneath his eyes, but god, the sight of him. Blond hair messy, lips so achingly kissable. Chris's heart fluttered, and the heaviness he'd been carrying dissipated. What he wouldn't give to have Warren there right now. To be able to brush the hair back from his forehead, hold him close, and promise that everything would be all right.

"While you watch, I'm gonna go rescue my poor credit card," Libby said while Chris studied the thumbnail, drinking in every detail of the man in it. "After that, I'm gonna take Jack to the cafeteria to snag some actual food, because who the hell brings someone raisins when they ask for a snack?"

While she spoke, she backed toward the curtain. Chris barely noticed. He was distracted imagining what Warren might say.

"We'll be back soon," Liberty said as she slipped through the curtain. "You're in a shared room, by the way, and Wren knows it, so don't get *too* excited. Okay. I'm off. Catch you later."

With that said, she was gone. Once Chris heard the door latch in her wake, he took a moment to calm his racing heart, then pressed play.

299

CHRIS

The first few seconds of the video were blurred. Chris bumped up the volume a few clicks in an attempt to get a feel for what was going on, but only heard the rush of air as it passed by the microphone. When the video stabilized, he realized why. Liberty grinned at the camera in the same toothy way she always did when she was up to no good, then scurried out of the frame, leaving a bamboozled Warren behind.

He was, for some reason, in a pantry. A shelf full of canned soup was visible in the shot.

"Um. Hey." Warren looked off to the side and scowled. There was a distant laugh from Liberty, followed by the sound of a closing door. Purportedly alone, Warren turned back to face the camera. The sour look on his face sweetened. Whatever his flavor, Chris was enamored. "It's me. Warren. You're probably wondering what I'm doing in a pantry, and, well, let's just say that it's better you don't ask. I live with an Owens. We'll leave it at that."

God, was it good to see him. Chris's cheeks hurt from smiling. He held the phone a little tighter and took in all of Warren's finer intricacies—the tilt of his head as he spoke, the mischievous curl of his lips, the eagerness in his eyes. The high-octane nature of their relationship had made them easy to overlook, but now that Chris had all the time in the world, he'd map Warren's body like astronomers mapped the stars. Not even his cosmic dust would be left behind.

"But anyway, enough about the pantry." Warren gestured at the shelf behind him, accidentally thwacking a can of soup in the process. The can was knocked onto its side, rolled off the edge of the shelf, and conked him on the head. The phone went flying. Chris was treated to a blurred video feed and the distant cries of a man assaulted by cream of tomato before the screen went black. The phone must have landed camera-down. Warren didn't rush to recover it. He cursed and shuffled about the room instead, disturbing at least one heavy wooden object and a couple more cans in the process, all of which hit the ground. Amid the tinny *clanks!* there came a distinct, "Oh, fuck you, *Campbell's!*"

"Are you okay in there?" came Liberty's voice. "It's not the potatoes again, is it?"

"No! It's the soup!"

"Ah. Soup. I should have known. The only thing condensed about it is its ability to do evil. Do you need backup? I can strap on some crackers and be there in like, three seconds."

"No. No, I'm fine. It just"—there was more clanking—"needs to stay on the shelf. I've got it under control."

Laughter and Chris's broken body did not pair well. Warren was no videographer, but if he tried hard and believed in himself, he'd make a fine comedian.

After a few more clinks as cans were forcefully set down, the camera flipped back around and there was Warren. He was no longer sitting beneath the shelf. Chris wasn't quite sure where he was, but it was somewhere without any condensed evil in sight. "Sorry. I was attacked. I'm better. Let's just forget that happened. This video was supposed to be serious, but I guess that's not happening now, is it?" He frowned. "Only it kind of has to, because the things I need to say aren't the kind of things I can joke about."

The video seemed to freeze, but right as Chris was about to tap the screen to see if it had gotten stuck, Warren shook his head and dragged a hand across his eyes.

"I thought I'd lost you," he admitted in a small, sad voice that instantly changed the tone of the conversation. Chris didn't feel much like laughing anymore. "I don't think I've ever been so scared. Seeing you on that stretcher broke me, and I'm still not all the way back together. I won't be until you're back home."

He stopped speaking to dab at his eyes again, but he wasn't the only one suffering—Chris blinked away the onset of tears.

"Um." Warren sniffled. "Uh. I told myself I wouldn't do this, but I guess you can't really tell your emotions what to do, huh? I feel like an idiot. I'm sorry I can't hold myself together. I'm making this all about me when you're the one who was hurt, and that wasn't my intention. I just... I just thought that we'd have more time. I save lives for a living, so you'd think I'd be aware that death doesn't discriminate, but apparently not only am I a stubborn, selfish asshole, but I'm willfully ignorant, too. You never think it'll happen to you or the people in your life, but it does, and I'm stupid for not realizing it sooner."

Warren's voice broke on the last word. He squeezed his eyes shut and puckered his lips, then shook his head and fought off whatever hard emotions were trying to break free.

"You remember how I said there was a thing I wanted to talk about?" he asked. "The one I said we'd talk about later, next time we were face to face? I shouldn't have waited. I should have called you and told you right then and there, but I didn't, because I thought we'd still have time. But then there you were at the station, tubes in your chest and—" Warren had to stop. Pain cracked his expression. His shoulders heaved through a silent sob. "And I almost never got a chance to tell you I love you. I've loved you for a long time, but I've been too stubborn to admit it."

The hospital was filled with noise, but Chris's world had gone quiet. It was only him, Warren, and the screen dividing them. Their two hearts were separated by a hundred miles, but in that moment they were united.

Chris's trembling lips pulled into a smile.

It was about time that big, college-educated brain of his figured it out. He only wished it hadn't taken an accident for it to happen.

Warren sobbed for real this time, then shook his head and continued. "I'm sorry it took me so long. I'm so fucking sorry. It's been hell thinking you might die having never known, but that's all on me. All of it. I'm the one who fucked up, and so I'm the one who's gonna move heaven and earth to prove how much I mean it." He breathed in deep. "We joked before about a wrestling match—how if I won, I'd get rights to your ass. Well, guess what? For the next month, you're gonna be flat on your ass while you recover, so I'm claiming victory on a medical technicality. I own your ass now. It's mine. But here's the thing..." Warren sniffled one last time, then lifted his chin and looked directly at the camera. Determination burned in his eyes. "I fucking hate topping."

Chris couldn't help it—he laughed. That was the Warren he knew. The one he loved. And god, did he love him.

"So I've been trying to think what else I can do to that ass of yours now that it officially belongs to me, and I've decided that instead of fucking it within an inch of our collective lives, I'm gonna spoil it. You won't know when, or where, or how, but you and Jack are going to be pampered, and until you get strong enough to win back what's rightfully yours, that's how it's gonna be.

"So consider this your official warning, Chris Donnelly." Warren grinned, and it was so full of adoration that it felt like he was right there with Chris, looking into his eyes. "You're mine now. You got that? Mine. And I'm gonna show you how much I care every chance I get, because tomorrow is never a promise."

Warren covered the camera with his palm, turning the screen black. The video ended shortly after. Chris replayed it as soon as it did. He needed to hear those words again. To prove to himself they were real.

I love you. I've loved you for a long time, but I've been too stubborn to admit it.

The magic was still there. Each replay, Warren invoked it again, and it was never less powerful than the time before. Chris traced the sides of the phone with his fingers, hoping that magic of his own doing would let Warren feel as loved as he felt in that moment.

He couldn't wait to go home.

47

WARREN

On the day Libby brought Chris home from the hospital, Warren had the day off work. With several minutes to spare before she made it back to town, he arrived at Chris's apartment complex and stationed himself outside of Chris's door, a bouquet of flowers cradled in his arm.

It wasn't the first time Warren had been to the apartment since Chris's hospitalization. He'd stopped by a few days before to screw the crooked numbers on Chris's apartment door back into place. Chris's landlord hadn't wanted to do shit-all about it, so Warren had taken measures into his own hands. It was the first of many small things he planned to do to make Chris's life better.

Time passed quickly. It wasn't long before the door to the stair-well opened. Jack came barreling out first, but wasn't paying attention and didn't see Warren standing down the hall before turning to make sure Libby and Chris were behind him. They were. Chris was leaning on Libby for support, and Libby was fussing over him as they slowly made their way into the hall.

Once they were through the door, Jack turned and spotted Warren. His eyes went wide. "Wren!" he gasped, rocketing down the hall to tackle him. "Wren, you're here!"

307

Warren ruffled his hair. "Did you think I wouldn't be?"

"I dunno. Maybe?" Jack looked up at him with big, sparkling eyes and a goofy grin. "You brought flowers with you."

"Sure did."

"For who?"

"Your dad." Warren had been on the fence about bringing Chris flowers at all, but the florist had assured him that it would be a sweet gesture, and the arrangement she'd put together had been too beautiful to turn down. She'd framed orange lilies, ocean breeze orchids, and white flowers Warren had no name for with vibrant green fronds that made their colors pop. Whether Chris liked them or not was irrelevant—it was the gesture behind them that counted.

And speaking of Chris, the man was eating Warren up with his eyes.

Warren arched a brow to acknowledge that he'd noticed, flashed Chris a smile, then redirected his focus on Jack and gestured at the bouquet. "Do you think he'll like them?"

Jack wrinkled his nose. "I dunno... Flowers are for girls."

"Where's the rule that says that?" Chris asked. He'd made it down the hall and come to stand behind his son, but when he spoke, he looked at Warren. "I think they're beautiful. I just wish we had somewhere to put them."

The statement hung open-ended, like Chris was waiting for someone to jump in and take the lead. Warren narrowed his eyes and mouthed, "What?" but Chris shook his head and tapped Libby's shin with the side of his foot. Libby glared at him, pouted, then seemed to catch on. Her eyes went wide.

"Oh. *Oh.*" She flapped her hands. "You mean you don't have a vase. Well, let me tell you, we have *so many vases* at our place that we're pretty much living in a vase emporium. Like, we have regular vases, but then also things you wouldn't even think were vases, but that actually totally are. Why don't you two strapping gentlemen stay here and babysit the flowers while Jack and I go to pick one out? There are so many it may take a while."

There were no vases in their household.

Warren squinted at Libby. She grinned at him, all teeth.

The lie worked. Jack, bright-eyed and bushy-tailed, dragged her away on a quest for the perfect flower receptacle. While he did, he chatted incessantly about how flowers were used as dye in Minecraft, and how he'd used them to alter the wool of a pen of sheep so they were his friend Billie's favorite color.

It was all very interesting, but Warren tuned it out. There was something else holding his attention—now that his son was gone, Chris had dropped his wholesome dad act and slipped into something a little more sinful.

"Well, well, well. If it isn't Reaves. Aren't you a sight for sore eyes," he said when they were alone. He set a hand on Warren's waist and gently guided him so his back was against the door. "You didn't have to bring me flowers, you know. Seeing you would have been more than enough."

"Did you not watch the part of the video where I told you that I was going to spoil your ass?" Warren tilted his head to the side and lifted his chin, inviting Chris in for a kiss. "If you think flowers are too much, you'd better recover fast, because this is just the beginning."

"Is that so?" Chris stepped forward, sandwiching the flowers between them. "You know I'm gonna have to get you back for this, right?"

"Wrong."

"You're a fool if you think I won't."

"And you're just as big a fool if you think I'm gonna let you." Warren pushed the flowers into Chris's arms, grinning all the while. "Now unless you want me to suck your dick out in the hallway, you'd better get this door unlocked."

"Is that supposed to be a threat?" He arched an eyebrow. "You need to up your game. After everything we did out in the parking lot, I have a feeling we'd both enjoy it."

"We've had this conversation already. I'm not into every kink, you pervert." Warren hooked his fingers under Chris's belt, holding him in place. "But I sure as hell am into every bit of you. Now open the door before I start getting mouthy."

"You mean to say you aren't being mouthy already?"

"Fuck you."

"Mm." Chris smiled and brushed his nose against Warren's. "There's the man I love. Fuck you, too. Fuck you hard, Reaves. Fuck you until you're screaming for me. Until I'm the only one who can give you what you need."

"It's too late. You already are."

Their back and forth was intoxicating, and the way it thickened and crackled in the air between them made it impossible to escape. Warren gave in and imbibed. High off the feeling—off love—he closed his eyes and kissed Chris like it was the very first time. Cellophane crinkled. The flowers were being crushed. If they didn't stop the bouquet would be ruined, but Warren had been waiting too long for this to care.

He was in love with Chris, and this was his chance to show it. He wouldn't ever take that for granted again.

Chris's mouth was firm, but sweet, and it knew what Warren wanted. The kiss it gave was slow and sensual, but it burned with unspoken need. Tears in his eyes, Warren matched it on every count.

"I love you," Chris uttered into the space between them when they paused to breathe. "I fucking love you, Warren."

Warren's smile stretched so wide it wobbled. "Not half as much as I love you."

It took Libby and Jack half an hour to make it back to the apartment. In that time, Chris unlocked the door, led Warren inside, and got comfortable on the couch. Warren helped himself to the floorspace between Chris's legs, dropped onto his knees, and welcomed him home in the best way he knew how—with his mouth. Chris was in no condition to be rough with him, but the weak moans of pleasure he made while Warren blew him were rewards unto themselves.

"Keep going," Chris groaned, and Warren could tell he was close. "Oh, fuck... keep going."

Warren looked up at him from his lap. Chris's face was pinched with pleasure, and he was breathing harder than his doctors would be pleased with. The sooner he finished him off, the better. With that in mind, Warren closed his eyes and bobbed his head, taking Chris all the way down. Chris pushed a sound of pleasure out through his teeth and carded his hands through Warren's hair, then grabbed it to keep him in place. It lacked the force sex between them usually had, but it turned Warren on all the same. Messy tears streaming down his cheeks, he choked and gagged while Chris finished inside him, then swallowed all the cum he gave.

Their relationship had changed, but that didn't mean their dynamic had to be left behind.

Which was a good thing, because the vase Jack had settled on was none other than an empty tube of Quaker Oats. No doubt Warren's jilted Oaty Daddy had been hoping this was his chance. Alas, it wasn't. With Chris, love and hot kinky sex went hand in hand.

48

WARREN

Warren woke up on Christmas morning in Chris's bed, snuggled up to his side. The house was quiet and everything was still, so Warren took advantage and enjoyed their closeness for a little longer. He draped one arm over Chris's bare stomach and rested his head next to his shoulder. If he hadn't been so sure that Jack would be bouncing off the walls before long, he would have gone back to sleep, but Christmas with an eight-year-old wasn't going to be the quiet, restful time it was when it was just him and Libby. All things considered, he was okay with that.

"Good morning," he whispered, pressing a kiss to Chris's shoulder. "What do you want for breakfast?"

Chris grumped and grumbled, but after a few more kisses began to stir. Most days Warren would have let him sleep, but today was the exception. It'd be kinder to rouse him like this than to leave it to Jack, who'd be all kinds of crazy. Santa had been good to him this year, and once he saw how many presents were under their little tree, there'd be no keeping him quiet. The literal mountain of presents was Warren's fault—not Chris's—but it felt important to make sure the kid had a good Christmas after the hell he'd been through. It was tough enough to have to move so far away from where you'd grown up, but it was worse doing it without a mom. Warren was no housewife, but since Free wasn't in the picture, he'd do everything he could to make sure Jack felt all the love she should have been there to give him.

"You awake now?" Warren asked a yawning Chris. "Let's try this again." He kissed along Chris's shoulder to his cheek. "What do you want for breakfast? It's Christmas, the one day of the year you're not on the naughty list. Tell me what you want and it's yours."

Chris turned his head and captured Warren's lips in a drowsy kiss. His voice was gritty from sleep. "You."

Oh, the nerve of him, flirting like that before Warren could get his morning wood under control. He indulged the feeling for a little while, kissing Chris slowly but surely until he was too close to giving in to temptation. "Sorry, but I'm not on the menu."

"Just one time wouldn't hurt."

"Yes, it would." Warren combed his fingers through Chris's bedhead and kissed the tip of his nose. "A surgeon was poking around inside your chest two weeks ago messing with your heart and lungs. I don't know about you, but I'd like to keep both those things healthy. It's bad enough I can't keep my mouth off your dick. I'm not about to let you have my ass when it might make your heart explode."

That got Chris's attention. He moved away just enough to look Warren in the eyes. "It would seriously explode?"

"No, but it might start spurting, and honestly, that's probably worse."

Chris made a face. Warren grinned at him.

Unfortunately, the threat of spurting organs weren't enough to deter him.

"What about if you get on top?"

It *was* tempting. Warren raked his teeth over his bottom lip. Chris had to be in cahoots with his morning wood. It was a pity he had to be the responsible one, because riding Chris sounded like an amazing way to spend Christmas morning. "Absolutely not."

"I promise I won't move." Chris sat up stiffly, ever careful of his ribs, and maneuvered himself onto his hands and knees to straddle Warren's thighs. The blankets tented to accommodate him, slipping down so they barely covered his ass. What Warren wouldn't give to see a picture of him from behind, all bare skin and rippling muscle, like a tiger getting ready to pin its prey, eager to take whatever it wanted. "All I'll do is lie there," he whispered, then turned his head and snagged Warren's bottom lip between his teeth. Warren's heart wasn't the only part of him that bite made throb. "I'll stay totally still and just watch as you ride me. So what do you say, Reaves? Will you be my Christmas present?"

"We shouldn't," Warren whispered, but he was so close to breaking that he couldn't say no.

Chris hummed in response and kissed him, which was when the bedroom door flung open and Jack rushed into the room. As exhausted as he'd been from wrapping presents last night, Warren had forgotten to lock it.

"*Dad!*" Jack exclaimed. An uncomfortable silence followed. When it became too much to bear, Jack asked in a much smaller, uncertain voice, "Dad?"

What was the opposite of a Christmas miracle? Because whatever it was, it was happening right the fuck now.

"Hey, champ," Chris said in far too normal a tone of voice for someone currently mounted on another human being. "Usually we knock before we open doors."

Jack's eyes were wide. He didn't speak. He only nodded.

Kids weren't in Warren's realm of expertise, but he knew if he opened his mouth, he'd end up regretting it. As mortified as he was, there was nothing he could do. Chris was on his own.

"You wanna talk about it?" Chris asked as he dismounted from Warren. Thanks to his ribs, it was a slow and tedious process that left nothing to the imagination. There'd be no faking their way out of this one. "It's okay if you're confused about it," Chris said as he sat

315

on the bed. "That's why questions exist. The more you ask, the more you know, and the less confused you'll be."

Jack's eyes darted from Chris to Warren and back again. At last, he said, "Is Wren your boyfriend?"

There was no way Chris would say yes. Jack was still little and not really old enough to understand. Chris would pull an excuse out of his ass, they'd move on with their lives, and everything would be *fine*.

Only that wasn't what happened.

Chris thought for a moment, then nodded. "He sure is."

Warren gawked at him.

There was another silence, this one slightly less uncomfortable. Jack lowered his head thoughtfully, then looked back up at them, his emotions guarded. "Okay. So does that mean that you're his boyfriend, too?"

"Yes."

Where was the eject button? If Jack hadn't been staring at him, Warren would have sunk down to hide beneath the blankets. Coming out to his boyfriend's son on Christmas morning was *not* his idea of a good time.

"And you love each other?" Jack asked, continuing his reign of terror.

Goodbye, world.

It'd been a slice.

Warren was all set to slide off the bed and let the monsters under it take him when Chris stopped him with his reply. It was short, certain, and sweetly genuine. "We do. We love each other very much."

Dumbfounded, Warren looked Chris's way. There was a smile on his face that matched the tone of his voice, and it did away with Warren's discomfort. Chris was so certain about him that he didn't think twice before telling his son, and that... that warmed Warren from the inside like nothing else. Stupidly in love with the man at his side, he slid his hand over Chris's and squeezed. The small way Chris's smile brightened made him swoon.

"Okay." Jack stood a little taller, like he was starting to understand and ready to fully engage. "It's kinda funny, because when you had Wren sleep over in your bed instead of on the couch I thought maybe it was because you were in love, but I wasn't really sure, so I didn't say anything. I'm happy you and Wren like each other so much, though. Does that mean you're gonna marry him?"

In Warren's mind, a new fantasy took center stage. In it, Chris shoved him into the wall, wrenched his arms over his head, and held him in place by the wrists with one hand. With the other, he slid a ring onto Warren's finger.

"You're mine now, Reaves," fantasy-Chris growled. "Mine."

Real-life Chris was a little less assertive. "I don't know yet," he admitted. "Probably."

Probably.

Warren was sure his cheeks had gone red from the way his face was burning.

Probably.

Like Chris had already thought about it.

Like he'd already made up his mind.

While Warren combusted from the inside out, Chris turned his hand around and wove their fingers together. It was such a simple thing to do, but Warren saw it for what it was—a way to show he was serious about laying his claim. He wanted to make Warren his.

"Okay," Jack said casually, like he hadn't just heard his father try to wife Warren up. "Can we go open presents now?"

"After breakfast," Chris said.

"Ugh. Okay. And then we'll go see Grandma and Grandpa, right, Dad? Since we live close now?"

"We're still waiting on our new car, so only if Warren will drive us." Chris squeezed his hand and looked him in the eyes. "You don't have to, but I'd love to have you there with us. I wanna show you off to my parents."

317

God, the heat pumping through his veins really was going to burn him up from the inside. Warren swallowed hard and nodded. He didn't think he could speak just yet—maybe later, in time to embarrass himself in front of Chris's parents.

God, he was going to meet *Chris's parents.*

This whole love business wasn't for the weak of heart.

But for all its flaws, love was worth it. Because of it, Warren would always remember the awkward conversations they had in bed that Christmas morning and how Jack had put on *Spider-Man* while they were unwrapping presents—how Walter and Debra Donnelly had welcomed him into their household with open arms. Later that night, full to bursting with it, he carried Jack up three flights of stairs to their apartment while Chris whispered sweet, sometimes lecherous things into his ear and cupped his ass.

"Merry Christmas, Reaves," Chris whispered against the ridge of Warren's ear after they'd tucked Jack into bed together. "I love you."

"Merry Christmas," Warren replied, and was strong enough of heart to say, "I love you, too."

49

CHRIS

One month was a long time to do nothing. Chris spent most of it sleeping, partly because recovery was kicking his ass, but also because if he spent all day awake, he'd go insane. Being homebound wasn't easy, and downtime was only fun when it was voluntary. Everything he wanted to do was beyond his capability.

Work out? Nope.

Scrub the stained grout in the bathroom? Forget it.

Bone his smoking-hot live-in nurse-slash-boyfriend who kept giving him bedroom eyes? Also no.

It was a good thing that boyfriend of his was attentive, because without him, Chris would have gone insane. Warren, thankfully, was good at keeping him occupied. If he wasn't challenging Chris with his smart mouth, it was only because he was too busy sucking Chris's cock.

Chris couldn't get enough.

After Jack went to bed for the night, Warren's mouth was what wore him out so he could sleep, and in the morning after Jack went to school, it was what woke him up and got him ready to face the day. Warren blew him in the living room, the bedroom, the shower. It got to the point where if Warren walked by, Chris's dick twitched in response. The man had him trained. Not that Chris minded. The more sex they had, the better. Chris only wished that Warren would give up his ass, but after their Christmas morning session had been interrupted, Warren hadn't been willing.

"It'll get too rough," he said whenever Chris brought it up—which was often. "I won't be able to control myself and I'll end up hurting you."

Chris wasn't opposed to a little pain, but Warren was the medical professional.

It didn't stop them from getting hot and heavy in other ways as he started to feel better.

Handjobs.

Blowjobs.

Fingering.

The first time Chris made Warren come by stroking his prostate, he was hooked. He'd spent the entirety of his adult life in a straight relationship, and while the female body was comparable in some regards, he had a lot to learn about how men liked to be touched in bed. Or, rather, how Warren liked to be touched. Chris wasn't interested in anyone else. Warren was the only one he wanted by his side.

Their not-quite-sex-fest came to an end the last full week of January, when Chris was cleared to go back to work. Penetrative sex, the doctor had told him, was back on the table, but he'd need to start slow and work his way back to more vigorous encounters. The problem was that Warren wasn't home when Chris got back from his appointment in Des Moines.

Upon finding the apartment empty, Chris sent Warren a text.

Chris: You coming home tonight?
Warren: No. I'm on tomorrow and Sunday, so I'll be staying here
Chris: Fuck
Warren: I'm guessing it went well?

320

Chris: Yeah. The doctor says I'm a-okay to get back to life as normal. I'll be going back to work on Monday
Warren: We'll have to make up for lost time after Jack goes to sleep, then ;)
Warren: I'll be home in time on Monday morning to drive Jack to school and get you in to work, no worries
Chris: Thanks. I love you. See you then.

Without Warren around, Chris shelved marathon sex and got to work on some of the other things on his to-do list. It wasn't the way he'd wanted to celebrate his return to normal, but he had to admit the sparkly white grout in the bathroom was kind of nice.

On Monday morning, Warren arrived home in time to drive Chris and Jack to where they needed to be. He dropped Jack off at school first, then headed for the station.

"Nothing much has changed since you left," Warren said on their way down Main Street. "Melody had an old exercise bike at her place that she replaced with a newer model over Christmas, so she brought the old one in for us to use. It's in the gym. If you don't go wild, it'd be good for you to use it on your lunch break. A moderate amount of exercise will help you heal. Just don't go using any equipment that's going to jostle your upper body too much, and stay away from lifting weights."

"I'm not gonna do anything stupid. I know I've still gotta take it easy, and that if I don't, I run the risk of hurting myself again. I'm not gonna let that happen. You've been spoiling my ass for too long for me to blow it on my first day back. I'm not gonna do anything that'll keep me from making that ass of yours mine."

Warren went pink. "You're doing better, but you're still not strong enough to best me in a wrestling match."

321

Chris raised an eyebrow and shrugged. "If I top you, it's pretty much the same thing."

Warren had no cheeky reply for that.

It didn't take much longer after that to make it to the station. Warren pulled into the parking lot, careful of the ice, and parked in his usual spot. Chris had assumed he'd idle there while they said goodbye, but Warren shifted into park and took the keys out of the ignition. When he unbuckled and opened the door, Chris decided it was time to say something. "What are you doing?"

"Helping you." Warren climbed out of the car and leaned in to continue the conversation. "It's a skating rink out here. I don't think anyone put salt down."

"So?"

"So I'm going to walk you inside."

"I'm not a kid," Chris grumbled as he, too, exited the vehicle. "I can take a little ice, Reaves. It's not all that far to the door."

"Don't care." Warren came around the car and took Chris by the arm. "Go ahead and call me paranoid. Until you're entirely back to normal, I'm not taking any chances."

"This is so unnecessary."

"Tell you what—funnel all that rage you feel over being treated nicely into owning my ass tonight." They reached the door leading into the station, which Warren cracked open. Its hinges squeaked. "The doctor cleared you to go back to work. He didn't clear you to take a tumble in a criminally icy parking lot. I'm a paramedic, Chris. Keeping people alive is kind of my shtick. You're crazy if you think I'm not gonna do everything I can to keep you safe when you're medically fragile."

"You're ridiculous."

"*You're* ridiculous."

Warren opened the door the rest of the way, admitting them into the short hallway leading to the common room. It was unexpectedly dark. For whatever reason, all the lights were out. When Warren shut the door, it went pitch black.

"Did everyone go back to bed?" Chris blinked a couple times as his eyes adjusted. "It's dark as hell in here."

"Oh, yeah. It was a pretty quiet night, so everyone decided to get some shuteye. It's about time I got everyone up. Let me get the light." Warren planted a hand on the small of Chris's back and steered him into the room. "All right, guys," Warren said when they arrived by the light switch. "Time to get up."

With a flip of a switch, the common room lit up. As it did, familiar faces popped up from all kinds of unexpected places. Meatball and Melody leapt out from behind the couch. Pete and the firefighters from the third shift—Jaime and Liam—rushed into the room from the gym, whipping noisemakers over their heads. Alicia and Gary burst out of the bunk room, bringing with them an army of brightly colored balloons that soared up to bump the ceiling. Sheriff Sinclair, wearing a hat made from streamers and packing tape, came out from his office. Even Kathleen made an appearance. She hobbled through the door of the sheriff's department, a pot of steaming coffee in hand, and only glared at Chris a little, which he took to mean that he'd live to see another day.

"Surprise!" Pete and his posse of firefighters cried as they stormed the room, noisemakers clacking. Kathleen turned her glare on them. It looked like Sheriff Sinclair was about to have a few more noise violations added to his mighty heap of paperwork.

Or maybe not.

Jaime and Liam swerved suddenly and circled her, acting as an annoying yet handsome distraction while Pete rushed Chris and clapped him on the arm. "Welcome back, you unstoppable force of nature, you. You had us all scared shitless. Great job."

"I don't understand," Chris admitted hesitantly. "What's going on?"

"Wren's been keeping us up to date with your recovery," Alicia explained. She and the other members of the staff had started to gather around Chris. Balloons trailed after them, bobbing across the ceiling. "We've all been rooting for your recovery, so now that you're back on your feet, it's time to celebrate."

Melody pumped her fist in the air. "Release the cake!"

Chris watched, stunned, as the crowd around him dispersed. Jaime and Liam took up cake duty in the kitchen where they bumped elbows with Kathleen, who'd set up a pseudo wet bar and was doling out mugs of her coveted coffee. Someone—Chris didn't know who—connected their phone to a Bluetooth speaker and started to DJ. Pete winked at Chris, nodded at Warren, then danced like a fool across the common room to the cake station, where he helped gather mismatched plates and cutlery in anticipation of a sugary feast.

"You doin' okay?" Warren asked in a whisper when Chris didn't move.

Chris nodded. It wasn't like him to cry, but there was a tightness in his chest that warned him tears might be on the horizon if he didn't pull himself together. It didn't seem real that all of this was for him. He'd come back to Lethridge out of desperation, knowing that even if he never managed to get back on his feet, Jack would be looked after and loved. He hadn't expected to find a community that would care for him and love him, too. He hadn't expected anything at all.

"Guess now you know why I had to walk you all the way inside to protect you from that big, bad ice," Warren said with a laugh. He stepped around Chris so they were face to face. The kindness in his eyes was so contrary to the way he'd been all those months ago when they'd still been at each other's throats.

So much had changed.

So damned much.

Full to bursting with happiness, Chris dragged Warren into his arms and hugged him tight. It didn't take a college education to figure out who was the mastermind behind the party. One of these days, Chris would get back at Warren for spoiling his ass so much, but before that could happen, they had some celebrating to do.

"Love you," Warren whispered. "Welcome back. We should probably get some cake before Pete scarfs it all down. The man's a menace."

It was too easy. Chris couldn't resist. "Takes one to know one."

"Fuck you," Warren said, sounding more in love than ever.

Chris gave all that love back to him and more when he replied, "Fuck you, too."

No sooner had Chris received his slice of cake than the door to the garage burst open. Mikey, the plucky paramedic who worked the shift before Warren's, rushed into the room while his partner, the much older Jay, trailed casually behind.

Thank god for Justin Timberlake, because without his golden voice, the station would have been dead silent.

"Hi!" Mikey squeaked as he flung off his coat and tried not to skid across the floor. Melting snow was packed into the treads of his boots, making small puddles wherever he stepped. "I'm so sorry we're late. Oh my god, was traffic bad. *So* bad. Like, I'm surprised you're all still here and not at the scene of some multi-car pileup accident kind of bad. Crazy, right?"

Chris glanced at Warren, whose expression said what everyone in the room wouldn't—that Mikey was full of shit. Traffic was never that backed up in their small town. The kid was hiding something.

"I'm really glad you're doing better, Chris," Mikey continued on to say as he arrived at the cake station. "When Jay and I heard the news, we couldn't believe it, and seeing Wren so sad really shook us up. I, um, I'm really glad that everything turned out okay. It's cute that you've got each other to lean on."

"Thanks."

"You're welcome." Mikey flashed him a big, sparkling smile. "So... have you been having fun?"

Before Chris could answer, Jay squeezed Mikey's shoulder and said in a pleasant but stern voice, "Go hang up your coat and tap the snow out of your boots, Mikey. You're making a mess of the floor."

Two men had never looked more different than small, slender Mikey and muscular, towering Jay. Fresh out of college and baby-faced, Mikey was the kind of guy who'd wear skinny jeans and baggy hoodies on his time off. In another life, he'd be famous on Instagram for his sweet, doe-like eyes, soft lips, and messy, don't-care hair. Next to him, Jay was even more imposing than he was alone. Not only was he physically intimidating, but he had the personality to back it up. Calm, collected, quiet, and meticulous, Jay was never mean, but he was all business all the time. It was strange to see him out of uniform.

It was stranger to see Mikey's face go bright red at being given the command.

With a little squeak of acknowledgment, Mikey scurried away to do what he was told. When he was gone, Jay stepped forward and extended a hand to Chris, which he shook. "It's good to see you back," he said. "How are you feeling?"

"Still sore, but better than I did a month ago."

"I'll bet." Jay arched a brow and glanced to the side in Mikey's direction. There was a hint of a smile on his face, like he'd seen something that amused him, but didn't want to let on. "We should go out for drinks sometime. Warren's been filling us in on your progress, but I'd be interested in hearing about your experience."

Chris spared a look at Mikey, who was stomping snow out of his boots. "Sure. When the ice melts, let's do it. I've got a feeling we'll have plenty to talk about."

CHRIS

The party didn't last long. Over cake and Kathleen's coveted coffee, the active emergency services team received a call. Once they'd gone, everyone else dispersed. Kathleen collected her coffeepot and shuffled back into her office. Meatball and Melody left one after the other, begging exhaustion—like Warren, they'd just come off a forty-eight-hour shift. The other guests followed their lead until only Pete, Warren, Chris, Mikey, and Jay remained.

"It's been a slice," Pete said as he slid off the couch and bowed low to Chris. At the lowest point of his bow, he flourished one hand dramatically and, while Warren wasn't looking, used it to abduct the last mouthful of cake from his plate. Pete righted himself, winked at Chris, and added, "I've gotta run. Good seeing you," before popping the pilfered cake in his mouth and booking it out of the station like his life depended on it.

Which it did.

It took Warren a second to realize what had happened, but when he went to spear his fork on the last of his cake and found it missing, he let loose with what Chris could only describe as a battle cry and flung his empty plate on the coffee table. He was on his feet and moving less than a second later. Pete cackled. Warren threw himself through the door, which slammed behind him. Kathleen stuck her head into the room and glared, but upon seeing no obvious wrongdoing, retreated into her lair and shut the door.

Mikey, who'd watched it all happen from his perch on the arm of the good armchair, snorted. He shoved the last of his cake into his mouth—likely to keep it safe from a drive-by cakenapping—and asked mid-chew, "They always like that?"

"Warren and Pete?" Chris shrugged a single shoulder. "Don't see much of them from the dispatch office, but from what I've heard—yes."

"And Kathleen doesn't write them up for disturbing the peace?"

"Not that I'm aware of."

"She must like them." He set his plate on his knee and scraped at the frosting with the side of his fork. "She writes me up like, at least once a shift. Sometimes more. And I don't do half the crazy stuff they seem to do. If I tried to chase Jay through the station, she'd probably detain me."

"I wouldn't be so sure." Jay took the plate from Mikey's lap and set it on the table. Mikey squeaked in protest when it was removed, but didn't otherwise argue. "I seem to recall a certain Post-It bandit never faced prosecution."

"Borrowing Post-Its for totally legit purposes is entirely different from scream-running through the station!"

"Hmm." Jay sipped at his coffee, letting his incredulity percolate. "I'll have to let Jaime know he should expect to find his car covered in Post-Its more often. I had no idea it was part of the job. I'll have to make up for lost time."

"Jay!"

Jay said nothing, but the satisfied quirk of his lips spoke for itself.

"Does anyone want more cake?" Mikey hopped down from his place on the armchair and shifted his weight from foot to foot, like he couldn't wait to get moving. "I'll make sure to leave some for

Caroline. She's the one working dispatch now, right? I haven't seen her around."

Chris nodded. "Yeah, Caroline's in the office right now. I'm gonna bring her a piece when I start my shift."

While they spoke, Jay braced his hands on his knees and rose. "And there will be more than enough cake for her, because one slice is all you've got time for today, Mikey. We need to go." After stretching his back and rolling his shoulders, Jay nodded politely at Chris. "Have a good first day back at work. I'll be in touch about drinks soon."

Chris returned the nod. "Sure. You know where to find me."

In the time it took them to say goodbye, a curious thing happened—Mikey disappeared. Chris could have sworn that he hadn't moved from his place on the armchair, but both he and his plate were gone. A quick search of the room revealed they'd stolen away to the kitchen, where Mikey was racing to serve himself a second slice of cake.

Jay sighed, then crossed the room and leaned in behind his partner to whisper something in his ear. Mikey's hand went still and his lips parted slightly. After a shocked moment, he mumbled something Chris couldn't make out, loaded his plate with cake, and was escorted out of the room. On his way, he waved at Chris, and Chris saw for himself the all too familiar starry look in his eyes. "See you later. Have a good first day back. Don't forget to look in your—"

Mikey slapped a hand over his mouth and shook his head, then rushed out of the room, Jay never far behind.

Odd. But not odd enough to linger on. There was something up with Mikey and Jay, and Chris looked forward to figuring out what it was over drinks one day. Until then, he had cleanup to do and a co-worker to relieve from duty.

Chris was rounding up the dirty dishes when Warren came back from exacting revenge. By the lack of severed head, it seemed Pete had escaped with his life.

"Did you have fun?" Chris asked.

329

Warren scowled. "No. That bastard locked himself in his car before I had a chance to get even and drove away laughing at me. Next time we're on shift, he's gonna get it." Without asking, he took the plates Chris had gathered and brought them into the kitchen. "Why don't you go start your shift? I'll get some cake plated for Caroline and rage-scrub these dishes to work my Pete-related anger out."

"You're not on the clock today."

"So?" Warren dumped the dishes in the sink and ran the water.

"So you should go home. You're coming off a forty-eight-hour shift. You need sleep."

"Need is a strong word. I can sleep later. After dishes." Warren waved him off. "Caroline deserves to go home, too. I was able to nap while things were slow overnight—she wasn't."

He had a point, but that didn't mean Chris liked it. He slid his hands into his pockets and eyed Warren while the sink filled. "One of these days I'm gonna get you back for all this. You know that, right?"

"You can try. But how about you plot your revenge in the dispatch office? Caroline is waiting. I'll be here this afternoon when your shift is over to drive you home. What do you want for dinner?"

"What I didn't get to eat on Christmas morning."

Warren plunged his hands into soapy water. "We'll have to see about that."

Something was rotten in the state of the dispatch office—namely, the drawer containing Chris's empty folder. It had been left ajar, open just enough that he caught a flash of something colorful inside. Curious, he opened it the rest of the way. What he'd seen had been Post-It notes in a rainbow of neon colors stuck haphazardly to his folder's top-facing cover. On each Post-It was a short message.

You do a great job!
Keep going.
Glad to have you on the team.
Kick butt today!

They were all written in the same hand. Not Warren's. Mikey's, maybe? Chris took the folder out to get a better look and noticed it was heavier than it should have been.

Cards and other stationary had been stuffed inside.

Chris took them out one by one.

The first was a letter from Sinclair written on the back of old, coffee-ringed paperwork writing Pete up for petty java-theft.

Next came a get-well card from Meatball, personalized with a terrible drawing of what was either human bones or lumpy dumb-bells—Chris couldn't tell which.

After that, a very proper note sealed in an addressed envelope from Kathleen, whose spidery handwriting was as neat as her glare was accusatory.

Not to be outdone, there were a few letters written to him on flowery stationary from Pete, who seemed to have raided Liberty's office supplies.

Chris read them one by one, laying them out across his desk until there was no room left, and he had to start stacking new letters on top of the old ones. Every person in the station had written something for him. A few—like Pete and Mikey—had written to him more than once. While every letter was different, they all touched on the same thing: how glad they were Chris was doing better. Some were more emotional than others. Alicia's letter, written in precise script, went into detail about how she'd felt when she realized who they'd just rescued on the day of the accident. Jay's was more subdued, but was heartfelt all the same.

The very last letter in the stack was from Warren.

*When I saw you on my stretcher, my world fell apart. I hope that on
days where you feel the same, these notes will help pull you back
together. We're here for you. We care about you. We're all so glad
you're home.*

Love always,
Warren

Chris laid the letter on the desk with the rest and sat in silence for a
long while, his hand cupped over his mouth and tears prickling the
back of his eyes.

Erika had told him that the community would remember the
kindness he showed them, but she'd never warned him about this.

When he'd pulled himself together, Chris took out his phone to
text Warren only to find that Warren had beaten him to the chase.

Warren: I love you. Have an amazing day at work. If you
need a pick-me-up, check your drawer
Warren: PS: I figured you might be tired, so I asked Libby if
she'd mind keeping Jack tonight. Pete's pissed, but that's what
he gets for stealing my cake, the bastard

God, the way those texts made him smile. Warmth spread
through Chris's chest.

The boy who'd tried to ruin his life had grown into the man
who'd put it back together.

Warren was the only one for him. Chris knew it now more
than ever.

Chris: I love you so fucking much
Chris: I can't wait to see you tonight

Warren: We'll be back together before you know it. Hold on. You've got this

Warren: Oh, and if you need a little something extra to help you get through your day... that thing you asked me to make for dinner?

Warren: It's officially on the table

WARREN

The table wasn't that evening's only official destination. The meal was introduced over the arm of the couch, where Chris shoved everything south of Warren's belt down and ate his ass until Warren was whimpering with need. Following that, appetizers were served on the counter dividing the kitchen from the living room—frottage, paired with refreshing cooling lube that Warren had strategically left out in the hopes Chris would be hungry for more.

He was.

Before either of them could come, Chris pulled away and grabbed Warren by the wrist. They stumbled their way to the table, kissing, eager for the main course.

When Warren's ass bumped the edge of the table, he hopped up onto it and used it for balance while he wrapped his legs around Chris. Chris didn't waste time. No sooner had Warren positioned himself than Chris's slick, girthy cock slipped between his cheeks. There was a bit of awkward fumbling as they found the right position, but the second Chris pushed inside, Warren forgot all of it.

The stretch as Chris filled him had been worth the wait.

"Fuck," Chris whispered against Warren's lips. "Fuck, baby... oh, *fuck,* are you tight."

Warren was too far gone to reply. The stretch. God, the stretch. He squeezed his eyes shut and wrapped his arms tightly around Chris's neck. They kissed harder than they had before.

He needed this.

Needed Chris.

Craved him like a drowning man craved air.

Thrived on the way Chris filled him.

The scratch of his stubble. The firmness of his chest. The strength he embodied.

Fucking perfection. All of it.

"Fuck me," Warren gasped as Chris began to pump. "Fuck me, fuck me, *fuck me.*"

One deep, urgent thrust after another, Chris complied.

Warren's toes curled. Tension ran down his thighs and through his groin, prompting him to tighten his body in a way that made Chris groan. Orgasm was close, and he milked it for everything it was worth, using the tension shooting through him to squeeze Chris's cock again and again.

"Come inside me," Warren begged breathlessly. "Wanna feel you. Need to feel you. Missed it so damn much."

Chris muffled a growl by sinking his teeth into the dip of Warren's neck and gave Warren everything he wanted. His dick thickened and throbbed, and Warren knew it was done. He came hard in response, then crumpled forward and rested his head on Chris's shoulder. His legs unlocked from Chris's waist. If it weren't for his hold on Chris's neck, he would have slumped onto the table.

A few moments passed while Warren caught his breath until at last he whispered, "You up for dessert?"

Chris nuzzled his way to Warren's neck and nipped it.

It was the best yes Warren had never heard.

Dessert was served in the bedroom amongst the rumpled sheets.

336

Warren had wanted to climb on top and ride Chris like they'd talked about on Christmas morning, but Chris had other plans. He crawled on hands and knees between Warren's legs and kissed him until Warren was supine. On paper, missionary didn't sound as exciting as jumping Chris's bones, but paper could go fuck itself. *Everything* could go fuck itself. Because with every slow, soulful kiss they shared, Chris upended Warren's notions of what made sex good.

There was nothing greedy about this.

Nothing rushed.

Nothing brutal.

But all of it was amazing in ways Warren had never thought vanilla foreplay could be.

"Love you," Chris murmured as he thumbed over Warren's slit, smoothing leaking precum over his tip. "God, I fucking love you. I can't believe you're mine."

"Then fuck me until you believe it."

Chris chuffed with laughter, helped Warren into position, and slid inside.

It wasn't often that Warren noticed things about penetration that weren't the ache of being stretched or the strange, sometimes uncomfortable fullness that came with being fucked. He liked it when it hurt. When it did, he could distill sex down to sensation and didn't have to think about the man he was sharing it with. It was selfish, sure, but it had meant that he could get off and leave without getting his heart involved.

It wasn't like that with Chris.

Warren closed his eyes. Stretched his neck. Arched his back. Chris was inside of him, moving slowly but inching deeper. All the sensations he was used to were there, but they were nuanced by layers of emotion he couldn't untangle. But that was what love was, wasn't it? So many different feelings wrapped indivisibly in each other. Happiness. Adoration. Need. Want. Lust. There was no clear indication where one ended and the other began, and so Warren took them all.

He'd never had sex like this before.

Had never known making love could feel so good.

"I'm gonna come," Warren uttered, voice almost too thin to carry. Tears had started to cluster beneath his eyelashes. He knew how to handle pain, but this? It was something else entirely. *"Chris..."*

"It's okay," Chris told him. The sound of his voice... god. It was deep and dark and chesty, the purr of a lion—dangerous, but sweet. "Come for me. Wanna feel it happen. Wanna know how completely you're mine."

Orgasm came. Warren tossed his head back and rode it out, taking Chris as deep as he could. Chris thrust into him in turn, too slow, too perfect. The sounds he made, those full-bodied, low-pitched groans of pleasure. God. It was a wet dream come to life—only this one didn't end right before things were about to get good.

When Chris came, Warren tightened around his cock in time with every pulse. The wet mess they made spilled between Warren's cheeks, but he loved it and moved with Chris until, sweaty and panting, they collapsed onto the sheets. Chris pulled out and lay next to him, prompting Warren to search for his hand and interlock their fingers. "That was amazing."

"Good, because we're just getting started."

Warren arched an incredulous brow. "I know you've got that big dick energy, but I'm calling bullshit. There's no way you're getting hard again for a while. I'm not. My dick is officially down for the count, and my ass isn't far behind."

"I never said right now." Chris was smiling at the ceiling, a distant but hopeful expression in his eyes. Warren had been all set to sass him, but seeing him look so happy knocked that urge back a peg or two. "I was thinking more in the grand scheme of things— the same way you spoiled me the last month, I'm going to spoil you."

"You don't owe me anything. I did what I did because I wanted to."

"And I'm doing what I'm doing for the same reason." Chris drew a long, filling breath through his nostrils, held it, and let it out slowly. His smile persisted throughout. "You're mine, Reaves. After what we just got up to, I think it's fair to say I've won your ass back fair and square. So, in retaliation for you spoiling me rotten, I've decided to make it my life's mission to spoil you."

On the inside, Warren swooned. On the outside, he played it cool. "Is that so?"

"Yup."

"I spoiled you rotten?"

"You did."

"I think you might be overexaggerating."

"And I think you're full of shit."

Warren grinned. Chris was a master at their little game of back and forth, and he recognized a setup when he saw one. "You know what? I'm not even going to try to defend myself. Fuck you."

"Fuck you harder."

"Fuck you with a rusty spoon."

"Calm down there, Salad Fingers. That's taking it one spoon too far."

Be still Warren's Newgrounds-obsessed teenage heart. As if he needed another reason to love the man. Brimming with the wild kind of joy that came from knowing he was in deep, Warren leaned in close to Chris's ear and whispered, "But the feeling of rust against my salad fingers is almost orgasmic."

"Which means my ass doesn't need to be involved."

"I said *almost.*"

"Christ." Chris plastered a hand over his face as Warren stifled a laugh. "If you fuck me with a rusty spoon, I am so not marrying your ass."

The game came screeching to a halt, and Warren lay very still. His pulse drummed in his ears. There it was again. That word. Marriage. Like Chris was so confident that Warren was his that it was a foregone conclusion.

Which it was.

But that was beside the point.

"You know, that's the second time you've brought up getting married." Warren rolled onto his back and lounged as casually as a man could given the circumstance, but his facade was starting to crack. A glimmer of hope sneaked into his voice. "I'm starting to think you're serious."

"I am."

"You know that's crazy, right?"

"I do." Chris paused thoughtfully. "I don't care, though. Fuck that. I've wasted enough of my life trying to make the best out of a miserable situation that was never gonna get better. I'm not gonna waste more of it putting my happiness on hold for bullshit reasons. Part of that is being transparent about how I feel. So, yeah. I'm gonna marry you one day. Not today. Not next month. Maybe not even next year. But I won that ass tonight, Reaves. You surrendered it to me. And now that it's mine, I'm keeping it forever. I'm never letting you go."

Chris was in luck. There'd be no struggle. Warren's ass had found the one to whom it belonged, and it would never stray.

EPILOGUE

CHRIS

January's bitter winds gave way to slushy February sleet. March steamrolled through at alarming speeds, and spring passed by in what felt like the blink of an eye. Summer came and went. Fall arrived. Come September the trees were still green, but there was a crisp quality to the air that hinted it wouldn't stay that way for long. Lethridge hadn't changed much that year, but Chris would never be the same.

"Dad?" Jack asked through a yawn. It was early, and they were in the car. School was back in session and his boy was a fifth grader now. Middle school was on the horizon. It still didn't feel real.

"Yeah?"

"Do you think they'll let Mom out so she can come for parent-teacher conferences?"

"I don't think so, champ. I'm sorry."

"Then do you think we can ask Wren to come instead?"

Chris was so taken aback by the question that at first, he couldn't respond. When he did find words, they weren't the right ones. "What?"

"Wren. Your boyfriend," Jack said, very matter-of-fact. "I know he's not technically my parent, but you love him, right? And that makes him part of the family."

Chris had to focus to make sure he didn't drive off the road. One accident was enough, thank you very much. "Yeah, I love him, but I don't understand what that has to do with parent-teacher conference night. There's no rule that says that both parents have to show up."

"I guess." Jack hummed in disappointment and tapped his fingers on the open car window. "Do you think that Wren would wanna be there, though? Would it make him happy if we asked him to come?"

When had Jack's heart gotten so big? Chris slowed as he approached the school and turned into the drop-off lane. There were a few cars ahead of him taking their time, so he idled and hooked his arm over the passenger's seat, turning at the waist to smile at his sweet boy. "I think it would."

"I think so, too." Jack smiled back. "If it's okay with you, I'll ask him. If he doesn't want to, he'll say no and that's okay because no matter what he says, he'll know that he's a part of our family, too."

The cars up ahead began to move. Chris twisted back around and followed them. "That's okay with me. It's a really nice thing for you to do."

"Thanks. I really want Wren to be happy with us. I like him a lot, and since Mom's not here anymore, I wanna make sure Wren feels like he's not doing anything wrong by being happy with us."

Over the past year, Jack had learned in bits and pieces what was going on with Free. He knew she was in prison for doing something bad, although he didn't know what it was, and that it was impossible for her to be the mom he needed her to be. It hadn't been easy. There'd been tears. It was hard to say goodbye to the idealized version of a person you'd loved with all your heart. But Jack was strong. He'd pulled through. And one day, when Free came around, Chris had a feeling Jack would use that same strength to forgive her. The road ahead wasn't easy for any of them, but all they could do was take it one day at a time.

342

Thank god Warren was there to support them along the way.

They arrived in the drop-off zone. Jack unbuckled and grabbed his backpack, but didn't fling open the door. Through the rearview mirror, Chris watched uncertainty drift across his face.

"I miss Mom," Jack admitted in a small voice that made Chris's heart ache. "But I'm also really happy that we get to have Wren be part of the family. Does that make me a bad person?"

"No. Not at all."

"Okay!" It was as simple as that. Jack smiled and leaned forward to kiss the back of Chris's head, then threw open the door and darted out of the vehicle. He stuck his head back inside, eyes bright, to say, "Love you. Have a really good day at work today."

If only all heartbreak could be so easily resolved. Chris smoothed the hair Jack had kissed out of place, smiling. "Have a good day at school, kid. I love you, too."

After Jack went to bed that evening, Chris received his nightly message from Warren. It was a time-honored tradition to give each other shit and flirt mercilessly once all innocent eyes were asleep, but tonight's text from Warren was suspiciously conservative.

Warren: Is Jack in bed?
Chris: … yes
Warren: Don't freak out

The lock on the front door clicked and in stepped Warren, looking like a dream in his soft gray sweatpants and fitted white t-shirt.

"Surprise," he said in a hushed voice as he stepped into the living room. "It's me. In person. Here in your living room. Abusing the spare key you gave me. Sounding suspiciously like Libby. God, I've been living with her for too long, haven't I?"

Chris cracked a grin. "Guess you have."

"Well, that sucks." Warren made a show of sitting on the couch next to Chris, crossing his legs beneath him so he could face Chris directly. "But never fear! I'll be sounding like myself again before long because Libby's moving in with Pete. The paperwork just finished processing—I bought her out today. The house is officially mine."

The news hit Chris hard. He sat up straighter, heart racing. "Are you fucking serious?"

"I am." Warren met his eyes and pared down the playful, Libby-like quality of his voice. "You know, your lease is up in October, and it's a big house to live in alone…"

"Are you asking me to move in with you?"

"No. I'm asking you and Jack." Warren placed a hand on Chris's thigh. "I'm not gonna waste any more of my life putting happiness on hold for bullshit reasons. Come live with me. Both of you. There's nothing holding us back anymore."

The nerve of him, using Chris's own words like that. If Jack hadn't been asleep, Chris would have burst out laughing. It wasn't because he found the situation funny, because it wasn't, but the racing excitement inside him needed to get out somehow. They'd been living apart, sustaining themselves on sleepovers for a few months shy of a year because of lease and mortgage bullshit, wanting more, but never able to make it work. All that was changing now. The clouds had lifted and the future looked fucking bright.

Enamored, Chris leaned in and kissed him. "When can we move in?"

Warren made a pitched, airy noise of excitement in response and kissed Chris hard, and the next thing Chris knew, they were lip to lip in a pile on the couch, Warren's sweats pulled scandalously low.

"Nope," Chris muttered. He yanked Warren's sweats back up. "Not in the living room. If you want to get naked, you come spend the night in my bedroom. But before I let you in, I need to know when you want us to move."

Warren's cheeks turned pink. "Libby's moving out now, so tonight, if you want. Not that you would, since Jack is sleeping and you're not packed, but—"

Chris silenced him with a crushing kiss, and by the time they were done, Warren's sweats were back to being scandalous. How terrible. Chris would have to punish them later by making them spend the night on his bedroom floor.

"I'll start packing this weekend," he said. "We don't have much. I figure we can start moving in slowly to help transition Jack between here and there. Not that he needs much time to adjust. He's used to the house. I think he'll be bouncing off the walls when he finds out we're gonna be living there, especially since we'll be living there with you. He wants to invite you to his parent-teacher conferences, you know. He's crazy about you."

The news did away with the flush of arousal in Warren's cheeks. He wiggled out from beneath Chris and sat up straight, adorably hopeful. "Really?"

"Yes, really." Chris sat up, too, folding his legs in the same way Warren had so they could sit facing each other. The little bit of pink left in Warren's cheeks was charming, and the way his hair was mussed made Chris itch to fix it, but god, was he gorgeous either way. "He's one hundred percent on board with us being a family. I was worried that the situation with Free would complicate things, but he's a good kid, and he's got a big heart. He loves you, and he's happy you're part of his life."

"I'm happy I'm a part of his life, too," Warren said, looking down at his lap. Chris followed his gaze and saw that Warren had taken out his phone and was doing something with it. More than that, his hands were trembling. Not much, but enough for Chris to notice.

"What's wrong?" Chris cupped one of Warren's hands to still it, worried that he'd said or done something to upset him. "You're shaking."

"I, um." Warren laughed nervously. "I guess I was waiting for you to find it for yourself, but it was dumb of me to think you'd even look, and, well… it feels right. This moment. Right now, here with you."

Warren turned his phone around and held it out to Chris. It was open to the Urban Dictionary entry that'd started it all—doucheweasel. Warren's viral entry was still the first one listed, although other entries had generated beneath it in years past.

"I'm not sure I understand." Chris went to pass the phone back to him, but Warren wouldn't take it. He pushed it back into Chris's hand.

"Check out the second entry," he said.

Doucheweasel

Gender-neutral word for a very sorry man who made a big mistake that almost cost him the love of his life.

"Did you hear about the doucheweasel who used Urban Dictionary to slander the hot AF guy he was secretly madly in love with?
"Yeah, what a fucking clown. Fuck that guy. He is kinda handsome, though…"

#ImSorry #ImTheAsshole #ILoveYouChris
#WillYouMarryMe

Chris snapped his gaze from the screen to Warren. In the time he'd spent reading, Warren had produced a ring. It was made of black tungsten, rose gold woven in a braid-like pattern down its center.

"I know you were planning to ask me, but you were taking too long." Warren's hands were still shaking and his eyes were glossy with tears. "So I figured I'd ask you. Will you marry me? I want what we have for the rest of my life. Fuck arguing with anyone else. You're the only one for me."

Chris laughed. It was choked and abrupt, but it came from the place deep inside of him where happiness welled, and it shone through in his voice. He pulled Warren to him and kissed him hard. The ring found its way to his finger. "Yes," he said through a grin when they stopped kissing to catch their breath. "I'll marry the hell out of you."

Warren's scandalous sweatpants spent that night on the bedroom floor, as they would almost every night after, forever and ever, for the rest of their lives.

ABOUT THE AUTHOR

Should you ever find yourself traveling down the gravel street of a quiet forest community in the Midwest, you may come across Emma Alcott—suburbanite by birth, but small-towner by choice.

Emma loves all things doctors say you should only enjoy in moderation, writing the stories of her heart, and traveling. Once upon a time, she fell in love with a man from another country and moved mountains in order to be with him. They've now been married for half a decade and have far too many fur-children.

Seriously.

Do you want a dog?

If you love Emma's books, you might also enjoy her work as her alter-ego, Piper Scott!

The Answer

Single Dad Sundays

Waking the Dragons Series

(with Susi Hawke)

Alpha Awakened

Alpha Ablaze

Alpha Deceived

Alpha Victorious

Rent-a-Dom Series

(with Susi Hawke)

Daddy Wanted

Master Wanted

Teacher Wanted

Beard Wanted

Redneck Unicorns Series

(with Susi Hawke)

Seriously H*rny

Dangerously H*rny

Forbidden Desires Series

(with Lynn Van Dorn, writing as Virginia Kelly)

Clutch

Bond

Mate

Forbidden Desires Spin-Off Series

(with Lynn Van Dorn, writing as Virginia Kelly)

Swallow

Magpie

Audio addict? See which of Piper's books are available on Audible. New titles are always always being added.

https://www.audible.com/author/Piper-Scott/B01MV2GNAJ

Made in the USA
Monee, IL
31 March 2022